wonderstorm

© 2021 Wonderstorm, Inc. The Dragon Prince™,
Wonderstorm™ and all related character names are trademarks
of Wonderstorm, Inc. Used under license.
All rights reserved.

Library of Congress Cataloging-in-Publication Data available

ISBN 978-1-338-66640-3

10 9 8 7 6 5 4 3 2 1   21 22 23 24 25

Printed in the U.S.A.   23

First printing 2021

Book design by Betsy Peterschmidt & Jessica Meltzer

Cover and frontispiece artwork by Katie De Sousa

Map artwork by Francesca Baerald

1 2021

THE
DRAGON
PRINCE

BOOK TWO: SKY

WRITTEN BY **AARON EHASZ** &
MELANIE McGANNEY EHASZ

CREATED BY **AARON EHASZ** &
JUSTIN RICHMOND

SCHOLASTIC INC.

SKY

It was a big world, and sometimes it felt daunting.

The girl was the granddaughter of the famous inventor who had built wings out of wax. And so, she knew the Warning Story better than anyone. It was the story of how her uncle had died because he didn't listen to Grandfather's warnings not to fly too high, and so his wings melted when he flew too close to the sun.

The girl told her mother that she wanted to fly more than anything. But her mother and all the other adults told the girl it was too dangerous. They told her over and over: Remember the Warning Story.

Nevertheless, she persisted.

The girl found the old wax wings, which had been hidden away. The wax was strong enough to hold the feathers, but the hot sun would melt the wax. So the girl strengthened the wax by adding her strongest glue, which she knew would stay solid even in the heat.

When the others saw her wearing the new-and-improved wings, they yelled at her to stop. "You'll fly too high!" they said.

Were they afraid she would fail, or were they afraid she would succeed?

With some luck and a strong breeze, the girl flapped her wings. Soon she was airborne. Soaring through the sky, she felt so free! And from high up there, the world looked . . . smaller. Not *small*, but just the right size. And the girl knew she could do anything, even change it.

PROLOGUE

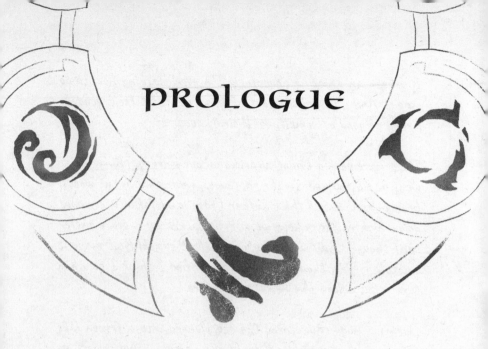

Dear King Harrow,

I hope you're not too worried about me and Ezran. It feels like a lifetime since we left home, but it's only been a week. We had to leave because we found something the world thought was destroyed—the egg of the Dragon Prince! I tried to tell you, but Lord Viren stopped me from entering your chambers. So, Ezran and I decided to take a journey across the world, carrying this precious egg home to its mother in Xadia. Bait tagged along, in case you were looking for him. We hope that when the Dragon Queen receives her egg from humans we will be able to stop the war.

It's been an amazing adventure. I'm even learning how to do magic! And I'm weirdly sort of good at it. It feels good to finally be good at something! Weirdly good.

There have been a ton of surprises on our journey. Things never went as we planned. In the past week, we've slept in the woods, been chased out of the Banther Lodge, and taken a rowboat down high rapids, where we were attacked by a sea monster that thought Bait would make a perfect snack! Bait made it out totally fine, though he was so terrified I think I saw him turn a few colors I've never seen before.

During a huge snowstorm, the egg plunged into a frozen lake for a few minutes and we thought all was lost . . . but something incredible happened. We managed to haul the egg up the Cursed Caldera, where we got some good advice and, well, to make a long story a little shorter, the egg hatched and now we're taking care of someone new! The Dragon Prince is here! He's the most powerful creature in the world, and he's just about the cutest thing I've ever seen.

This journey hasn't always been easy—in fact, it's probably the hardest thing I've ever done. But we haven't done it alone. We've been traveling with a new friend, Rayla—a Moonshadow elf. Nothing I believed about elves is true. Rayla is kind and good. She's fearless, fast, and strong . . .

But I'll stop talking about her because there's something I have to say to you. Ezran keeps telling me that you would want me to call you "Dad." I know you're not my first dad, my dad-dad... he's gone. But maybe Ezran is right, and you would be okay with this? Let me start this letter again.

Dear Dad,

I love you and I miss you. Ezran and I will take good care of each other until we see you again.

Love,
Callum

CHAPTER 1
A FEW MORE DAYS

Come and get it, everyone!"

Callum's ears perked up. There was a gnawing hole in his stomach where food should have been. It seemed like Lujanne had been preparing breakfast for ages. *Wasn't she a mage? Couldn't she just conjure something up?*

Callum hurried over to the long wooden table nestled in the clearing. He took a seat and looked around the caldera for Rayla. It still felt strange to be friends with a Moonshadow elf, especially an assassin sent to kill his little brother. But he and Ezran—the two princes of Katolis—were still alive and Rayla was now one of the best friends Callum had ever had. He didn't see her, though. Maybe she was sleeping in for once.

"'Morning, Callum!" Ezran said, coming up behind his brother. "Boy, am I hungry! But I think Bait is even hungrier."

Ezran motioned to the pet glow toad at his feet.

Callum glanced at Bait, marveling at his little brother's ability to perceive what animals were feeling. Callum himself could usually tell Bait's mood by the hue of his color-changing skin, but Bait's teal-spotted yellow skin hadn't changed—he was just as grumpy as ever. (Of course, those who knew Bait well knew that underneath the façade of "grump" there was great loyalty, courage, and even grumpy love.)

"Oh, his skin didn't give him away," Ezran said. "And he didn't tell me in glow toad either. He communicated with the universal language—tummy growling!" Ezran chuckled. "But I think Zym is the hungriest of all."

Azymondias, the Dragon Prince whom they all called "Zym," romped over to Ezran and Callum. Only a week ago, this adorable, puppy-like dragon with long eyelashes and a tender heart was inside an egg. And now he was out—hatched and healthy! It was a little hard to believe that Zym was destined to become a massive, epic archdragon. Callum patted the dragon on the head, and Zym immediately nipped at his fingers.

"Hang on, buddy," Callum said. "Breakfast is coming."

"Whoa! Ava! Come back here, girl!"

A huge wolf burst into the clearing, followed by Ellis. Ellis was the brave girl who'd led them up the Cursed Caldera in search of the Moon mage Lujanne. Years ago, Lujanne had healed Ellis's wolf pet, Ava. Ava was massive, but despite her size, she was as tame (and as fluffy) as a kitten. She was missing a leg due to an old injury, but she didn't seem to notice or care. Ava gave Zym a big lick on the cheek.

Callum sighed, feeling lucky they'd met all these new people and creatures on their journey. After all, Zym might not ever have hatched if Callum and Ezran hadn't met Ellis and Ava and Lujanne.

He also felt lucky he was about to consume the most tantalizing dishes he had ever seen.

"Elves and humans over here," Lujanne said, pointing to the garland-covered table. "And those with three or more legs can sit there, with Phoe-Phoe." Lujanne gestured to a nearby clearing where her pet, the immense moon phoenix Phoe-Phoe, was standing. Phoe-Phoe guarded four large bowls with her spread feathers, but Callum could see that the dishes were heaped with squiggling worm-things. Ava, Zym, and Bait hopped over to Phoe-Phoe and immediately began chowing down.

"You named your pet 'Phoe-Phoe'?" Ellis asked Lujanne in her squeaky voice.

"She's a moon phoenix," Lujanne said. "Her name is short for Phoenix-Phoenix."

Phoe-Phoe squawked and flapped her brilliant blue wings when she heard her own name.

"Can we try whatever we want?" Callum asked, greedily eyeing an iced chocolate cake. Ezran had already helped himself to a plate of cookies, but Callum didn't want to be rude.

"Of course, dear," Lujanne said sweetly. "The choice is all yours."

"You have the best food up here," Ezran garbled. His mouth was full and he clutched pastries in both hands. "What's your secret?"

"Well..." Lujanne started. She tapped a long, shapely fingernail on her tan cheek. Her lip twitched. "My secret is ... that it's all fake." She smiled.

"What do you mean, fake?" Callum asked as he sank his teeth into a crispy layered pastry. Nothing had ever tasted more flaky, more buttery, more delectable than this delicate tower of delight.

"You know, fake," she said. "They're delicious illusions."

Callum nodded while he chewed, although he had no idea what Lujanne was talking about.

"You're actually eating grubs," Lujanne said, still smiling sweetly.

Callum froze midbite, and then placed the exquisite treat he was holding back on the table. He tried to stay focused on the melt-in-your-mouth flaky goodness, but now that he knew it was a spell, he was starting to detect the writhing larvae that were apparently being disguised by the illusion.

"Oh, you must mean 'grub'?" Ezran asked. He brushed a few long dark curls out of his eyes. "Like as in, 'Wow, this is some good grub!'"

Callum looked over at Ezran. His kid brother was still eating with gusto. He wanted to explain to Ezran that there was no cultural misunderstanding over the word *grubs*, but he was too nauseated.

"Um ... no," Lujanne said. "Do you see what Phoe-Phoe is eating?"

Callum looked over at the pet area, where the four animals had their heads buried in squirming worms. All Callum could hope was that Ezran would swallow his last bite before he realized the unpleasant truth.

"That bowl of worms?" Ezran asked tentatively.

"Those are grubs," Lujanne said. "Technically not worms, but insect larvae. Extremely nutritious!"

Ezran clutched his stomach. Nearby, Ellis continued to chew what appeared to be a slice of blueberry chocolate pie.

"I don't care," Ellis said. "Worms. Flies. Yesterday's garbage. This illusion pie is the best I've ever had." She cut herself another slice as Ezran quietly vomited onto the grass.

"Hey, everybody!" Rayla called out, jumping down from a hilltop and waving both hands.

Rayla! Callum stood up, desperate to move on from the whole grubs situation.

"Well, you're in a good mood," Ellis said to Rayla.

"It does feel good to have two working hands again," Rayla said. Her pointy ears wiggled with excitement. When she caught sight of Ava with only three legs, she looked a little sheepish. "Uh, no offense, Ava." But Ava just panted happily and returned to her grubs.

"Guess what, folks—I can slish and slash with both swords again," Rayla said. She hurled herself up a craggy rock, swung both blades around in an exuberant whirl, and then quickly folded them away. "I can also clap, do handstands, and do that thing when you finish a nice song and dance." Rayla clapped, tumbled into a handstand, and finished off with perfect form, waving both hands in the air.

"That's so great, Rayla!" Ezran exclaimed.

Callum was relieved Rayla's hand had fully healed. Just a few days ago, it had turned a deep and disturbing shade of purple, constricted by a tight binding on her wrist. Rayla had magically bound herself to killing the human prince, Ezran. But of course, that was before they had gotten to know each other. When Rayla decided she would not follow through on her assassin's duty, the unbreakable binding became tighter and tighter until it seemed her hand might fall off. But the little dragon Zym had solved the problem by nibbling off the binding with his baby teeth! Easy for Zym, but a true miracle for anyone who wasn't a legendary dragon.

"And how's everybody else feeling?" Rayla asked, cupping her now healthy hand to her ear.

She received a chorus of enthusiastic responses.

"Glad to hear everyone is feeling good!" Rayla went on. She looked around mischievously. Then her voice turned from playful to deadly serious. "'Cause it's time to go."

"What? Why?" Callum asked. "We barely just got to the Moon Nexus."

Everyone else groaned in agreement. If nothing else, Callum thought saving and hatching a dragon egg might buy him three or four days of rest and relaxation.

But Rayla ignored the griping. "Danger is coming for us, I know it. The longer we stay here, the higher the risk," she told them. "I'm not trying to scare you all, I'm just being realistic."

"She's right," Lujanne said. "The night the Dragon Prince was born, I sensed something amiss." She shook her head. "Those strange purple wisps that were drawn to the newborn dragon that night—pretty as they were, there were dark forces behind them that are now probably pursuing you."

"Nobody likes dark forces! Which is why—" Rayla signaled it was time to go by swinging both hands toward the foot of the mountain.

"Making good use of those two hands, huh?" Ezran said.

Callum smiled. His little brother had inherited their mother's sense of humor. Her jokes had often been accompanied by an encouraging smile, as Ezran's was now.

"You bet I am," Rayla said. "Besides, we've got precious cargo to deliver. War is coming, like the world's never seen, unless we get the wee dragon home to his mom."

"But Zym—he's so widdle. He still needs to learn how to fly," Ezran said.

"Ez is right," Callum said. He was also reluctant to leave the relative safety of the Moon Nexus while Zym was still so fragile. Plus, he was hoping to learn some Moon magic while they were here.

"Ezran seems to have a special connection to the dragonling," Lujanne said thoughtfully. She turned to Ezran. "Perhaps you could teach him to fly?"

"Me?" Ezran asked. "But I don't know how to fly."

Callum nodded encouragingly at his little brother. He was sure Ezran was the right person for the job, despite his lack of wings.

"I could try," Ezran finally said.

"Good. We'll be stronger as a group if Zym can fly," Callum said. "And even stronger if I knew more magic. Maybe you could teach me some Moon magic, Lujanne?"

"I could show you some things," she said.

"Ummm, Lujanne, I thought you were on my side?" Rayla said. "Remember, dark forces, purple wisps?"

Lujanne shrugged noncommittally.

"A few more days, Rayla—that's all we're asking," Callum pleaded. "I wrote a letter to my stepfather to catch him up on everything. I think there's a real chance that he'll send us help if he can. We should hang out for that."

"A letter to your stepfather? The . . . king?" Rayla asked.

"Yes. That's what I said," Callum replied. He noticed Rayla's face turn even paler than usual. She could clearly use some rest too.

"Fine," Rayla relented. "We'll stay one extra day—one! But I'm serious about the danger. I'll keep patrolling. Everyone else, stay on your toes." She looked intently at each member of the group, her eyes landing on Zym. "Except you. You work on getting *off* those toes!" She flapped her hands like wings, and the baby dragon seemed to smile in reply.

Callum was glad Rayla was going to continue patrolling to keep them safe—but he was even gladder that he now might have enough time to learn some Moon magic.

CHAPTER 2
THE BREACH

*G*ren will find and protect the princes. He has to.

This was the single thought running through General Amaya's head as she rushed away from Katolis toward the Breach. She'd had to leave the princes' safety in the hands of her trusted interpreter, Commander Gren, for without her leadership at the Breach, the humans' secret passageway into the magical land of Xadia would become vulnerable.

Amaya dug her heels into her horse until the rhythm of its hooves hitting the ground was almost as fast as her heartbeat. Protecting the Breach was a huge responsibility. Centuries ago, after all humans were driven out of Xadia, the continent had literally been divided in two as the great dragons scorched a deep scar into the earth and filled it with a river of molten lava. But humans had discovered a hidden feature: Beneath an epic lavafall, a slight ridge protruded from the cliff's face, forming a treacherous path across the molten river—a singular, secret link to Xadia! The Breach was a closely guarded secret of the kingdom of Katolis, and humans controlled outposts on both sides of the passage. It was critical that elves and dragons never learned of the secret passage bridging the continent's divide.

Amaya slowed her horse as she approached the Breach. She needed to cross the path to reach the outpost on the Xadia side, which was hidden within the walls of the cliff itself.

As she started down the path, the sky was so dark, it was hard to believe it was morning. She trod carefully, scanning the scene for anything amiss.

Amaya had been born deaf, but she'd learned to hear with her eyes in situations like this. She took in every detail and every movement, no matter how small. Her mind constructed a perfectly detailed map of everything in front of and behind her—and in every direction, for that matter—so that she could detect any change or variation instantly.

Amaya turned her horse in a circle, looking for anything of importance, being careful to avoid the blasts of steam that rose from natural vents in the ground. Had her horse's ears just flitted to the left?

Amaya whipped her own head in that direction and trotted slowly toward a large vent. There wasn't much steam coming out, considering the size of the hole. She dismounted and leaned in to examine it. *This was curious—*

She suddenly felt vibrations on the pathway floor behind her.

They were decidedly *not* her horse's footsteps. In an instant, she leaped off her horse and whirled to face the three figures who had followed her down the path. All three wore fire-red armor that set off their mahogany skin tone. Amaya recognized them in an instant.

Sunfire elves.

The warriors raised their swords and rushed the general.

They were fierce, determined elves, and it was three on one, but Amaya's strength, experience, and mighty shield outmatched all three. One by one, she fought each elf to the edge of the path until each one fell screaming into the fire pit below.

Out of breath but alert, Amaya looked up. Apparently, she wasn't done.

A female warrior wearing a golden headdress stood a few feet away, her armor glinting in the firelight. Her yellow-gold face paint highlighted her dark brown eyes and fierce expression. She had a hand on her sword, but she stood still—calm and confident. Amaya was sure she was facing a Sunfire knight, one of the most elite fighters in all of Xadia. She felt a twinge of intimidation, but steeled herself for battle.

They locked eyes. Then, with a slow, steady hand, the knight reached for her sword in its runed sheath. Amaya gritted her teeth; she recognized the weapon as a glowing Sunforge blade. One of the rarest weapons in the world, the blade's heat alone could kill.

It suddenly seemed to Amaya that she and the knight had been sizing each other up for hours—it was time to break the standoff.

"AHHHHHHHHH!" she cried. She lowered her head and charged the knight.

The two warriors clashed. The Sunforge blade sliced through Amaya's sword like a hot knife through butter, breaking it in two. Amaya would have to rely on her shield now.

The knight came at Amaya multiple times, swinging the heavy blade with ease. The general dodged each of the elf's dangerous swings, but the hot orange glow of the blade was so bright, it was nearly blinding. At one point, her shield took a hit from the blade that left it with a smoldering gash in its surface.

Amaya noticed that the Sunfire knight's confidence seemed to grow with each swing of her blade. The general knew that those who feel invulnerable sometimes neglect their other senses—a mistake Amaya herself would never make.

Your blade may be invincible, Amaya silently said to the knight as she dodged swings of the blade. *But you are not. Watch and learn.*

Amaya bided her time till there was some space between her and the knight. Then Amaya stood tall and beckoned the knight to approach her.

Sure enough, the knight took the bait. When she charged forward, Amaya was ready: She slammed the knight in the torso with a side kick that sent her flying backward. The knight landed on her back, skidding to a halt just inches from the lava.

It was a small victory, and Amaya knew her weapons would not hold up against a Sunforge blade forever. She took this opportunity to mount her horse and race back the way she came.

"Dragons! The Xadian threat grows every day," Viren said as he slammed his fists down on the battle table. "Wake up!"

It was early in the morning, but he had been up for hours, strategizing about the kingdom's future, *caring* about the kingdom's future. Some of the other council members were still rubbing sleep from their eyes.

Viren, the high mage, had called this meeting of the council in the throne room to discuss the next steps for the kingdom of Katolis. The princes had both disappeared; there was an empty throne and no clear successor. The council would listen to him. He would make them understand that King Harrow's assassination was only the first incident in what was surely a full-scale war.

"There have been sightings of terrifying shadows in the clouds, flying high above the towns and cities of Katolis—war dragons!" he yelled.

A skeptical council member waved his hand in Viren's face. "Whoa, whoa, whoa—*war* dragons? How can you tell they're 'war' dragons and not just . . . you know, regular dragons?"

Viren laughed derisively. Such a question could only come from an ignoramus. He looked at the other council members and shook his head, trying to bring them into his confidence.

"Gigantic destructive beasts are circling at the edge of our kingdom," he said. "They're not our friends. It's naive to ignore this. They're waiting to strike! We must take action."

Viren frowned at the soft murmuring around the table.

Finally, High Cleric Opeli spoke. "No, we should wait. Xadia sent assassins, and they took the king's life," she said.

"Yes," cried Viren. This was exactly his point. Did Opeli want to sit around waiting to be attacked again? "And we must answer Xadia with force."

"But there hasn't been even the slightest skirmish since then," Opeli said. "Maybe the assassination was it. They've had their revenge, and everything will just . . . settle down now. Perhaps anything we do would escalate a situation that is actually waning."

"Settle down?!" Viren scoffed. "Can't you see the danger we're in? General Amaya reported that elven forces are gathering on the Xadian side of the Breach. We must be prepared to fight, and we won't be able to fight them alone." He ran his hand through his hair. "I can only hope I am not alone in thinking we must call for a summit of the Pentarchy." Viren knew that as this conflict escalated, it was critical that all five of the human kingdoms combined their strength. He looked around at the council members, trying to get a read on their inclinations.

Opeli, as usual, stood strong against Viren.

"You're out of order, Lord Viren," Opeli said. "Only a king or queen can call for a summit. Frankly, I doubt the other rulers will even look at a message that doesn't bear the king's seal." She crossed her arms.

"But this is a crisis of historic proportions!" Viren yelled. How could Opeli not understand the calamity? "Humanity could face extinction if we don't work with the other four kingdoms to do something!"

"None of that matters while we have no king," Opeli said. She leaned in and stared Viren down. "Therefore, our top—and only—priority must be finding the princes. Until we do, our hands are tied."

Another skeptical council member grinned, agreeing with Opeli. Another one yawned.

"It seems the council is still divided," Viren said, "and perhaps not alert enough to make this decision." He shot an accusing glare at the yawner. "The council shall convene again when everyone is properly prepared for this discussion."

Viren left the room before anyone could protest. He did not agree with Opeli when it came to the princes. His hands weren't tied in their absence—quite the opposite, in fact. However, Opeli did make one good point: The only way to get the attention of the other four kingdoms would be with letters bearing the king's seal.

Viren strode across the courtyard and ascended the stairs to King Harrow's chambers. When he reached the top, he shuddered involuntarily at the scene before him. Arrows, elven and king's guard alike, stuck out of the king's chamber doors. Dried, crusted blood splattered the walls. For a moment, Viren found himself reliving the night of the final battle; screams and chaos roiled in his ears. He shook his head to clear the visions, and then entered the king's bedroom.

Although someone had attempted to clean up around the tower, the king's bedroom had been left untouched. The bed was unmade. Harrow's belongings were broken and scattered about. An arrow stuck out of the cracked face of a large pendulum clock, freezing it at the time of the attack. The balcony door was partially open, and the curtains fluttered softly in the breeze. In the corner, the king's songbird, Pip, stood silently in its cage. Viren walked over.

"Good for you, surviving the attack," Viren told the bird. Pip did not respond.

Viren held one hand over his face to stifle a sob—and sank onto the unmade bed. *I miss you so much already, dear friend*—

He ran his hand over the soft bedclothes, trying to soothe himself, but his hand stopped on a hard object—a small painting in a frame. He picked it up and came face-to-face with a royal family portrait of Harrow, Queen Sarai, young Callum, and baby Ezran. This was certainly one of the very last things the king saw before the assassins came.

Viren felt a pain budding in his chest, a mix of sadness, regret, guilt, and loss. He willed the emotions back down inside before they could grow out of control though. He hadn't come here for sentimental reasons.

He placed the portrait back on the bed, then walked over to Harrow's desk and tugged on the wooden drawer in the middle, the one he'd seen the king pull paper and quills from a million times.

"Locked," Viren muttered to himself. He shook off a final pang of guilt, and then uttered a basic spell. The drawer shot open, revealing the king's seal on a stack of paper next to a ball of red wax. Viren pocketed what he needed and left the chamber.

CHAPTER 3
A SECRET AND
A SPARK

That afternoon, Callum accompanied Lujanne to a place she called the Moonhenge. They must have climbed two thousand stairs, and at this point, Callum was *feeling the burn*, as Soren might say. If he'd known he'd be expending this much physical energy, he might have forced himself to eat more of those grubs-disguised-as-food this morning.

Actually, he would not have done that.

"What, you're not impressed?" Lujanne asked, gesturing to their surroundings.

Callum looked around. Shimmering pools of water surrounded a collection of ruins—the remains of structures that had clearly once formed the perimeter of a moon-shaped building. A gushing, marvelous waterfall reflected the light of a faintly visible daytime moon. It was peaceful and awesome and supernatural. Callum breathed in the ancient majesty of the place.

"Lujanne, thank you so much for agreeing to show me stuff!" he said. Claudia had taught him some magical tidbits here and there, but learning from an elf felt authentic, like he was a true apprentice. "I can't believe I'm going to learn magic from a real mage."

"How do you know I'm real?" Lujanne asked mysteriously.

"Uh . . ." Callum didn't know how to respond, but he was ready to put up with just about anything from someone who would teach him magic.

"Don't worry, I'm real," Lujanne said with a little laugh. "Come on, this way." Callum hurried to keep up with her.

"This is the Moonhenge," Lujanne continued. "It's a special place that magically connects with the Moon Nexus at the top of the caldera.

"Thousands of years ago, when Xadia was one land, this place physically embodied a very deep magic. The architecture, the design, every aspect of this place was itself a magical symbol, like a massive intricate rune. The ancient ancestors of Moonshadow elves performed fantastic rituals here. Would you care to take a peek?"

Without waiting for Callum's answer, Lujanne chanted a spell: "Historia viventem." She traced a rune in the air as she spoke the ancient words and made a sweeping gesture with her arm.

Callum waited quietly, but nothing happened. *Maybe Lujanne is just a fake, like her gross grubs banquet—*

Suddenly, Callum felt an ice-cold wave run through his body. When he blinked, he was staring at the back of an ancient elf—it seemed a ghost had just passed through him! Then the cracked ruins began to glow electric blue. Before Callum's eyes, the cracked stones resealed themselves, and the ancient structures grew into their former grandeur, though they were made of only faint ghostly light. Two moonlit chapels reached high into a dark sky. It was as if Callum was looking into the distant past, a spectator at an event that had occurred over a thousand years ago. Dozens of translucent elf ghosts walked through the phantom Moonhenge, lost in their own world.

"Legends say those ancient elves could use the power of the Moonhenge to open a portal through the Moon Nexus to another plane," Lujanne said. "It was a shimmering world beyond life and death. Or perhaps it was a plane between life and death? Beyond or between, either way, this was one strange plane, and very dangerous."

Callum didn't care which description was correct; this place captured his imagination. A world on the other side of life and death sounded like the type of place where he might be reunited with his mother.

He watched the sparkling elf illusions dance. Some were playing beautiful stringed instruments.

"But it's ruins now—what happened?" Callum asked.

Lujanne released the spell and the illusions evaporated, leaving only rubble.

"The Moon druids destroyed it themselves—when Xadia was divided in two," she said. "The Moon Nexus happened to be on the side of the continent that was designated for humans. And so the Moon druids decided it was safer to disable this magical place."

"That's so sad," Callum said. The more he heard about fighting and war, the less sense it made to him. Now, because of the fighting, no one could enjoy this special place. It wasn't even worth thinking about reuniting with his mother—this portal had closed forever.

"Ever since the portal closed, there has always been a Guardian of the Moon Nexus—a mage like myself," Lujanne said. "It is the guardian's duty to prevent humans from discovering the Nexus."

"What happens when humans do discover it?" Callum asked. He shuddered to think that he was now part of a very small group. "Do you . . ." Callum drew his finger across his throat and gulped. Lujanne seemed lovely to him, but he was starting to believe that anyone was capable of just about anything.

Lujanne laughed at Callum's question. "Nah, why kill them when you can break their brains with insane illusions," she said. "I've got some real mind melters—they would completely freak your bean! Interested?"

"Um, I'll pass," Callum said. He had little interest in having his mind melted. Or in having his bean freaked, for that matter.

"Suit yourself," Lujanne said as she continued on the path. "Follow me."

As the sun set, the pair walked along a path that led up from the Moonhenge to the edge of the caldera. Lujanne's energy was boundless—Callum had trouble keeping up.

"Though primal magic is everywhere, it may be weaker or stronger at different times and places," Lujanne said. "The Ocean is strongest at high tide. The Sky is strongest in a storm. And the Moon is strongest—"

"When it's full!" Callum said, a proud smile on his face.

"Please don't interrupt," Lujanne said, and Callum's face fell. "But yes. And there's more. There are six special places where the magic of primal energies is most pure and powerful in this world. Such a place is called a Nexus. This is the Moon Nexus. Look."

She gestured to the caldera spread out in front of them. It was an enormous circular crater filled with sparkling blue water. Callum gasped. The caldera was a miracle of nature. The clear blue water shimmered pink and orange in the waning afternoon light. Something about the lake reminded Callum of the moon.

"The Moon Nexus reflects the moon perfectly," Lujanne continued. "When the moon is full, its light completely fills the lake. Moonlight is already a reflection, each and every ray of light reflected off the moon itself. Moon reflects sun, as death reflects life." She closed her eyes as if lost in her deep—if somewhat confusing—thought.

Callum agreed the scenery was beautiful and awesome . . . but it didn't have anything to do with why he'd asked for Lujanne's help. He needed some practical teachings in the ways of magic. He decided to be straightforward.

"I love this!" Callum said. "I love learning about magic. But I want you to teach me to do some Moon magic. Maybe some hands-on learning, something easy to start me off . . . some kind of moonbeam, or a moon ray?"

Lujanne gave Callum a hard look. "Humans can't do magic."

Callum didn't want to be rude to Lujanne, but she was wrong. "Um . . . I did do magic."

"Right, with a primal stone," Lujanne said. "But then you smashed it, so now you're just a standard human again." She giggled.

Callum felt his face fall, as well as all his hopes for the future.

"But look on the bright side," Lujanne said. She wiggled her four-fingered elven hands at Callum to demonstrate her point. "You humans have those extra fingers. The tiny ones—what do you call them? Pinkos?"

"I know other humans who do magic," Callum said. He stared glumly at his useless pinkies.

Lujanne sucked in her breath and shook her head. "We do not call that practice magic," she said, refusing even to say the words *dark magic*. "It's an atrocity."

Callum hung his head. "This can't be. I thought magic was . . . my thing. I was good at it."

"It looks like you could use some cake," Lujanne said, producing a delicious-looking slice of vanilla cake out of nowhere.

"That's really a plate of worms," Callum said.

"Oh. You're too smart for old Lujanne's illusions." She put the cake behind her back and immediately whipped out a bowl. "How about some nice old-fashioned iced cream, then? Hmm?"

Meanwhile, much farther down the hillsides of the Cursed Caldera, Ezran geared up to give Zym a lecture on flying. Ava and Ellis had joined to watch the practice, and Ezran felt pressure to succeed. Bait was there too, a stern expression on his face.

Ezran placed Zym on top of a small boulder and readied himself to give the little dragon some firm but kind words. But it was hard to concentrate with Bait staring at them like that. Was he maybe jealous? Ezran thought the glow toad would radiate a bit green if he were seriously jealous, but it might be worth reassuring him anyway.

"Hey, Bait, you know you're my best bud, right?" Ezran asked. "I've known you practically forever." He scratched Bait under the chin, and the grumpy glow toad stopped glaring.

Zym looked down at the little crowd, wide-eyed and innocent.

"Okay, Zym. It's time to buckle down and get to work," Ezran said. He put his hands on his hips.

Bait grumbled in agreement.

"Flying is a natural and beautiful thing," Ezran said. "Now, that doesn't mean it's going to be easy—"

Again, Bait grumbled in agreement. This time, Ezran turned to look at him. "You don't need to keep doing that," he said.

Bait narrowed his eyes at Ezran and made a defiant grumble, which Ezran had sense enough to ignore. Ezran's father always liked to say "pick your battles" when he wanted Ezran to overlook something small that was bothering him. This seemed to be one of those instances.

"Ready, Zym?" Ezran asked. "Wings out! And ... FLAP!" Ezran stretched his arms out and demonstrated flapping as best as a human could. "Come on! You have to flap those wings." He jumped up and down, but Zym didn't seem to be catching on.

The little dragon tilted his head to the side . . . and toppled over from the weight of his own head!

Ellis laughed. Bait rolled his eyes.

"Oh no—are you okay?" Ezran asked. He pulled Zym back up into a standing position and made sure he was holding his head up straight.

"One more time," Ezran said. "We'll try it nice and slow. Flaaaa . . . aaaap . . ." Ezran raised and lowered his arms in slow motion. This time, Zym wiggled his ears in response and broke out into a grin.

Ezran laughed. "That's not flying, but it's a very, very good start." Ezran had also learned from his father the power of encouragement.

"That was a good try!" Ellis shouted.

Zym leaped on Ezran and licked him. Ezran giggled.

But then Ezran stopped laughing. He could feel eyes on him. Slowly, Ezran turned to face Bait, who had somehow raised the level of his stare from intense to super intense. How was it possible for a glow toad to express so much disgust with a simple look?

"Let's take a break," Ezran said to Zym. "Everyone meet back here in ten minutes. I have an idea."

A few minutes later, Ezran returned to the flight practice boulder. Since he didn't know how to fly himself, he thought he should find someone with real-life experience to guide Zym. "And . . . we're back. This time we're here with a special guest. She's mystical, magical, Moon-powered, and she knows how to fly. Please welcome: Phoe-Phoe!"

Ellis clapped as Lujanne's moon phoenix stepped forward daintily.

"Ready, Phoe-Phoe?" Ezran said. "Show him how it's done."

Phoe-Phoe spread her enormous blue wings and flapped them. Almost effortlessly, she took flight.

"See?" Ezran said. "It's pretty easy." He felt a little bad saying that, not having any idea how to do it himself. But Zym tentatively opened his wings in imitation of Phoe-Phoe.

"Yes! Yes, that's right," Ezran said. At least Zym had picked up the idea of flying. "Now I'm going to show you what flying feels like." With Zym's wings spread, Ezran hoisted the baby dragon above his head. Then he began running in circles. "See? Can you feel it? Can you feel the *whoosh* of the air beneath your wings?"

"Oooooo-eeeeeee," Zym chirped.

"He's doing it!" Ellis said. "He's amazing."

"Yes, yes—he's amazing," Ezran said. He ran faster and faster. He was going to do it; he would teach this baby dragon to fly. As his excitement peaked, Ezran realized it was time to let Zym try on his own. It was time to let him soar.

Ezran sprinted forward in a burst of speed, and then stopped short and let go of Zym. *Fly, Zym, fly!* Ezran thought.

For a moment, the baby dragon careened through the air. It really looked like he was flying! But the truth was, he'd just been propelled forward by Ezran's sudden stop. A few seconds later, and—

FRRRUMMMFFFFF. Zym landed in some bushes and disappeared beneath the leaves.

"Ezran!" Ellis shouted. "You killed the Dragon Prince!"

"Oh no. I'm so stupid," Ezran said. He ran over to the bushes and frantically dug through them. "Oh no, oh no, oh no."

Finally, Ezran unearthed a dazed Zym.

"I'm so sorry, Zym," Ezran said. "I wasn't trying to hurt you, I promise. Are you okay?"

Zym broke into a huge smile and panted happily. Ezran hugged him.

When he pulled away, he caught Bait rolling his eyes at Phoe-Phoe.

Ezran would have to do better.

"Come on, buddy," Ezran said. "Let's try again."

That evening, Callum returned to the courtyard near camp. After all the time he'd spent with Lujanne, he was thrilled to see Rayla, Ezran, and Zym.

But it turned out Rayla was on her way out.

"Hey—where are you going?" Callum called as she sprinted through the courtyard.

"I need to patrol for dark forces," Rayla called back.

Callum stared after her. He wished she didn't have to keep risking her life for them like this.

"Rayla says we have to leave tomorrow," Ezran said.

"Seriously?" Callum asked. "So, I guess Zym can fly now?" Callum was impressed. He hadn't learned any magic, but at least Zym had learned to fly. He gave the little dragon a big smile.

"Uh, no, not yet," Ezran said. "I'm doing my best." Zym lowered his head. "And so are you, Zym. I know you are!"

"I guess we all had a tough day," Callum said.

"Yeah," Ezran replied. "Lots of jumping and flapping, but no flying." He patted Zym on the head. "But we'll get it. No matter how impossible it seems, we believe in ourselves and we're not giving up!"

Zym looked up at Ezran with a smile of gratitude that made Callum feel silly for being so easily disheartened. Ezran had a wise way about him, especially for someone so young.

"You know what?" Callum said. "I'm not giving up either. I'm gonna go give Lujanne a piece of my mind. But you know, nicely." He stood up and strode back the way he came.

This time, Callum stomped up the endless stairs to the Moon Temple. Apparently, learning magic required a person to be in excellent physical condition. He'd have to get some tips from Soren.

When he arrived at the temple, it appeared to be empty. But soon he spotted Phoe-Phoe flying through the night sky with Lujanne on her back. The pair landed softly in front of the temple.

"You're wrong," Callum called to Lujanne from the shadows.

Lujanne jumped. "Callum! What are you doing here? It's late."

"I'm never giving up," Callum said. He started pacing. "Growing up, I was supposed to learn horseback riding, sword fighting, archery, battle tactics . . . but I was so bad at everything."

"But then . . . you didn't give up? And you got good?" Lujanne asked. She dismounted Phoe-Phoe.

"Well, no—I gave all those up," Callum said. He could see

Lujanne was missing the point. "But then I tried magic, and it felt right! It felt like I was finally good at something. I *will* learn magic. It's who I am."

"I admire your determination, Callum," Lujanne said. "But learning magic is not your destiny. You can't do primal magic because you weren't born connected to a primal source."

"I don't get it. What do you mean 'connected'?" Callum asked.

Lujanne stroked Phoe-Phoe's feathers. The phoenix nuzzled her hand as she explained. "In Xadia, all creatures and elves and dragons are born connected to a primal source," Lujanne said. "They have a piece of it inside them—we call that piece an arcanum."

Okay, Callum thought. *Now we're getting somewhere. I'm learning things. Xadian creatures are born with an arcanum. Which means—*

"Wait," Callum said. "What's an arcanum?"

"It's like . . . the secret of the primal, or its meaning," Lujanne said.

"The secret of the primal?" Callum shook his head. He was already confused again.

"Yes," Lujanne said. "That secret becomes a spark—the tiniest possible flicker of a primal source inside you, but enough to ignite the world with its magic!"

All right. I think I maybe sort of kind of get it, Callum thought. *Every primal source has a secret.*

"So, what is it? What's the arcanum of the Moon?" Callum asked.

"It's something I just . . . know," Lujanne said. "It's not easily put into words. Knowing it in my own heart, it's an idea and a feeling more basic than a single word. But I couldn't explain it with ten thousand words if I tried."

"Well, try! Please?" Callum begged. He was ready to learn, and Lujanne just kept giving him these non-explanations.

"Very well," Lujanne said. She closed her eyes. "The arcanum of the Moon is about understanding the relationship between appearances—"

Callum felt a tap on his shoulder. When he turned around, he saw a copy of Lujanne!

"—and reality," said the Lujanne copy.

Callum swallowed. This elf just got weirder and weirder.

"Most people believe that reality is truth and appearances are deceiving," Lujanne said.

Then a third copy of Lujanne emerged out of nowhere. "But those of us who know the Moon arcanum understand we can only truly know the appearance itself. You can never touch the so-called reality that lies just beyond the reach of your own perception." Each of the three identical Moon mages smiled, done with their shared lecture.

Callum closed his eyes and shook his head. When he opened his eyes, there was only one Lujanne. This was not the type of magic he'd been hoping to learn.

"I'm confused," Callum said.

"I don't blame you! After all, you're only human," Lujanne replied.

Callum felt even more discouraged than before. He decided he'd had enough of the elven mage for one night.

When he returned to the camp, Ezran, Bait, and Zym were all

sleeping soundly. Callum lay down in his humongous bed, but he was too worked up to sleep. He grabbed the rune cube, which would illuminate on a specific side when it detected magic of that type, and held it toward Bait. The Sun rune glowed. Then he moved it toward Zym, and the Sky rune glowed. When he moved the cube close to his chest, it went dark.

Callum was suddenly exhausted. He pulled the cube tight against his body, curled up into a ball, and fell asleep.

Out in the forest, Rayla was on high alert with her blades out. "'Oh, can't we stay a bit longer so I can learn some magic tricks?'" she muttered, doing her best impression of Callum. "And oh, 'I wanna play around with the wee dragon!'" She shook her head. "Humans."

She joked, but Rayla's conscience was heavy. Callum's words from breakfast this morning were ringing in her ears: *I wrote a letter to my stepfather to catch him up on everything.*

Callum had given Rayla yet another perfect opportunity to tell the truth: The king was dead, killed by the other Moonshadow assassins. She'd probably had a half dozen opportunities to come clean in the last day. What was stopping her? She was supposed to be Callum and Ezran's friend.

Rayla shook her head again, this time trying to erase the guilty thought from her mind. Right now, her job was to be the protector. She had to focus. And again, the princes were the only reason they were still here on this cursed mountain.

Rayla peered around a corner, inspecting the path as she

walked. "Only the noble elf cares about keeping us all alive, apparently. There's something out here, I know it. Something ba—" She stopped. *Was that music?*

The melody was quite beautiful. It sounded like a wood instrument, a lute or flute or piccolo—something like that. Where was it coming from? Something wasn't right.

Rayla yawned. She had been patrolling all day, and the music was so soothing. Her eyes seemed to be getting very heavy. Maybe she could rest, just for a little while.

No! Rayla told herself. Yes, she'd been patrolling all day, but she shouldn't be *this* tired. She'd forced down all that imaginary food earlier so she'd be alert for her patrol, but now it felt like her whole body was filling with sand. Something wasn't right.

And yet, it would feel so good just to lie down . . .

Rayla saw a blue rosebush nearby and quickly plucked a rose. She lay down, holding the rose tight, and closed her eyes.

Claudia quietly stepped into the glade, playing the last measures of the entrancing song on her ocarina. When she finished, she lowered the instrument and looked at her sleeping victim. Her heart swelled with the knowledge that she was close to the dragon egg. She would complete her mission, retrieve the egg, and make her father, Viren, so proud. But the chance to kill the elf who'd kidnapped the princes? She hadn't expected this little gem to fall into her lap. She motioned to her brother, Soren, who stepped out of the nearby brush.

Claudia nodded at Soren. "Do it," she whispered.

Soren just squinted at the elf, unresponsive to Claudia's command. Claudia rolled her eyes. She had offered Soren normal earplugs to block the sleep spell, but Soren had insisted on rolling up pieces of bread from an old sandwich. He said it was a "super-effective" trick he'd learned at sleepaway camp.

"Soren! You need to take your ear-ball things out!" Claudia whispered.

"What?" Soren asked a bit too loudly.

"Your ear bread!" Claudia whisper-yelled.

"I cannot hear you!" Soren practically shouted. He pointed to his ears. "I have the bread-plugs in! Told you they were better than any magic earplugs!"

Claudia moved closer to her brother and exaggerated her pronunciation so he could read her lips. "The sleep spell is over. You don't need the bread anymore."

Soren nodded. "Just tell me when the sleep spell is over so I can take out my bread-plugs."

Ugh. Did she have to do everything *herself?* Claudia reached over and plucked the wads from Soren's ears.

"It's over. The spell is done," she told him. "You don't need these anymore."

Soren seemed oddly annoyed. "Maybe I don't need them, Claudia. But I still want them."

She handed the two damp, mushy balls of bread to Soren, who joyfully popped them into his mouth.

Claudia just shook her head.

CHAPTER 4
OLD FRIENDS, NEW ENEMIES

Misty gray clouds speckled the nighttime sky in Katolis, all but covering up the moonlight. Viren passed through the dark courtyard swiftly on his way to the rookery. It was a place he rarely visited. Viren didn't care for crows, their loud cawing and their stinking messes.

Several fires lit the rookery halls. Viren wrinkled his nose when he saw dozens of cages dangling from the ceiling, each harboring a captive crow. Crow droppings dripped to the ground at regular intervals, making tiny *splat* sounds. Viren shuddered. Over the years, he had forced a servant (and occasionally Soren) to ferry his mail down to the filthy rookery. And so, Viren was at a bit of a loss when he arrived carrying a tray of four sealed scrolls to be mailed. What's more, his nerves were frayed—of all his concealments and deceptions, using the king's seal ranked among his most treacherous.

Nevertheless, when Viren saw a young man feeding the crows, he cleared his throat and spoke in a steady voice.

"Ahem. Crow Lord," Viren said.

But the man in the chamber didn't turn around or show any sign of having heard Viren.

"Crow Lord. Sir! You!" Viren boomed.

There was a long pause, and finally the man turned around. He was young—not much older than Soren—and wore his black hair slicked up and spiky. His nails were painted a shade of purple so dark it looked black. His tunic was pale, untucked, and covered in bird droppings. Viren looked at him disdainfully.

"Sorry, I heard you calling for the Crow Lord—he's not here right now," the young man said.

"Then who are you?" Viren asked with a withering sigh. In his experience, it was common courtesy to respond when there were only two people in the room.

"Oh! Well, I'm the Crow *Master*," the young man said eagerly. He said the word *master* slowly and with emphasis as if he were speaking to a child.

Viren stared at the Crow Master. *How different could this be from Crow Lord?*

"I'm sort of like the assistant Crow Lord. I recently got promoted," the young man said, clearly pleased with himself.

"Congratulations," Viren said. *He* could muster a few manners when necessary; what was wrong with this youth? "Are you able to send the mail, Crow Master?"

"Sure, sure, of course," he said in a high-pitched tone that suggested he had never sent the mail before.

Viren presented his tray of scrolls to the Crow Master. As he reached his hand out to receive the tray, the Crow Master suddenly backed away.

"Um. These seem to bear the king's seal." It was a statement, but his voice went up at the end as if he were asking a question.

"Yes," said Viren. He was prepared for the Crow Master to recognize the king's seal and maintained an easy expression.

"Um. Um. The king is ... you know," the young man stammered. Then he began to painfully spell aloud: "D ... E ... A ..." The young man looked both ways as if to check that no one else was listening before whispering the final letter: "D." He pushed the tray back to Viren and shook his head. "I can't send these."

Viren considered the best tactic to take with this apprentice and settled on a combination of empathy mingled with intimidation. "I understand your dilemma," he said, not unkindly. "You were recently promoted, and you are trying to do a good job."

"Yes. Yes, exactly!" the Crow Master said.

"But let me be clear, Crow Master," Viren said. "You will send these to the leaders of the other four kingdoms immediately." He paused and leaned in. "The king was very D-E-A-R to me, and I am fulfilling his dying wishes by delivering his final missives. If you dare refuse, you will face ... a consequence."

"Wh-what consequence?"

Viren felt confident that pointed ambiguity would create

more motivation here than any specific threat could. He narrowed his eyes, and responded, "You know."

The Crow Master's lower lip trembled at Viren's sudden change in tone.

"Now that I think about it . . . I'm just going to go ahead and take care of these for you," the Crow Master said.

"I thought you might," Viren said with a triumphant twinkle in his gray eyes.

Ouch. Rayla was starting to rethink this rose plan. But stabbing herself with a thorn was a small price to pay to avoid falling asleep and never waking up. Whenever she felt the magic of the strange music pulling her toward sleep, she pushed the point of the thorn that much harder into her hand to counteract it.

Rayla felt the presence of two bodies hovering over her. Then she heard that awful raspy voice. It was the dark mage from the castle—the girl who'd sent the smoke wolves after them. That mage must have been tracking the princes and followed them here.

Rayla made out more whispers, a male voice and clanking armor. The mage had brought some sort of warrior with her for extra protection. Rayla kept her eyes closed and her breath steady, hoping they would believe she had fallen for the sleep spell.

"Go on. Do it, Soren. What are you waiting for?" the dark mage asked. "She's a Moonshadow elf. And she kidnapped the princes. You just have to—"

"I know, Claudia," the male voice responded. "I've just never attacked someone who's sleeping before. It doesn't seem . . . sporting."

Sporting? Since when was killing a sport? What was wrong with this warrior? Rayla refocused on her breathing. She had to stay alive and protect the princes.

"You want me to *wake* her?" the mage asked. Rayla detected some exasperation in her voice.

Then silence. Rayla slit open her eyes just enough to see this Soren character raise his sword high in the air.

"Wake her," he whispered, poised to slice Rayla in two.

"And how long do you need her to be awake for it to be sporting?" the mage asked. "Ten seconds? Five?"

Adrenaline pumped through Rayla as she waited for the answer.

"One second," he said quickly. "One second is sporting."

Rayla tensed all her muscles.

"Okay, on three," the mage said. "One . . . two . . ."

In an instant, Rayla grabbed the swordsman by the ankle and yanked him off his feet. His weapon clattered to the ground. Rayla leaped to her feet and faced her attackers.

"But how did you resist the sleep spell?" the dark mage asked her.

Rayla smirked and opened her fist. "Oh, I used this lovely rose to help me stay awake," she said. Rayla buried her nose in the azure bloom and breathed deeply. A trickle of blood ran down her hand. "Hard to sleep with a thorn poking at you." Then she tossed the rose away and unfurled her blades.

Soren and Rayla circled each other like two wolves vying for a single alpha spot. Soren twirled his sword back and forth and over his head. He was clearly nimble and skilled.

"Are we gonna fight, or is this a talent show?" Rayla asked. She'd never seen such a ridiculous display of bravado. *How hard could it be to defeat this silly show-off?* Rayla took a deep breath and ran headlong at him. She knew she was faster than he was, especially with all that armor weighing him down.

But when they clashed, Soren's strength surprised her. He hurled his sword against her blades, and Rayla found herself backing up. She sprinted backward to get some space and then took a running leap, coming down on Soren from above.

But before Rayla's legs connected with his skull, Soren kicked her in the stomach. She flew backward, hands on her gut. She'd had the wind knocked out of her, but Rayla got back on her feet. She charged and swept at Soren's ankles with her blades, ready to sever them from his body.

Soren was ready for her—he jumped up and then landed on the blades, pinning them to the ground. Rayla struggled, but she could see Soren was off-balance. She did a backflip, freeing her blades, and he fell to the ground. Rayla hooked his sword with her blade and flung it away, disarming him. Then she pointed her blade at his heart.

"Gosh, I wish I had learned some of those sword acrobatics," Rayla said. "Too bad you won't be able to teach me after I've ended you with my blades." As soon as she finished this guy off, Rayla would crush that dark mage. The princes would never even have to know about the encounter.

But the mage was signaling to Soren, who was back on his feet and running at Rayla. He tackled Rayla hard and shoved her into an enormous puddle of thick, mucky mud. Rayla scrambled to her feet as the mage crushed something in her hands—was it a bird? A *live bird*?—and then flung the resulting goo on Rayla's blades. *Gross*, Rayla thought, as the mage began chanting.

"What's this goo?" she demanded.

"Just wait," Claudia whispered. "Latem eht taeh hcuot gninrub," she chanted. Rayla's blades began to glow orange. Soon, they were red hot. With a scream, she dropped her weapons. Before she knew what had happened, Rayla found herself staring at the point of Soren's sword.

"Any last words, elf?" Soren asked.

This idiot sure was dramatic. "Does 'hot mud' count as words?" Rayla asked.

"What do you mean?" Soren asked.

Rayla kicked some hot mud into Soren's face, blinding him. But before she could enjoy her moment of triumph, she heard a scream.

"STOPPPP!!!"

Callum had woken up with a jolt. He felt like he'd just fallen asleep, but there was a commotion outside, not far from the camp. He jumped out of bed and ran toward the noise. When he reached the caldera, he could barely believe his eyes. Claudia and Soren were here! And they were facing off against Rayla, who was kicking mud as hard as she could at Soren.

"STOPPPP!!! Don't fight each other! You're not enemies!" Callum yelled. He ran in between Rayla and Soren, waving his arms like a maniac.

To Callum's relief, everyone stopped fighting. Callum wondered what Claudia and Soren were doing here, but he didn't really have time to ask.

"We found you!" Claudia said. She ran over to embrace Callum.

"Hey, Callum, your friends tried to kill me," Rayla said.

Callum sidestepped Claudia's embrace and looked at her for an explanation.

"She kidnapped you! We were just trying to help," Claudia said.

"The elf threw mud in my face," Soren yelled at Callum. "Some got in my mouth."

Callum stifled a laugh. "Okay, okay, everybody! Knock it off a second. Just let me explain," Callum said. He avoided eye contact with Rayla. It was clear she was furious. Her arms were crossed and her lips pressed together so tightly they were white.

"First," Callum said, "Claudia and Soren, I don't know what you're doing here, but I'm really glad to see you."

"Are you kidding?!" Rayla shouted. "They attacked me. How can you be glad—"

"Buhp-buhp-buhp—Rayla, pipe down," he said. "Yeah, they're two of my oldest friends, and I am glad to see them. But I'm *not* glad to see you trying to murder my new friend, Rayla, who happens to be—"

"She's an elf!" Soren jumped in.

"Yeah…" Callum started. *How could he explain his new friendship?* "But she's a 'good' elf."

"What do you mean, 'but a good elf'?" Rayla asked Callum. "Do you know any bad elves?"

Callum continued to avoid Rayla's gaze. He had to be careful—he'd offended Rayla before when he'd told her his mistaken beliefs about elves.

"Callum, she kidnapped you and Prince Ezran. How can she be 'good'?" Claudia demanded.

Callum shook his head.

"There was no kidnapping; we went with her by choice. Listen, it's late—let's all just get some rest and cool off." Callum grabbed Rayla's mud-covered hands and pulled her onto dry land. "If in the morning I can't convince you that we're all on the same side here, you can fight each other then. Agreed?"

"Fine," Rayla said. "Agreed."

Callum looked expectantly at Soren and Claudia, who seemed to be communicating silently with each other.

Finally, Claudia nodded. "Fine," she said.

"Whatever. Guess we'll kill you in the morning," Soren said to Rayla.

"That's more like it," Callum said. He was very confident he could head off any violence in the morning. Well, fairly confident. Somewhat confident. "Come on, I'll show you guys where you can stay tonight." He walked briskly ahead of everyone else toward the moon camp.

After a moment, Claudia caught up with him. "That was very assertive, Callum," she said. "The way you handled that situation."

"Oh, I guess," he said, shrugging casually. He was all jittery though, like he always was when Claudia was around. It was a sort of pleasant uneasiness that he hadn't felt at all in the past week. Then he thought about Claudia's primal stone. She would probably want that back. It would be best to tell her right away that he had smashed it. Maybe she would forgive him once he explained he really had no choice, and that smashing the orb was the only way to save the dragon egg so Zym could hatch. Callum opened his mouth.

"Your hair's a little messy," Claudia teased, interrupting Callum's train of thought. She licked two fingers and tucked a stray wisp behind his ear. "There you go," she said.

Callum's brain froze, and his face got hot. *What was it he'd wanted to tell Claudia?* He hoped Rayla hadn't witnessed Claudia stroking his head. He glanced over his shoulder.

Rayla was staring at him.

Well, *glaring* was more like it.

CHAPTER 5
THE POWER
OF PANCAKES

I t was very early morning, but Viren had been awake for hours, thinking. Finally, he got out of bed and entered his study, shutting the door firmly behind him. He crossed to the sheep portrait and swung it open to the secret passage that led to his other, less official, study.

Harrow had given Viren the freedom to build his offices as he liked. "I want you to do your best work," he'd said. So Viren modeled the passage to his secret study after the stylings of his old mentor, Kpp'Ar. His mentor loved to integrate secrets and puzzles into architecture—he thought of it as a man-made magic.

A few minutes later, Viren was descending the spiral staircase into his secret study. Commander Gren stood chained to the wall near the entrance. Viren had almost forgotten that he'd imprisoned General Amaya's interpreter only a few minutes after promising the general that Gren would lead the search for the princes. A shadow of a smile passed over Viren's lips at the memory.

The prisoner had grown a layer of stubble over his goofy face, but otherwise looked no worse for wear.

"Good morning," Gren said.

Viren ignored him.

"I . . . I assume it's morning," Gren continued, stammering. "Come to think of it, I have no idea what time of day it is."

Viren sighed. Gren was the least of his problems. He continued down the hallway to the cell where the Moonshadow elf Runaan had been held.

"Good whatever time it is," he heard Gren call out after him.

Viren returned to the rune mirror in Runaan's former cell. When he'd stolen the human-sized mirror from the Dragon Queen's lair a few months ago, he'd known it was special and powerful. But it wasn't until Runaan, the leader of the elven assassins, refused to tell him the mirror's purpose that the weight of its power dawned on Viren. Had Runaan been too awed to reveal the mirror's true nature? Was he too horrified?

Whatever his reasoning, the Moonshadow elf had chosen a fate worse than death over revealing the mirror's secrets. Out of anger and frustration, Viren had captured Runaan inside one of his cursed coins, where the elf would remain trapped forever.

Viren glanced at Runaan's empty shackles, which were still locked shut. Then he swirled his hand at a candelabra, lighting all the candles simultaneously. He had a single goal for the day—to unravel the enigma of the mirror.

"Today is a special day, mystery mirror! It is the day you

finally reveal your secrets to me," he said to his own reflection. He lifted a small glass vial from his robes. Dark black fluid had settled at the bottom of the vial. "This true-sight serum will strip away all illusions and allow me to see you for what you really are."

Viren had hesitated to use this serum, but after numerous failed attempts to uncover the magic of the mirror, he had no other recourse. He held the last of an unusual liquid that he had inherited from Kpp'Ar. The liquid was a rare serum that the Oracles of Ophidia were said to have used long before the fall of Elarion in order to see through the illusions of the world. They would harvest venom from the fangs of eyeless vipers; and it was said that the venom had to be extracted on a moonless night. All it took was a single stray beam of moonlight to taint the serum and bring out its most dangerous qualities. Instead of clearing one's illusions, a dose of tainted serum would drive a person into a permanent, irrecoverable madness.

Viren removed the wooden stopper with care.

"Neddih si tahw laever eye gniees eurt," Viren chanted. The liquid immediately responded, bubbling and gurgling like hot tar. Viren grimaced. *Was something going wrong?* Was the serum supposed to become hot and boil like this? Perhaps this was a warning that the serum was tainted. But he knew this was his only chance—he was out of options.

Viren leaned his head back and pulled his lower eyelid down. He stared directly at the vial as he tilted it toward his iris. The moment a small black drop touched his eye, he felt a terrible searing sensation, and purple smoke hissed from his cornea.

Viren gasped in agony. Then he steeled himself and repeated the process on the other eye. The burning pain seemed to shoot from the pupil all the way through his skull. Viren could no longer retain his composure—he screamed and clutched at his face. Had he blinded himself?

After a few seconds, the pain began to recede. Viren blinked open his eyes. He wasn't blind, but his vision was fuzzy. There was a soft purple glow around the room, and Viren could make out his face in the mirror. His pupils were white. As his eyes adjusted, Viren saw a negative image of the room reflected in the mirror. This was unusual, but hardly the reveal he had hoped for. There was no new information! Viren hurled the empty vial on the ground, smashing it into tiny pieces.

"Nothing, nothing, nothing!" he shouted, pointing a finger at the mirror. "You're powerless, useless! I thought you were going to be something special . . . something important!"

Viren froze when he saw himself ranting in the mirror. Was *he* nothing?

He shoved the mirror away, and then grabbed a candelabra and hurled it across the room. The small flames licked at the books and scrolls scattered around the floor. The books began to catch fire. Viren watched the growing blaze with mild disinterest. After a few seconds, he closed his fist to extinguish the inferno.

The cell remained smoky as the last embers faded into darkness. But then Viren noticed the room was no longer completely dark. A dim light emanated from the mirror.

"What's this?" Viren said.

He walked around to look directly into the mirror. It no longer bore his reflection. From the dark room Viren now stood in, the shimmering glass revealed another room entirely. It looked like a parlor or library—shelves lined with books and plush chairs carefully placed around a marble floor.

Viren gasped. "What is this place?"

Soren had passed a fitful night's sleep in one of the small stone huts scattered about the grounds of the so-called Moon Nexus . . . whatever that was. *Quaint*, thought Soren, taking in the dome-shaped ceiling and the circular tables and windows.

Soren had spent most of the night alternating between trying to figure out how Callum had become friends with an elf and fantasizing about chopping off the head of said elf.

Soren glanced over at his sister. Claudia sat slumped at a half-moon-shaped granite table. It looked like she'd had even less sleep than he had.

"Hey, Clauds, did you know that the circles under your eyes are almost as dark as your hair today?" Soren asked. He wasn't sure what kind of response he'd been hoping for, but all he got was a grunt. "Well, anyhoo, I've totally figured out what's going on—why the princes have gotten so chummy with the elf." Soren couldn't believe he was just remembering about Moonshadow Madness. It was a horrible disease he'd learned about at that summer training camp his dad used to send him to. A counselor had told Soren all about how an elf could bite a human during a full moon and, from then on, the human would do the elf's bidding.

"Don't talk to me until I've had my hot brown morning potion," his sister snapped. Her eyes were still half-closed. Soren stood by politely as Claudia took a long sip from a steaming cup. Once her eyes had fully opened, she turned her gaze on Soren and sighed.

"Okay. Go on."

Soren couldn't wait to tell Claudia his theory. "She must have bitten them, and now they both have Moonshadow Madness!"

Claudia opened her eyes as wide as they would go. "What?!"

"I know it sounds crazy, but I've been thinking about it all night, and that's the most logical explanation," Soren said.

"Soren, I've never heard of Moonshadow Madness. Where did you hear about it?" Claudia asked.

Soren paused. "Camp," he said.

"AHAHAHA." Claudia laughed long and hard. Then she stood up and swatted Soren's shoulder. He was starting to feel less secure about his theory.

"Whatever. So you don't agree," he said. "We still need to do something—Dad gave us a mission."

"To bring the princes home," Claudia said, her face growing serious.

"Right," Soren said. Then he thought about the cryptic conversation he'd had with his father. The one where his father suggested it might not be so bad if the princes came home dead. "To bring them home," he repeated. "Unless a terrible accident occurs. Accidentally."

Claudia looked at him like he was speaking another language. "What?"

"Nothing. My point is . . ." Soren trailed off as he formulated a plan. "I have an idea." He snapped his fingers. "We should stuff the princes in sacks!"

"Soren! They're our friends," Claudia said. "We should try persuasion first. Use our words, not our muscles."

"So you're saying . . . we need to butter them up?" Soren asked.

Instead of responding, Claudia tapped her nose. She always did that when she had an idea, ever since she was a little kid. Soren found it endearing, but their dad thought it was stupid, so Soren usually pretended he thought it was stupid too.

But Dad wasn't here. He tapped his own nose and smiled at Claudia.

"Let's hear it," he said. "What's your brilliant idea?"

"Pancakes!" Claudia shouted. "Pancakes with butter."

A strange odor woke Rayla from a deep sleep. Then she relaxed. It was just the scent of buttery pancakes. By the time she got outside, the whole gang was already sitting at the Cursed Caldera's communal table. Callum's mage-friend, Claudia, was serving up the pancakes. Rayla scowled.

"Go on, try one," Soren said. "Or are you scared?"

Rayla wasn't scared. She was suspicious. Rayla moved a small stack of the golden cakes onto her plate. She stared at Soren as she stuffed a piece into her mouth. She didn't care what it tasted like. The sweet pancake melted like a soft cloud on her tongue.

"I have to admit . . . these are good," Rayla said.

Soren snickered.

"Impossibly fluffy, right?" Claudia asked.

"Exactly," Ellis agreed. "How do you get them so light?"

"The secret is separating the eggs, and beating the whites into a stiff meringue," Claudia said in her lecture tone.

"Wait, who are you?" Soren asked Ellis. "And what are you doing here?"

"I'm Ellis," she said. "I led the princes and Rayla up the mountain to meet Lujanne. I met her a couple of years ago. You see my pet?" Ellis pointed over toward an enormous wolf, who was gnawing on a large tree branch.

"Uh, that beast is your pet?" Soren asked.

"Yes, it's a wolf. Her name is Ava!" Rayla snapped. "Ava only had three legs and Ellis's dad wanted to kill her. So Lujanne created an illusion—a fourth leg so that humans would accept her."

"I only see three legs," Soren said, munching on the pancakes.

"The fourth leg only appears when she wears her Moonstone collar," Rayla said. "As I mentioned, the fourth leg is just an illusion. And you know what else isn't real?" Rayla said leadingly.

Everyone stayed silent, waiting anxiously.

"These pancakes." Rayla spat her half-chewed bite onto the ground. "There's something off about them."

"Oh, a hint of dark magic never did any harm," Claudia said, winking at Rayla.

Rayla seethed. She knew it. She wondered what creature had to die to make these pancakes so delectable.

"So," Claudia began, "now that we know you're not kidnapped, you guys should come back home. With the dragon egg, of course." She batted her eyes at Callum.

Of course. Claudia has an agenda. There was no way the princes would fall for this. Rayla caught Callum and Ezran looking at each other.

"Actually, there's no dragon egg," Callum said. Then he whispered something to Ezran, who immediately left the table.

"What?! What happened to the egg?" Claudia said. Her expression had changed from sugary sweetness to outright panic.

"You'll understand in a second," Callum said.

"Oh no," Rayla muttered. The princes were too trusting.

Ezran returned to the table holding Zym. Rayla watched in horror as Claudia put two and two together.

"Oh my, oh my, it's sooooo cuuuuute!" Claudia squealed. "It's a baby dwagon!" She stuck her hand out toward Zym.

Rayla jumped out of her seat and threw herself between Ezran and Claudia, who was about to pet the dragonling.

"Whoa—what happened to 'it's not an egg, it's a powerful weapon'?" Rayla said, recalling the argument they'd had in that dungeon in Katolis. Back then, Claudia seemed unable or unwilling to see the egg as anything more than a dark magic tool.

"Still true," Claudia said without taking her eyes off Zym. She seemed unconcerned by her own hypocrisy. "Someday, it could bring death and destruction raining down on all of us. But right now, he's so widdle!" Claudia reached out to stroke Zym's head but Rayla slapped her hand away.

"Well, get a good look, because we're headed to Xadia to return him to his mother," Rayla said.

"Rayla's right. We can't go home yet. This mission is too

important," Callum said. Rayla was relieved. Callum hadn't completely lost his head over this Claudia person.

Soren jumped in. "But the thing is . . . Callum and Ezran do need to come home," he said.

Rayla thought she saw Soren wink at Claudia.

"Because the king—your dad—really misses you," Soren said.

Rayla felt the blood drain from her face and nausea settle in her stomach. The king was dead. Soren had to know that. He was lying to the princes.

Rayla seethed. Why hadn't she just told them about the king? If she said something now, it would be her word against Soren's.

Claudia slammed the door to their hut closed. She couldn't wait to give Soren a piece of her mind. But when she spun around to yell at him, she saw him standing there, grinning like a fool.

"What are you so happy about?" Claudia sputtered.

"Did you catch that intense look I got from the elf?" Soren asked. "I think she's into me . . ." He stroked his chin thoughtfully.

"She's not *into* you, she's onto you!" Claudia said. She was trying to keep her voice down, but she was furious. "The princes' dad is dead, and you lied about it," she hissed. She felt terrible for Callum and Ezran. "They're our friends! It's wrong."

She thought Soren would back down immediately and apologize, but instead he flared up.

"You squash innocent creatures to make magic pancakes!" Soren shouted.

Claudia shrugged and shook her head. What did dark magic

have to do with lying to their friends? "How are we going to look Callum and Ezran in the eye when they find out we knew all along their dad was dead?"

"Look, all I know is I tried it your way," Soren said. He sat down in a moon chair and kicked his legs up on the table. "Using words . . . And now you don't like the way that turned out. Maybe it's time for my way—punching and stuff." He slammed a balled-up fist into his open palm.

"Ugh." Soren really did not get it. "No. Give me one more day to convince Callum to leave with us. I'm going to rely on something that's even stronger than muscles."

"Some kind of *magic* muscles?" Soren asked.

"*Trust.* You can think of it as a magic muscle if that helps you," Claudia said. Callum adored her. She knew she could get him on her side.

"Trust." Soren thought for a moment. "You know what, Clauds? I think trust building is a great idea." He drummed his fingers on the table mischievously.

Claudia didn't have time to wonder what he was up to.

"Glad you agree. I'm going to talk to Callum."

Claudia rushed out of the hut before Soren could change his mind.

"I'm telling you, we can't trust them," Rayla said. This was about the tenth time she'd tried to turn Callum against Claudia and Soren.

Callum was sick of hearing bad things about his friends, but he tried to understand where Rayla was coming from. "Look, I get it—you don't like Claudia. She tried to kill you. Twice! Once with lightning. Once with smoke wolves. And she put you to sleep so her brother could stab you. So maybe it was three times. But on the other hand . . ." Callum immediately realized he was not prepared with anything "on the other hand."

"Yes?"

"Uh . . . she made you pancakes!" He was grasping, and they both knew it. "All right, you're probably right not to like her. But remember, until today she thought you were trying to hurt me and Ezran."

"That's not it, Callum. I know they're lying to you. I know because . . ." Rayla suddenly became oddly serious and hesitant.

"Because what?" Callum asked. But before she could answer, he heard a light rap on the door.

"Knock, kno-ock." Callum smiled at the sound of Claudia's throaty voice.

Rayla narrowed her eyes at him. Callum rushed over to the door and opened it.

"Oh! Hi, Claudia," Callum said. "What are you doing here?" His stomach was in knots. Claudia might be looking for her primal stone. Which unfortunately no longer existed.

"Um, I wondered if you would go for a walk with me," Claudia said. "I really want to see the Moon Temple." She peeked over Callum's shoulder.

"Sure thing," Callum said. He felt a little relieved. He turned to look over his shoulder. "Rayla, can we finish this conversation later?"

"Whatever you say, Callum," Rayla responded.

Claudia grabbed Callum's hand and pulled him down out of the hut and along the path toward the temple.

"So, are you two . . . Did I interrupt something? Between you and . . . your elf?" Claudia asked, lifting her eyebrows slightly.

"What, me and Rayla? Nooo!" Callum said nervously. He didn't want Claudia to think there was anything romantic between him and Rayla. "I don't think of her that way. I think of her more as . . . an assassin. An assassin-friend," Callum said. It would be horrible if Claudia got the wrong idea.

"Oh, yeah, yeah, yeah," Claudia said. She waved one hand in the air. "No, I totally have friends like that." She said it casually, but she slowed down her pace and Callum could tell she was relieved.

"So, uh, you wanted to . . . talk?" Callum asked. For some reason, Callum illustrated the word *talk* by moving his hand like a puppet. Why did he always find himself doing strange and awkward things around Claudia? Probably better just to put his hands away for now. He shoved them in his pockets, but that felt awkward too. He scratched his head, and then his elbow. His elbow! Had it always been this pointy? Why, oh why, had he been born with such pointy elbows?

"Yes. I need to tell you about some things that happened back at home," Claudia said. "Good things, bad things . . ."

Good things, bad things, Callum thought. Claudia's primal stone was a good thing. He had broken it, which was a bad thing. Callum suddenly felt very anxious about this, and knew it was only a matter of time until Claudia discovered the truth. His anxiety was like a growing bubble, and Callum thought perhaps he could simply pop it. "I broke your primal stone," Callum blurted out.

"What did you say?" Claudia asked. She sounded truly shocked.

"Sorry, I broke it. I broke your primal stone. I've been feeling really terrible about it," Callum said. Popping the bubble had not released his anxiety.

"But how did you break—"

"I smashed it," Callum said. "Yup." He closed his eyes, hoping she wouldn't get angry with him. When he opened his eyes, Claudia was smiling.

"Hmm. Well—accidents happen," Claudia said.

"Oh, well . . . I did it on purpose," Callum said. Callum wanted to slap himself on the forehead. He didn't have to tell Claudia he smashed it on purpose. He was always doing that—going overboard with the information.

"I'm sure you had a good reason, Callum," Claudia said. She shrugged and brushed her long hair away from her face. Callum couldn't believe it—Claudia was still smiling at him. Suddenly, he could breathe again.

"I did! I really did have a good reason. You're the best, Claudia . . . I know this doesn't exactly make up for it, but I thought maybe you would let me show you around all the magic Moon places and stuff?"

"I would definitely let you," Claudia said.

"What?" Had he heard her right? "Great!" Callum said. "This way."

A few minutes later, they'd reached an incredible castle-like structure.

"This is the Moon Temple," Callum said. "Isn't it amazing? Like a work of art?" He wondered if Claudia would appreciate it in the same way.

The building was all silver, with a half dozen sparkling spires and grand gazebos nestled into the grounds. Everything was surrounded by a moat and waterfalls.

"It's incredible," Claudia said breathlessly. "Can you show me the inside?"

"Sure!" Callum said. He led her up hundreds of shimmering stairs, across the moat. They entered the temple through the central atrium, where light shone through moon-shaped windows illuminating green garlanded archways. Butterflies glided gently along. The towering walls of the atrium were made of granite, and hundreds of runes had been etched into them.

Callum looked over at Claudia. The ethereal beauty seemed to have caught her by surprise.

"This place is breathtaking," she murmured.

"Yeah, I wonder what all these runes do," Callum said, staring up at them. The runes glowed in the dim light.

"They're probably the most incredible spells," Claudia said. "I barely recognize any of them."

"I would love to try new spells," Callum said. "It's just too bad humans can't do magic without a primal stone."

Claudia was looking at him like he was nuts. "What are you talking about?" she asked. "We can do magic. I've shown you magic. You've seen what my dad can do."

Callum shook his head. "No, I meant primal magic. That's what I'm interested in now. Not, you know . . ." Claudia squinted back at him, waiting for Callum to finish his thought aloud. Perhaps she knew what he was suggesting, but she was going to make Callum say it. "Your kind of magic," he said, hanging his head.

"Oh? My kind of magic?" Claudia asked. Callum knew he hadn't phrased it right. And now he'd managed to offend Claudia.

"Dark magic," Callum whispered.

Claudia was frowning now.

She lowered her voice. "Do you always whisper when you're being judgmental?" she asked.

"Sorry, I didn't mean it that way," Callum said. He didn't want Claudia to feel bad. "It's just, I loved learning magic—and I feel sad now that I can't."

"But you can. If you want to," Claudia said. She removed her dark magic spell book from her bag and held it out to Callum.

He shook his head. "I want to learn primal magic," he said. "But you have to be born with that magic inside you." Claudia looked really annoyed. Maybe showing her around the Moon Temple had been a bad idea. "Let's go outside," he suggested.

"That's the great thing about dark magic," Claudia said, ignoring Callum's suggestion. "You just take creatures that are born with magic inside—and squeeze it out of them." Just then, an exquisite giant moon moth fluttered up and perched gently on Claudia's shoulder. For a moment, Callum feared Claudia might demonstrate her point on the delicate creature. Instead, she gently nuzzled it.

Callum gulped.

"You're doing it again, Prince Judgyface," Claudia said. "Look, here's how I think about it. Humans weren't born with magic— we were born with nothing—but we still found a way to do amazing things. That's what dark magic is really about."

Claudia was explaining things in a way that actually kind of made sense. Callum had sometimes felt like nothing himself, and he had sometimes felt powerless. Magic made him feel different. Maybe being able to do amazing things was worth it?

But deep down, Callum knew dark magic required killing. You had to kill a magic creature and take something that belonged to it naturally in order to do those amazing things Claudia was talking about. "I'm sorry. It's just not for me," Callum said.

Claudia shrugged.

"Come on," Callum said. "There's something else I want to show you."

Together, they descended into the Moonhenge. The moss-covered rocks looked a little shabby to Callum now that he was trying to impress someone. "There's not that much to see here," he said. "But I thought you might be interested."

Claudia was thrilled. "Ruins! I love ancient ruins!!"

"Really? Me too!" Callum said. He couldn't believe they had this interest in common. It was almost enough to forget about the dark magic disagreement. He watched, mesmerized, as Claudia ran to the middle of the Moonhenge and started spinning, her skirts twirling around her.

"If you close your eyes, you can imagine what it was like," she said softly. Her eyelids fluttered shut. "Everything was so magical back then . . . It's beautiful."

"Yeah . . . beautiful," he said. Forget the ruins. He couldn't take his eyes off Claudia.

She opened one eye. "Hey—your eyes aren't closed," she said. "No fair."

Callum felt his face turn red as a cherry. Then Claudia breezed over to him, tilted her head, crossed her eyes, and made a fish face. Callum relaxed a little. Claudia completed the face with an enormous snort. They both started laughing.

"You think this is great?" Callum asked. "Wait until you see the Moon Nexus."

"Let's go!" Claudia said. "Lead the way."

Callum started toward a nearby path, and then stopped.

"Actually, hold on. We should come back tonight after the moon rises," he said. It would be spectacular at night.

"Great. It's a date," Claudia said. She waved goodbye and headed back toward the huts, leaving Callum wondering at the possibilities the evening held in store.

CHAPTER 6
THE SLIDEY-SLING GO-FAST ROPE OF TERROR

The sun was getting high in the sky, and Soren realized he'd made little progress on his mission to capture (or was it kill?) the princes. Claudia had gone off to flex her "trust muscles" at Callum, so Soren would go to work on Ezran.

Out the window of his room, Soren could see the young prince playing with his little dragon. They appeared to be wrestling. The grumpy glow toad, the weird girl, and her three-legged dog were hanging out too. Soren left the hut and walked over to join them.

Soren had an idea. These kids looked up to him. Trusted him even. Maybe he could convince them to play a game...a dangerous game.

But would that be wrong?

You can't hurt Ezran, Soren, he said to himself. *He's just a kid. A little runt.* He stopped and turned back toward his hut. But as he started back up the path, he pictured his father's disappointed face. He could almost hear his father's voice in his head, scowling as he uttered a single word: *failure.*

Soren stopped in his tracks. He couldn't purposely hurt Ezran. *On the other hand, if there was an accident because Ezran was doing something dangerous and stupid . . . Well, that would be on Ezran.*

Soren turned around again and approached the young prince and his friends. Everyone stopped talking and looked at him. Soren plastered a big cheesy grin on his face. Then he tried to high-five Bait, who turned the other way. *Why was the grumpy gremlin rejecting him?* Soren felt a little hurt.

"I have an idea for something super fun," Soren said. The younger kids looked excited. "Super fun, but also incredibly dangerous in which some potential accidents may occur—but so fun! Who's in?!" He felt even less guilty about this plan now that he'd included a disclaimer.

"What is it?" Ezran asked.

"I'm in!" Ellis shouted.

Little kids were so gullible. Soren led Ezran and Ellis to an overlook high above the tree line. Soren hammered a peg into a tree with his scabbard. Then he wrapped a thick rope around the peg, coiled up the slack, and hurled the remaining rope across a ravine, aiming for a tall tree many feet below them.

"Hang on, gang," Soren said. "I'll be right back." Soren hurtled down a rocky path to get to the bottom of the ravine. When he located the other end of the rope, Soren wound it securely around a tree. He looked up. Ezran and Ellis were waving at him.

Soren waved, and then sprinted back up the hillside at top speed. It was too bad he hadn't thought through the strategy of this plan. Luckily, he was in excellent physical condition. He was nearly out of breath by the time he got to the top, but Soren knew he was in great shape and would never be truly out of breath. *There's always more breath where that came from,* he told himself in any situation that required prolonged physical effort.

Back up top, Soren found a plank of wood and attached it to the rope, like the seat of a swing.

"Hop on!" Soren shouted to Ezran.

Ezran sat gingerly on the wooden swing, holding Zym on his lap.

"So, you just zip across this line?" Ezran asked.

"Exactly," Soren said. "You just zip down the line!"

"What do you call this thing?" Ezran asked.

"You mean this line? That you zip on?" Soren thought hard for a moment. "I call it the slidey-sling go-fast rope."

"That is a good name," Ezran said. Then he looked at the peg in the tree. "Are you sure it's going to hold?"

Soren gave Ezran a look as if to ask, *Don't you trust me?*

"It's not me," Ezran said. "Zym is nervous. He's just a baby."

"It's totally fine," Soren said. "Would I steer you wrong? I'm planning to take a ride right after you. Plus, that little dragon needs to feel the air in his wings."

"Soren's right," Ezran said. "Zym, this is your chance to see what flying feels like."

Soren held the swing steady while eyeing the peg that held up the rope. It looked nice and loose.

"Whenever you're ready, guys," Soren said.

Ezran shoved off with his hands in the air, squealing with delight.

"Yayyyyyyyy!" Ezran shouted, his eyes wide and filled with joy.

Zym had closed his eyes to enjoy the wind on his face.

Immediately, Soren turned back to the peg—and nearly jumped out of his armor. Rayla was standing next to the tree, examining the rope. Her arms were crossed.

"Watchu thinkin' about?" Rayla asked. She smiled.

"Nothing," Soren said. "Watchu thinking about?"

"I'm thinkin' . . . you should go next," Rayla said.

Was Soren imagining things, or had Rayla's lips curled into an evil smirk? He gulped.

"Go ahead," Rayla said. "Unless you think it's not safe for some reason?" She was asking the question in that way people did when they didn't totally mean what they were saying.

"We made it!" Ezran yelled from down below. "But Zym never even opened his eyes!"

"Obviously, it's perfectly safe," Soren said. "Let me just, uh, double-check this peg." He hammered it into the tree with all his might.

"I bet," Rayla said. "Go on, now."

Soren thrust the sword in its scabbard over the zip line. Then he grabbed an end in each hand, creating a makeshift rig he could slide down on. He took a deep breath and then kicked himself off the ledge.

"Having fun yet?" Rayla called out to him. When Soren looked back at Rayla, she flicked open her blade and touched it to the rope.

Soren shuddered. That elf was scary. She gave Soren a mean smile and poked at the rope with her blade.

TWANG.

Soren was really starting to hate that elf.

Rayla ran to Callum's hut as fast as she could. She'd been right all along. Soren and Claudia were up to no good. If she hadn't shown up at that zip line when she did, who knows what would have happened to Ezran and Zym? She pushed open the door and entered without knocking.

"Callum! Callum! We can't trust Soren and Claudia," she yelled.

But the dorm was empty. Callum was gone. Probably on his date with Claudia. Rayla was too late.

This was a disaster. Callum trusted Claudia. It was Rayla who was the newcomer and the one who had to prove herself. Plus, there was the problem that she hadn't been completely honest with Callum. She wasn't as deceitful as Soren, who had outright lied about the king, but she wasn't any better than Claudia. She wanted to come clean to Callum, but she didn't know where to begin. Rayla needed advice.

"I'll ask Lujanne," she said out loud, heading for the Moon Temple.

She found Lujanne sitting in the atrium, meditating.

"Lujanne—I need your help," she panted.

"If wisdom is what you seek, I shall do my best to fake it,"

Lujanne said. Then she giggled and stood up. "That's an old illusionist joke."

"Right," Rayla said. She didn't have time for jokes. "I need my friend to trust me, but he doesn't. And I think it's my fault. I've been keeping a secret from him. Hiding the truth."

"Rayla, look at the moon," Lujanne said.

Obediently, Rayla gazed out a window at the half-moon.

"Light only falls on half its face right now, but that doesn't mean the other half isn't there," Lujanne said. "And it is the same with you—there are parts you keep hidden."

"But if I want my friend to trust me, don't I have to stop hiding the truth?" Rayla asked.

"Real trust is about accepting even the dark parts we will never know," Lujanne replied.

Rayla looked down. "No—no, I don't think that's right. Lying and hiding the truth aren't that different. Strong relationships need honesty—the full truth."

Lujanne chuckled. "Oh, now you sound like my first four husbands."

Rayla looked Lujanne in the eye. "I'm afraid of hurting him, but I owe him the truth. I can't leave Callum in the dark any longer—I have to tell him what happened to his dad."

"I'm glad my wisdom helped," Lujanne said with a wink.

"Ummmm, it didn't," Rayla said. "It was wrong." This was one nutty Moon mage.

"Was it wrong? Or was it just differently true?" Lujanne asked.

Rayla shook her head and walked out. She didn't have time for puzzles either.

Chapter 7
Shadows Holding Hands

Claudia had only a few minutes left before she had to meet Callum at the Moon Nexus. She was standing in front of the mirror, fiddling with her long dark hair. She couldn't decide if she wanted to leave it down or put it up. Did the white lily headband look ridiculous or charming? Dating was so stressful.

"Hey, are you doing something different with your hair? Some kind of a . . . braid-bag flower-dealie?" Soren asked.

"Yeah, it's cute—so what?" She tried to ignore Soren's narrowed eyes and decided once and for all she would wear her hair up, with the flowers. Then she dashed out the door and hurried to the Moon Nexus. She didn't want to keep Callum waiting.

Claudia steeled herself. This was a date—sure—but she planned to tell Callum about King Harrow. Hurting him would be unbearably difficult, but she had to show Callum she was a true friend. She twirled her hair anxiously, playing out the scene in her mind.

"Hi, Claudia," said Callum, smiling.

His hair was slicked back and he smelled clean. This date was really going to happen.

"Hi," Claudia said softly. Callum's face fell a little, and Claudia realized she had sounded too serious—maybe even off-putting. She smiled at him.

"The moon is so bright tonight. You can see our shadows," Callum said. He pointed to the ground, and Claudia followed with her eyes. Their shadow hands were almost touching. Callum moved his hand a little bit so that their shadows were holding hands.

Claudia sucked in her breath. Was he doing it intentionally?

"Hey. Did your shadow hand just hold my shadow hand?"

"Did it?" Callum said, a little mischievously.

Claudia laughed and grabbed Callum's real hand. "Come on. Take me to see the Nexus!"

"We're almost there," Callum said. "This way." He led Claudia up the path to a small stone overlook.

"Wow. It's like the moon, but more . . . here," Claudia said.

Luminous green trees surrounded the entire lake, enclosing it protectively. The stars twinkled in the water, and the reflection of the half-moon spread out like a silky white sheet across the lake. It was very romantic.

"So, Claudia," Callum said.

"Yeah?" she asked.

"I've known you for so long," Callum said.

It was kind of a cheesy comment, but Claudia knew how he felt. "Yeah, me too," she said.

"Well, you've known yourself your whole life," Callum said.

"HAHAHA." Sometimes Callum said the most ridiculous things. She loved him for it. But Claudia could tell he was feeling a little embarrassed, so she gave him a playful pinch on the arm. "Callum, you always make me laugh," she said.

"You make me laugh too," Callum said. "And you make me think. You make me see the world in a different way."

Claudia looked at him and smiled.

"Wow," Callum said. "I . . . I suddenly don't have any more words."

"That's okay. We can just . . . be here. Without words," she said.

Callum nodded. Claudia sat very still until she saw Callum close his eyes. She did the same thing. Slowly, she started to lean in toward him.

Claudia could feel Callum's warm breath on her face, and she breathed in deeply. She wanted to kiss him like she'd never wanted anything before.

Callum's face drew a little closer. But as much as she wanted to, Claudia couldn't kiss him. It felt too much like a betrayal. She pulled back abruptly.

"Wait, Callum. I need to tell you something."

CHAPTER 8
WEEP-RIDDEN

The half-moon shimmered high above the Moon Nexus, but Callum no longer saw the beauty in it. His head was down as he walked back toward the huts, his shoulders shaking with silent sobs of disbelief at the news of his stepfather's death.

And there, standing in front of his dorm, was the last person he wanted to see. Rayla. *That liar.*

"Callum?" she said. "I'm so glad you're here. I need to tell you something," she began.

Callum held up his hand to stop her.

"I know. I know what happened. He's gone. Claudia told me."

"Oh no," Rayla said.

Callum turned around and started to pace. Rayla was following him silently, and Callum was glad he didn't have to look at her. He didn't know if he could be nice to her right now.

"Callum, I'm sorry," Rayla called out. "I tried to tell you the king was dead."

The king. Callum scoffed. Rayla didn't know anything. "My stepdad!" Callum yelled. "He was more than just the king to me."

"Your stepdad. I know," Rayla said. "I really tried, but I could never find the right way. And whenever I tried, I messed it up, and the next time was harder, until . . ."

"Rayla, just stop. I can't talk about this right now," Callum said. She sounded sorry, but he didn't really care. "All I can think about is how I'm going to tell Ezran our father is gone." Ezran was just a few years older than Callum had been when their mother had died. Callum knew from experience there was no good way to break this news to him.

"I'm sorry, Callum. I'm so, so sorry," Rayla repeated.

But Callum ignored her. He started walking faster, trying to leave her behind.

His stepfather had tried to prepare him for this moment. *The letter!* Callum suddenly remembered the letter King Harrow had given him, the letter Callum had misplaced. The king had given Callum that letter and told him only to open it if he died.

"Stupid!" Callum shouted at himself. How could he have lost something so important? Now he would never know his stepfather's last words to him. He wanted to be near his little brother. He glanced over his shoulder and was relieved to see that Rayla was no longer following him.

Callum's heart ached when he glimpsed Ezran sleeping

peacefully on his bed, the moonlight shining on his coffee-colored skin. For a moment, Callum stood in the doorway, watching the rhythmic rise and fall of Ezran's chest. Then he sat down on the bed and reached to wake him, but Ezran rolled over in his sleep.

Callum lowered his hand. He would let Ezran have one last night of dreamless sleep. But there would be no sleep for Callum. He lay down near his brother and tried to picture his stepfather's smiling face.

"Well, it's about time," Soren said when Claudia walked in. "Did you have fun on your little date?" Soren had been bored senseless. He'd invented a little game where he timed how long his sword could spin on its point. Three seconds. Three seconds was the time to beat.

But Claudia didn't reply. She just sighed as she pulled the wilting flowers out of her hair. Soren shook his head. His sister had her mysterious ways.

"Clauds? Hey, anybody there?" Soren asked. Then he took a closer look and realized she was crying.

"Holy swords. What happened? What did he do to you?" Soren yelled.

"Soren, relax," Claudia said. She put one hand on his shoulder. "You don't have to get so worked up. Nothing happened . . . Callum would never hurt me."

"Oh," Soren said. He was confused. He sheathed his sword. "Then how come you're all . . . weep-ridden?"

"That's not an emotion, Soren," Claudia said. "I told Callum about the king. It was super emotional."

"You told him?" Soren couldn't believe it. "Well, did it work? Is he going to come back with us?"

"I think he might. He's really mad that Rayla didn't tell him. I don't think he trusts her anymore."

"Um, well, good work," Soren said. He felt a little bad for Claudia. "Are you okay?"

"Yeah, Soren. I'm going to be fine," she said.

"Because . . . you're my sister, as you know. I'm always here for you . . . to punch someone, or whatever you need," he assured her.

"I know," said Claudia, trying to smile.

"Good," Soren said. "We still have to bring the princes back with us. Whatever it takes—whatever happens. I need to know that all this emotion-y stuff won't get in the way of doing what we came here to do." No matter what, Soren needed Claudia to be in shape for this mission.

"It won't get in the way," she said. "I can do it."

"Atta girl," Soren said. He gave Claudia a little punch on her arm. "You're such a daddy's girl. You'd never let the old guy down."

CHAPTER 9
KING HARROW'S LETTER

Ezran opened his mouth in an enormous yawn and peeked at the early morning sky. It was pink. Good. That meant there was still time to catch a little more sleep. He flipped over onto his stomach. But then he saw Callum's brown hair poking out over the side of his bed. What was his brother doing sitting on the floor?

"Callum?" Ezran asked sleepily. He leaned up on one arm to make sure he was seeing things correctly.

"Morning, Ez," Callum said.

"I had another weird dream," Ezran said. "I was running from that giant hippo . . . the one made of taffy, remember?"

"I think so?" Callum said.

Ezran shook his head at Callum's poor memory. The taffy hippo was one of the strangest recurring dreams he'd ever had.

"Only this time, there was someone riding on the hippo's back. When I turned around, I saw it was the baker! You know... Barius, the one who doesn't like me!"

"He'd like you if you stopped stealing his jelly tarts," Callum said.

Ezran chose to ignore his brother's remark.

"The baker said I was wanted for crimes against dessert," he continued. "And to make the hippo chase me, the baker told him I was jelly-filled!"

Ezran didn't know anyone else who dreamed about hippos— let alone ones made of taffy. He desperately wanted Callum's help figuring out this dream.

"I was a pastry fugitive, Callum," Ezran said. "It was terrible. And the worst part was... the baker was right." Ezran's eyes filled with horror. "I was light, flaky, crispy. I was delicious. What do you think it means?"

Callum's eyes were watery and red and tired looking.

"Ez, let's go for a walk," he said.

"Sure," Ezran said. Maybe Callum could analyze the dream more clearly once they were outside.

The two brothers started out along the Moon Temple grounds. Ezran was still waiting for Callum's analysis.

"So, Ezran, I wanted to talk to you about... life. And growing up. And how sometimes there are... changes... you don't expect..." Callum began.

Ezran raised an eyebrow. What was up with Callum? Where was he going with this? Callum had been out late with Claudia last night—maybe he wanted to talk to Ezran about dating.

Ugh. This was going to be so awkward. Better get it over with.

"Is this the talk about 'sandwiches'?" Ezran asked.

"Sandwiches?" Callum asked.

"Yeah, remember a few nights after we left the castle and you were hugging that loaf of bread while you were sleeping and, um, telling the bread how you felt about it? Then when I asked what your dream was about, you said, 'Peanut butter sandwiches.'" Ezran knew that peanut butter sandwiches were Claudia's favorite, but he decided not to mention her specifically. "You said one day when I was older we would have a heart-to-heart talk about 'sandwiches.'"

Callum jumped. "No! No, not that! Definitely not that."

Callum cleared his throat, and Ezran waited with growing impatience.

"Ezran," Callum said, "for a long time, I treated you like a little kid. And that wasn't fair. You've grown up so much, and I'm really proud of you."

"Oh. Yeah . . ." Ezran said. Ezran was pretty sure he could see where this conversation was going now. Callum was disappointed that Zym hadn't learned to fly yet. This was going to be a pep talk.

"But when you grow up, sometimes . . . you must face things you're not ready for," Callum said.

Ezran stared at the ground. "I know," he said.

"You . . . know?" Callum asked. He seemed surprised and maybe a little relieved. Ezran decided to take the pressure off his brother and own up to his shortcomings.

"I know everyone's counting on me to teach Zym to fly," Ezran said. "And flying is just the beginning. Someone's gonna have to teach Zym all the things he's supposed to do. Everything he's supposed to be." Ezran paused and looked up. Phoe-Phoe was flying in circles high above the Moonhenge ruins, her fluorescent blue feathers lighting up the early morning sky. It was hard to imagine Zym ever soaring through the air like that.

"And he's meant to learn it all from a big, strong king of the dragons! But he doesn't have that. All he's got is . . . me," Ezran concluded.

He felt Callum's hand on his shoulder.

"Hey, don't be so hard on yourself, Ez," Callum said. "I know it'll be tough, but no matter what, you've got us. Me, and Rayla— probably Bait. We're all here for you."

"Thanks, Callum. That means a lot," Ezran said. "But I really wish Dad was here."

Ezran was surprised when Callum didn't immediately agree—wasn't it just yesterday he'd sent their father a letter? But Callum had suddenly tensed when Ezran mentioned their dad.

"I keep wondering what would HE do? What would HE say to Zym? When I was little and I wasn't listening to him, Dad would say . . . 'Ezran, you're a handful!'" Ezran puffed up his chest, put his hands on his hips, and executed his very best impression of his father trying to be stern. He was pleased to see Callum giggle.

"So," Ez continued, "I tried that with Zym. I said, 'Azymondias, you're a handful!' But Zym doesn't understand. He doesn't even have hands." Ezran sighed. "I guess I just miss Dad. He'd know what to do . . . you know?"

But again, Callum didn't say anything about their dad.

"Callum? What's wrong?" Ezran asked. He locked eyes with his big brother, trying to read the thoughts in his mind.

Then Callum knelt down and hugged Ezran tight. "Nothing, Ez," he said. "I just really miss him too."

Back in Runaan's former cell, Viren hastily swept up the ashes and singed scrolls and papers from the fire he had started. He growled under his breath, angry with himself for his lack of control. It was difficult to clean the room as carefully as he desired in the dark, but he had no choice—the nature of this mirror appeared to be that its dim world was only visible to Viren if he kept his side of the mirror even darker. Every few seconds, he glanced back at the mirror, afraid he might miss something. But the view remained the same—a cozy study with many bookcases, an unlit fireplace, and a desk. The room was meticulously clean and tidy, but there was no sign of any inhabitant.

When he finally finished sweeping, Viren yanked a nearby chair in front of the mirror and sat down on it with a huff. He removed a tall candle from his cloak and sparked a flame with his fingertips. *Why carry matches when a quick spell was just as effective?* He used the flame to soften the base of the candle and drip a few drops of wax onto the arm of the chair. Then he pressed the candle upright onto the melted wax, making sure it was secure.

With another snap of his fingers, Viren lit the candle's wick, turned to the mirror, and leaned forward to watch. A single candle's light was all the faintly glowing world beyond the mirror would allow—anything brighter and Viren would find himself gazing at his own reflection.

For hours, Viren sat there, staring at the room. As exciting as it was to extract this secret from the mirror, watching an empty room was becoming dull. Viren rubbed his eyes and held back a yawn.

COUGH COUGH COUGH.

Viren woke in a choking fit. The candle had gone out, and he was breathing puffs of smoke. When he saw the melted heap of wax on the chair, he realized he must have been asleep for hours. He waved the smoke away from his face and ran his hands through his hair. Something flickered in the corner of his eye.

Viren snapped to attention and lurched toward the mirror. There had been some barely perceptible movement in the mirror's room. But Viren had missed it. *Did a door close? Did someone leave? Why did he have to fall asleep?*

"Was there someone there...?" Viren said to the mirror. He peered even closer, looking for even the smallest hint of change in the room. His eyes scanned the bookcases, chairs, and floor. Then he saw it. A flame was now blazing in the parlor's fireplace!

Callum felt like a coward. He'd had the chance to tell Ezran about their dad, and instead of doing the right thing, he'd allowed the words to sit frozen on his tongue. Callum loved

Ezran with all his heart, yet he couldn't bring himself to cause pain to his little brother. They had a long journey ahead to return Zym to his mom. Maybe it simply wasn't necessary for Ezran to carry that pain and grief across the world with him? Or was Callum just making excuses to avoid a painful conversation?

Callum would have to carry the sorrow for the both of them. He remembered how his stepdad had told him about his mother's death—gently and kindly. He realized now just how brave King Harrow had been.

It's not Rayla's fault, he reflected. *I have to find her and tell her I understand.*

Callum wandered over to the outdoor area near the Moon Temple, where Rayla was sitting alone at a table, her head resting on her folded arms. It looked like she might have spent the night there.

Callum wasn't angry anymore. He stood by Rayla awkwardly for a moment, and then sat down and touched her elbow. She looked up at him.

"I couldn't do it," Callum said. "I couldn't tell him."

"Callum . . ." Rayla turned to face him.

"And I understand why you couldn't tell me," Callum said. "When you care about someone, it's hard to hurt them. Even when what you're telling them is the truth."

"I still should've told you," Rayla said. "You had the right to know."

"I think maybe I did know," Callum said. "Deep down, I knew. I just hoped . . . if I didn't think about it, maybe somehow it wouldn't be true. But he's gone. He's really gone." Callum's insides churned. He couldn't hold back the tears any longer.

Rayla grabbed him and pulled him into a tight hug.

He relaxed into her embrace, thinking about how hard yesterday must have been for her.

Then Callum remembered something. Soren had said King Harrow wanted them home. Was Soren just trying to protect their feelings the same way Rayla was?

"Wait," Callum said, pulling away. "So yesterday, when Soren said that Dad wanted us home, he was lying. And you knew he was lying."

"Yeah. He lied," Rayla said. "I didn't know what to do—I thought if I told you then, you would just think it was my word against Soren's. And you've known Soren much longer than you've known me."

"Well, maybe Soren was also trying to protect our feelings," Callum ventured. He avoided Rayla's gaze while he defended Soren. Even so, he could feel her incredulous look boring through his body.

"Oh, right," Rayla said. "He definitely seems like a thoughtful, sensitive, feelings-protecty kind of guy. He's a softy, that one."

"Yeah, you're right, that's not really his style," Callum said. It was getting hard to see Soren's side of the story.

"Look, Callum. We don't have a choice anymore. We've got to leave. And we've got to do it now—get as far away from Claudia and Soren as we can before they even realize we're gone. They're up to something dangerous."

"Whoa, wait a minute," Callum said. He held up both hands. "They're still my friends."

"But they lied to you," Rayla said. Her voice was fierce. "You don't owe them a polite goodbye."

"Soren lied to me," Callum said. "But Claudia told me the truth. We can't just leave them."

"Leave?"

Callum whipped his head around in time to see Claudia at the door of her hut.

"But where would you go?" she asked.

Callum felt a little rattled. Claudia was walking slowly toward him and Rayla, with Soren not far behind.

Callum glanced at Rayla. She nodded.

"Yeah. I'm sorry," Callum said. He spoke only to Claudia and ignored Soren. "We've decided. We're leaving today. This mission, taking the Dragon Prince back to Xadia, it's the most important thing we'll ever do. We can't go home with you." He waited for them to argue, but Claudia just nodded.

"Are you sure?" Soren asked. "Your dad is gonna be really disappointed—"

"Soren! What is wrong with you?!" Claudia asked. She slapped him on the shoulder. She seemed genuinely furious with her brother.

"I'm just trying to—"

"Don't! Stop it, Soren!" Claudia shouted.

"Ugh, fine. Do what you want," Soren said. He turned away and stormed off through the trees.

"I'm sorry about him," Claudia said. "But before you go . . .

Callum, I have something I need to give you. In private."

"Oh. Uh, all right," Callum said. This was a surprise. He could sense Rayla's impatience growing.

Claudia smiled at Callum, and he felt the butterflies in his stomach again.

"Come with me," she said.

"I'll meet you in a few minutes," Callum told Rayla. He followed Claudia quickly before Rayla had a chance to stop them.

Claudia went straight into her hut, but Callum lingered by the door.

"So, closed door? Open door? What's, uh, what do you—"

"Closed is fine," Claudia said.

"Closed. Good. Okay." Callum shut the door and waited.

"I have something for you. Something I wanted to give you last night, actually."

Callum's thoughts raced. He closed his eyes and leaned forward just slightly, instantly feeling as nervous as he had been in the moonlight beside the lake. Then he heard what sounded like Claudia digging around in her bag.

"Where is it?" she said, sounding frustrated. "Aha!"

Callum opened his eyes. With a huge smile on her face, Claudia presented Callum with a scroll—a scroll bearing the king's seal. It was Callum's lost letter from his stepdad.

"Where did you find that?" Callum asked, his eyes wide. For the first time since he'd learned about his stepfather's death, he felt a flicker of hope. He thought he'd never see the letter again.

Callum took the letter from Claudia's outstretched hand and gently ran his fingers over the unbroken royal seal.

"That's . . . my letter. From him," Callum said. "You didn't open it?"

"Why would I do that?" Claudia asked as if it had never occurred to her. "It's for you."

Callum smiled and nodded. Even if Soren was a jerk, he knew he could trust Claudia.

"Though, I mean, for the record, I could have opened it and easily resealed it with magic," Claudia said. "My kind of magic," she added with a wink.

"Wait—did you?" Callum asked.

"Did I?" Claudia said with a mysterious smile. "We may never know! But no."

Now Callum was confused. A moment before he had trusted Claudia completely, but now he thought there was a . . . 5 percent chance she had read the letter? Maybe a 10 percent chance.

"So, are you going to open it?" Claudia asked.

Callum stared down at the letter. "No. I don't think I'm ready yet. But thank you, Claudia."

"You're welcome. So . . . I guess this is goodbye," she said.

Callum looked up from the letter. Without saying anything, he hugged Claudia and then turned to leave. It was time to press on to Xadia.

"Wait, Callum," Claudia said.

He paused, his hand on the door, his back to Claudia. "What is it?"

"I just have one thing I want to ask you," she said.

CHAPTER 10
THE MAGE
IN THE MIRROR

G et in the backpack, Zym," Ezran commanded in his most serious voice. But the dragonling slipped out of Ezran's grip and scampered away.

Callum had just burst in the door and announced it was time to get packing for Xadia if they were going to make it out by the next morning. Three seconds later, he'd disappeared again. Callum was always doing this—he never gave Ezran any warning. Ezran was frustrated—it had been hard enough lugging that heavy egg around in his backpack, but a live dragon was a different story altogether. Ezran had gingerly tried to push Zym into his pack headfirst. Zym wiggled and squirmed, twisting out of Ezran's grasp. Ezran found it impossible to keep the bag open while guiding Zym's flailing legs into the bag.

"Zym! Come on! You loved it in there as an egg," Ezran coaxed.

Eventually, with a little more coaxing and a lot more squirming, Ezran managed to stuff Zym into the bag.

Rayla poked her head through the hut door and stared at the brown sack on the floor.

"Rayla, look," Ezran said. "He can't fly yet, but he should be safe in my bag."

"There's nothing in there, Ezran," Rayla said.

"What?" Ezran looked down. The bag was empty. Zym was on the other side of the room!

"Hey, Zym! How'd you do that?" Ezran asked. He looked in the bag again. This time, Bait poked his head out. "Bait! You're not helping."

Rayla laughed.

Then Callum came in, holding something in his hand. He avoided eye contact with Rayla and Ezran.

"How was Claudia?" Rayla asked in a not-so-nice voice. "Let me guess. Once she had you alone she tried to manipulate you and convince you to go back home again?"

Ezran frowned. He hated when Rayla and Callum fought about Claudia. He tried to focus on pulling Bait out of the bag. But the glow toad had made himself quite comfortable at the bottom of the sack.

"No. She didn't try to manipulate me," Callum said. "Actually, Claudia really understands how important it is to get Zym back to Xadia."

Uh-oh, Ezran thought. *Here's where Rayla gets super defensive.*

"Oh. That's unexpected," Rayla said. "But good."

Ezran was relieved to hear Rayla back down.

"In fact, she understands it so well that she and Soren want to come with us," Callum said to Rayla.

"That's great!" Ezran said. "Maybe Claudia can help me get Zym in this sack with some magic." The more people they added to their journey, the safer Ezran felt. Soren was amazingly strong and Claudia could do anything with magic. He didn't understand why Rayla looked so unhappy with this turn of events.

"WHAT?" Rayla asked Callum. "That's the worst possible plan."

"How is it bad?" Callum asked. "They're offering to help."

"Or . . . it's a trap," Rayla said, looking Callum in the eye. "I know you trust them," she said to Callum. "But if we let them come with us, by the time we know the truth, it'll be too late."

Ezran froze. It seemed like Callum and Rayla were having a secret conversation even though he was in the room. "Why wouldn't we trust Claudia and Soren?" he asked.

"Do you understand? We'll lose everything," Rayla said to Callum.

"So, what are we supposed to do? How can we figure out if it's help or a trap?" Callum asked.

"I do have an idea," Rayla said. "Will you follow my lead?"

"I did it!" Ezran yelled. He'd finally stuffed that stubborn dragon into the sack. The bag bulged and strained as Zym struggled inside it. But Callum and Rayla weren't paying attention.

"I'll follow your lead," Callum said to Rayla.

Ezran wasn't sure what was going on, but he decided that if Callum was following Rayla's lead, he would follow Callum's. Not that either one of them had given him any choice in the matter.

Just then Zym poked his head out of the flap and gave Ezran a big goofy dragon smile. "See! I told you it would be nice and cozy in there," Ezran said.

Rayla thought Callum was delusional about Claudia, but she also knew she still had to earn his trust. Callum didn't seem angry anymore that she had kept the king's death a secret. Nonetheless, she was going to have to prove that she was a better friend than Claudia. Luckily, Rayla had an idea—she just needed a little bit of help making it happen.

"Knock knock," Rayla said, rapping on the wall of the Moon Temple. She could see Lujanne sitting there, legs crossed, eyes closed. She looked like she was in some sort of trance. Meditation was the one subject in Rayla's assassin training that she'd never been any good at. Runaan had always said meditation was about achieving focus, and that the goal was to achieve the unflinching momentum and singularity of purpose of the point of an arrow. Runaan's joke about Rayla meditating was that she had achieved the singularity of purpose of a wet noodle.

"Knock knock," she said to Lujanne at a volume that would break even the most transcendent trance. Rayla caught one of Lujanne's eyes open the tiniest sliver. She tapped her foot loudly on the temple floor.

"Can I help you?" Lujanne asked, opening her second eye. She looked annoyed.

"I'm sorry, were you meditating or something?" Rayla said. She opened her eyes wide and batted her lashes innocently.

"I *was*," Lujanne said.

"So, you're done. Good," Rayla said. She walked closer to Lujanne. "We're leaving. Heading out for Xadia. And the other humans—Soren and Claudia—they're coming with us."

Rayla wasn't sure, but she thought she caught Lujanne raise an eyebrow.

"And you're unhappy with that," Lujanne said. "Moonshadow elf to Moonshadow elf."

Rayla nodded. "Callum trusts them, but I know they're hiding something."

Lujanne looked up at the sky pensively. "You see, Rayla, to every truth, there is a dark, shadowed side. Consider the half-moon—"

"You already did this," Rayla said. "You gave me this speech before."

"Oh. Have I?" Lujanne said. She didn't look the least bit embarrassed.

"Yeah," Rayla said. "I think I've got all the moon-themed advice I need."

"Oh," Lujanne said. She sounded a little disappointed. "Moon themes are really all I've got . . . unless you're in need of a spooky monster or some fake food."

"Actually," Rayla said. "There *is* something you can help me with along those lines. An illusion would help me reveal Claudia's and Soren's darker side."

"Whatever I can do," Lujanne said.

It was late at night, but Viren was drinking cup after cup of hot brown morning potion. He lifted the cup to his lips with shaking hands and sipped the potion wearily. Viren had been up for what seemed like days, but he would not rest until he had learned more about the room in the mirror.

And then he saw something. In the mirror, the light beneath the door went dim, and the doorknob began to turn. Viren stared without blinking. Finally, the door swung open, and a mysterious stranger entered the room.

Viren sucked in his breath and blinked his eyes. He'd been up so long he thought he might be hallucinating. But the figure didn't disappear. It glided into the room. A sweeping, midnight-blue cloak decorated with shimmering stars and gold trim draped its shoulders.

The figure's face was obscured from Viren. It quickly made its way over to a bookcase. As it selected a single volume, the cloak slipped back, revealing an arm covered in twinkling star tattoos. Viren watched, rapt. He held his breath and leaned forward in his chair. But once the figure had the book, it turned to leave the room. Viren stood up, spilling his hot brown morning potion.

"No, no, no—come back here!" he yelled. He couldn't let this mystery slip away.

But the figure was gone. Viren slid back into the chair, defeated.

"Who are you?" he asked the empty mirror.

CHAPTER 11
THE TRAP

Soren joined the crew gathered near the Moon Temple. Claudia was there with Lujanne and Ellis. Ava the three-legged dog stood nearby, panting. *Where were the prince and step-prince?* Running late, Soren supposed. He decided to fill the time with some intense preparatory stretches.

"Where are Callum and Ezran?" Claudia asked. Soren lunged forward, feeling a burn in his quadriceps.

"Oh! They'll be here soon," Lujanne said. "I think Ezran's still packing up his dragon."

Figures, Soren thought. The crown runt wasn't strong enough to control a tiny dragon. He pulled one arm across his chest and breathed into the stretch.

"It has been a pleasure to have you all here," Lujanne said. "I truly have enjoyed you all sneaking past my defenses and desecrating this sacred place these past few days. It will be lonely—quiet, but lonely—without you."

Soren wasn't sure what "desecrating" meant, but he felt a little bad for the lonely mage who appeared to love their company. It seemed like the wolf girl felt bad for her too because she jumped up into Lujanne's arms.

"I'll miss you so much, Lujanne," Ellis said. Lujanne knelt to hug her.

"Ellis, you will always be welcome here," Lujanne said. The wolf barked happily. "And you too, little one," Lujanne said, patting the enormous wolf on its fluffy head. "And here's the Moonstone collar I gave you so long ago." Lujanne pulled out a thick blue collar decorated with half-moon jewels and slipped it around the wolf's neck. A sparkly blue stone hung from the center of the collar.

"You don't need the illusion any longer," she said to Ava. "But I hope it serves as a reminder that someone is always looking out for you." As she removed her hands from the collar, it glowed a brilliant gold, pulsing with magic.

Soren stopped stretching—he wanted to see the wolf's fourth leg grow back. But nothing happened. Moon magic was boring.

When Soren looked up, he saw the princes approaching.

"Finally," Soren said.

"Okay! Everyone's here now! We can all hit the road!" Rayla said.

Even though Soren hated Rayla, her excitement was a little contagious. He jumped up and down a little. "All right! Time to go to the magical land and do whatever!"

Claudia and Soren walked behind the princes, Rayla, Ellis, Ava, and Bait. As they descended the slope of the great caldera, the trees thinned out and the mountain's cool mist dissipated. When she was sure the others were out of earshot, Claudia turned to her brother with an expectant look.

"So, you're ready to do this the Soren way, right?" he asked her. He flexed a bicep in Claudia's face, and she winced.

Claudia was resigned. She had wanted the princes to return to Katolis willingly, but she would do whatever it took.

"Yes. There's no other way," she said.

"Good. Then when it's time to strike, I'll give the signal," Soren said.

"What's the signal?" Claudia asked. She did not recall any discussion about a signal, but Soren sure did look proud of himself.

"The signal . . . is me attacking the elf," Soren said.

Claudia rolled her eyes, but focused her energy on Rayla, who had just glanced back at them.

"It's going to be a long journey," Rayla shouted. "Let me just go around this bush corner and see if I can find some berries or something . . ."

Rayla wandered off the trail. Claudia couldn't believe the opportunity. She looked at Soren and widened her eyes until they seemed about to burst out of the sockets.

"I should go now?" Soren whispered.

Claudia nodded vigorously. She watched as Soren went

through the bushes behind Rayla. Then Claudia approached the princes from behind. She raised her arm, allowing her sleeve to fall backward toward her shoulder. She was wearing two identical bracelets: emerald-eyed snakes entwined with chains. Claudia felt the dark magic surge inside her as she began to chant: "Meht dnib leets gnirehtils . . ."

The bracelets began to glow. To her delight, they transformed into two magical snakes with bright green eyes. She bent her knees and lowered her arms to the ground, releasing the snakes in the direction of the princes.

At the last second, Callum and Ezran turned around, but it was too late for them. The snakes coiled around the princes' legs, tripping them, and then wrapped themselves around the boys' bodies before transforming into heavy chains. As Ezran fell to the ground, Zym tumbled out of his arms.

Claudia had executed the spell perfectly. The only thing left was to get rid of that wolf. Claudia glanced in Ava's direction, but the wolf was so spooked by the snakes she'd fled on her own. As Ellis chased after Ava, Claudia couldn't believe her luck.

Zym stood alone, unhindered by chains but aware of the danger. Claudia ran toward him with an open brown sack. The little dragon tried to get away, running on his tiny legs, but he didn't stand a chance. With a few long strides, Claudia had caught up with him. Quivering in her shadow, Zym cried desperately and flit his tiny wings—but he still couldn't fly.

Claudia caught a look of horror on Ezran's face as she stepped past Zym to cut him off. The dragon fumbled to a terrified halt.

"I'm sorry, little guy," Claudia said. She did feel bad for the tiny dragon. "You have to come with me." And with that, she dropped the sack over Zym's head.

Mission complete. She couldn't wait to get back to Katolis to show her father—he would be so proud. She looked around for Soren, hoping he'd finished off Rayla by now.

After Rayla left the path, Soren spotted her at once. Maybe elves weren't so stealthy after all. Rayla was leaning over a bush picking berries, with no idea what was about to become of her.

Soren smiled. Then he closed in, allowing his shadow to fall over Rayla. He whipped his heavy blade directly at her head, but just missed. At the last possible moment, Rayla dodged to the side and regained her balance. Then she whipped out her own blades.

"Oh no. It's a trap!" Rayla said.

"Yup," Soren smirked, even though the elf didn't sound as surprised as he'd hoped.

"But why ever would you do that?" Rayla asked. "I thought we were friends."

"Sorry, but no. I'm just a nice guy and people get the wrong idea sometimes," Soren said.

"You don't speak sarcasm so good, do you?" Rayla asked.

"No, I do not," Soren said. Then he lowered his head and charged.

Viren's eyes never left the mirror, and eventually, his attention paid off. The mysterious figure returned to the room and walked directly toward him. *Could it see him?* Viren wasn't sure. The figure's gaze was intent.

Viren stood up and looked closely at the figure. It had deep blue skin and pointed ears and horns. Its star-dappled hands had only four fingers. A four-pointed silver star was emblazoned on the figure's chest. Viren couldn't believe it—he was staring at a Startouch elf!

"An elf? You're an elf?" Viren said to the mirror. The figure walked directly toward the mirror, and Viren tensed. The elf's eyes focused on Viren, and he held out his own hand to touch the mirror. *Was he visible now?*

The figure stared thoughtfully, eyes narrowed, and seemed about to wave back at Viren. But then the elf straightened his collar and tugged down his tunic, confident and satisfied. Viren relaxed. "You can't see me. On your side, it's just an ordinary mirror..." He smiled, glad to have the advantage once again.

CHAPTER 12
THE TRICK

"Whoomph!"

Claudia heard Soren and Rayla fighting, but she couldn't see them, so there was no way to know whether the battle was almost over. Claudia had hoped Soren would have ended things by now. Still, judging from the crushing sounds of Soren's heavy sword, Rayla was on the defensive.

Claudia scrambled to get closer to the fight. She left the princes chained up on the dusty ground. They weren't going anywhere.

"What? You're running away?" Soren asked Rayla.

Rayla quickly swung herself up into the branches of a tree.

"Hey! Do either of the tiny princes want to fight? This elf's a coward!" Soren shouted.

"Just finish it, Soren," Claudia called out. Neither Callum nor

Ezran responded to Soren's taunting, but Claudia wasn't surprised. Guilt-ridden, she looked over at Callum. He wouldn't even return her gaze. She walked back over to him.

"I'm sorry, Callum," Claudia said. "I know this feels like a betrayal, but I can't let you go. I have to do what's right—I have to take you back home."

Callum kept his stony silence. Claudia couldn't stand it; she wished he would fight back.

"Please don't give me the silent treatment, Callum. Say something! Say you hate me. Say anything!"

Still, he said nothing. This behavior was unnerving. Claudia bent down so she was face-to-face with Callum. But the look in his eyes was vacant, as if he were an empty vessel.

Claudia looked at Ezran and saw the same vacant stare.

Claudia started to feel dizzy. These bodies in chains—they weren't the princes.

"Soren, something's wrong! This is a trick!" Claudia shouted.

But it was Rayla who responded with a hearty chuckle from her spot way up in a tree. "A trick? Us? No!"

Claudia knew it! Rayla had undermined them.

"Wait, she's using sarcasm, Claudia," Soren called out. He jumped with excitement.

Claudia slapped her palm on her forehead. What a time for Soren to finally comprehend the rhetorical use of derision.

"That's right!" Rayla said triumphantly.

"What did you do, elf?" Soren asked.

"I can't wait for the look on your big stupid face when you see this," Rayla said. Then she winked at Claudia.

"Ellis! Show them!" Rayla hollered.

Claudia watched, furious, as Ellis emerged from the bushes where she'd been hiding with Ava. The little girl tugged the Moonstone collar from Ava's neck. Claudia watched, eyes wide, as the collar released the spell. The chained "princes" shimmered with silver magic and then disappeared. The chains binding them clattered to the ground.

"Goodness, they're . . . illusions," Claudia said. Lujanne must have enchanted the Moonstone collar. How could she have fallen for such a simple trick?

"What?! You're saying they're not real?" Soren asked.

"That's what 'illusion' means, Soren," Claudia said. She was out of patience with her brother.

Infuriated, Soren lunged for Ellis and Ava, who dodged him easily. Claudia shook her head. Speed was not her brother's strong suit; he had no chance of keeping up.

"Not even close," Ellis squealed. "Woo-hoo!"

"Where are the real princes?" Soren asked breathlessly. He stopped running.

"We're up here!" Ezran shouted from way up high.

There was a bright flash of blue light. Claudia looked up. Phoe-Phoe flew overhead, carrying Callum and Ezran on her back.

When they saw the escaped princes, Ellis cheered and Ava howled. Rayla reached up from her tree branch and grabbed Phoe-Phoe's talon, which hoisted her up into the sky.

"Claudia! They're getting away," Soren said.

Claudia looked up into the sky toward the escaping moon

phoenix. Maybe they had tricked her, but they would pay for showing off.

"No, Soren. They're not," she said. Claudia opened a bag containing a mummified tentacle. She dropped it into her hand, crushed it, and uttered an incantation: "Nwod meht gard psarg gnih tirw."

Claudia's eyes turned black, and dark energy enveloped her arm, taking the form of a massive tentacle. It writhed and expanded until it was several times her size. Then Claudia snarled and thrust the tentacle at the moon phoenix. It coiled around the terrified bird.

"Claudia, please," Callum begged from atop Phoe-Phoe. "Don't do this."

But Claudia only tightened her grip. She didn't feel so sorry for Callum anymore. Slowly but surely, she dragged the bird and its passengers toward the ground.

"AHHHHH!" Claudia suddenly cried out in pain. Out of nowhere, a metal chain wrapped around her hand. She looked back and saw a tracker—maybe one of General Amaya's men—holding the chain. He gave a strong yank, wrenching Claudia's arm backward into a strange angle.

"Stop! Let them go!" the tracker shouted.

Claudia dropped the gnarled tentacle, which crumbled to dust. Immediately the spell dissipated, releasing Phoe-Phoe. The magical bird regained flight and soared into the sky, taking Rayla, Callum, and Ezran with her.

"What are you doing?" Claudia asked.

"Protecting them from you," the tracker said evenly.

Claudia felt her eyes turning back to normal. She glared at the tracker and tried to pull away, but the chain held her arm tight.

Claudia desperately tried to come up with a spell to get her out of this situation—some magic to get her out of this literal bind. *Think, Claudia, think.* Then Soren's blade sliced through the chain, and it fell to the ground, severed and useless.

"Big mistake, Chain Man," Soren said. He knocked the tracker on the back of the head with a rock.

Corvus had been tied up and taken prisoner by the brother-sister duo, but he didn't care. His arms were bound and he was scowling, but he knew he had saved the princes.

"You know you're going to pay for this, traitor," the brother said.

"Traitor?" This idiot had to be kidding. Corvus had done nothing but follow orders from the princes' aunt. "General Amaya sent me to protect the princes of Katolis—and you just tried to kidnap them. Please tell me who the traitor is," Corvus said.

The blond kid seemed to consider this point. He looked to his sister for guidance.

"Everyone who votes this guy is a traitor, raise their hand," the brother said. He raised his own hand. Then his sister raised hers.

"Two against one. Traitor," the brother said. He tied a gag over Corvus's mouth.

"What are we gonna do?" the sister moaned. She slapped her hand against her forehead. "We betrayed our friends, and it was all for nothing."

Corvus couldn't agree more, but it was hard to voice his opinion with the gag.

"It wasn't *totally* for nothing, Sis," the brother said with a smile.

"What do you mean?" she asked. She followed her brother's gaze to the wriggling brown sack on the ground, and her face brightened. "The dragon! We still have the dragon!"

Corvus froze. He had only been focused on the princes. He hadn't even thought about the baby dragon.

The brother picked up the bag and began to open it. "Come on out, you little—"

But much to Corvus's relief, a couple of moon moths flew out of the bag and into the doofus's face. There was no dragon inside. The brother flailed and swatted as the moths relentlessly fluttered around his head.

Ezran looked down from his seat on Phoe-Phoe. Ellis was sitting on Ava's back, waving and cheering.

"Goodbye! Good luck! Come back someday!" Ellis shouted. Ava barked enthusiastically.

Then Ezran's eyes met Claudia's. Her expression flickered with guilt. Now Ezran understood what Rayla and Callum had been talking about back at the huts. Claudia and Soren weren't their friends after all. Ezran was sad, but he wasn't shocked. He'd always put a lot of trust in Rayla.

Rayla punched Callum lightly on the arm. Her white hair was whipping around wildly in the wind.

"We got 'em! I was right," she said.

"Yeah. You were right," Callum repeated. But he wasn't smiling. In fact, the way Callum was staring out at the sky made Ezran think his big brother might cry.

"I'm sorry. I wish I wasn't right," Rayla said. She put one hand on Callum's shoulder.

"Thanks for saying that, Rayla," Callum said.

Ezran coaxed Zym out of his backpack. "It's okay, Zym," he said. "It's safe to come out now."

Zym seemed nervous, but he crept out of the backpack into Ezran's arms. The tiny dragon shuddered when he noticed he was thousands of feet up in the sky. Ezran knew his little buddy was scared, but he couldn't help but see an opportunity.

"Hey—we're up in the sky! Wanna see how flying feels?" Ezran asked. He patted Zym to reassure him, and then lifted him carefully into the wind. "Come on, spread your wings."

Slowly, Zym unfurled his wings. The strong wind beat against their upturned faces. Ezran could feel the dragon's fear falling away.

CHAPTER 13
CRASHING
AND LEARNING

It was the first time Callum had ever slept on the back of a flying moon phoenix. *Add that one to the list.* Initially, he thought there was no way he'd sleep, but the bird's immense wings flapped methodically in the air, creating a smooth, rhythmic lullaby.

But now Callum was awake and restless. He couldn't stop thinking about Claudia, how he had trusted her, maybe even—

Don't think it, Callum. He shook his head, trying to lose the thought because he knew it would hurt. *Maybe even loved her.* The idea twisted inside him and made him ache. Nothing would ever be the same. He had to do something to move on!

Callum closed his eyes and crossed his legs. He had seen Lujanne slip into a deep meditation in this pose, and he would try to do the same. Callum began watching his thoughts go by and very soon, his mind started to clear. He felt the breeze pass over him as Phoe-Phoe glided effortlessly through the sky. The wind was cool, and the air was fresh.

He would never get over Claudia's betrayal. Callum felt anger rise, but then exhaled the anger into the sky. *He had to complete his mission.* He exhaled the anxiety in the air. *This was working.* The air felt suddenly warmer.

"Ahem," Rayla said. Callum opened one eye. Rayla was breathing in his face. He closed the eye.

"Ahhhhhh-hhaaaaa," Rayla yawned. "What are you doing?"

Trying to get her out of my head, Callum thought. *Trying to forget someone who meant so much to me.* He looked away from Rayla, not ready to admit the truth. "I'm meditating upon the meaning of Sky," he said.

"That's more boring than anything I would have guessed," Rayla said, stretching her arms overhead.

"I'm trying to connect to the arcanum—like Lujanne said. So I can use Sky magic again." Callum immediately felt guilty for lying to Rayla, but for some reason he couldn't tell her the truth. She had been right about not trusting Claudia, and that made it even harder to be vulnerable with her about this. But one thing was true—maybe meditating on the meaning of Sky wasn't such a bad idea?

"Didn't she also say you have to be born with the arcana-whatsit to do magic?" Rayla asked.

"Actually, no," Callum said. "She said you had to connect to the primal—and that magical creatures are born with a connection. But I don't see why I can't make my own connection."

"By sitting weird and humming?" Rayla asked.

"Right. Seems reasonable," Callum said. He ignored the teasing and resumed his meditation. He hoped she would get the message and keep quiet for a little while.

"Hey. Is it just me, or are we losing altitude?" Rayla interrupted again.

This time Callum opened his eyes. "What? No way. I'm extremely attuned to slight changes in air flowwwww. Ahhhhh." Callum gripped Phoe-Phoe's bright feathers as she careened downward toward the earth at breakneck speed.

"Wuuuuhhh!" The sudden plummet woke up Ezran and Zym too. They hung on for dear life as Phoe-Phoe plunged through the clouds, rapidly approaching the ground below. If ever there was a time for Ezran to use his talking-to-animals powers . . .

"Ezran, what's going on?!" Callum yelled through the rushing air. "Is she crashing?"

"I don't know," Ezran said. "It looks like she's headed for the edge of that cliff."

Ezran was right—if Phoe-Phoe didn't correct her angle . . .

Thwummmp.

They landed hard on the cliff top, and Phoe-Phoe skidded to a stop, coming to a halt just inches from the edge. With the momentum of the sudden stop, Zym lost his grip and flew toward the brink. Ezran reached for Zym but missed and started to fall as well. Stunned, Callum watched as Rayla dug her feet into the ground and grabbed Zym and Ezran, one hand for each.

"It's nice having both hands again," she said calmly.

Callum just nodded, afraid even to breathe.

Disheveled and exhausted, Viren continued to watch the unusual room on the other side of the mirror. Even in the candlelight, the room was getting dimmer. The elven figure studied one of the leather-bound tomes, but Viren could tell it was becoming too dark to read. The Startouch elf removed one of the candles from the wall near the mirror—but then stopped and stood perfectly still.

After a tense moment, the elf moved to the desk and picked up a candle snuffer. Slowly, the elf circled the room, extinguishing each candle along the wall. Then he snuffed out the last candle in his hand, and the room went pitch-black.

Viren strained to make out anything. He blinked repeatedly and pressed his face up to the mirror, but there was nothing to see. The only thing Viren heard was the sound of his own anxious breath, rapid and shallow.

Then a pale, four-fingered hand emerged from the darkness and pressed its palm against the other side of the mirror. The suddenness of it startled Viren. Though it seemed to be only a fraction of an inch from his face, Viren knew this mirror-place was probably hundreds or thousands of miles away, if it was even in this world at all. Still, it was shocking.

Viren jumped back. "Who . . . are you?" he asked. He looked up and down at the beautiful, elegant, mysterious elf figure. And for the first time, the Mirror Mage looked back at him. With both sides of the mirror now dim, they could both see into the other's side.

The Mirror Mage didn't respond, but he gave Viren the

once-over. Viren looked down at his clothes and glanced at the dark room he was standing in. Was the elf considering his worthiness? Viren's stomach was in knots.

Then the Mirror Mage moved his gaze to the wall, where Viren's staff was leaning against a shelf. The mage's expression softened. A hint of a smile passed his lips. After another moment, he turned and left the room. Viren stood up in a panic.

"What is it? Where are you going?!" Viren shouted. He considered himself a patient man—in fact, his ability to play the long game was one of his finer qualities. But the elf's strange behavior was making him crazed with curiosity.

A little while later, the Mirror Mage returned to view, carrying a small ornate chest. The chest had four short golden legs. Delicate golden carvings of foliage wrapped around its edges. The top and sides of the chest were clear crystal. Viren felt that he had seen this object somewhere before. Perhaps during his studies as a young mage? Yes, he could see it perfectly in his memory—a chest that could have been this one's twin, or sibling at least, belonged to Kpp'Ar. Certainly it was among the irreplaceable relics his mentor had destroyed during the profligate tantrum he called his repentance.

The elf opened the chest and removed a few items. First, he withdrew a spherical rock, which appeared to be a geode. Then came a luxurious kerchief of violet silk, a spool of gold thread and a needle, a mallet, a pestle, a crystal goblet of water, and finally a sharp, thin knife. He gestured to the objects, then toward Viren as if to say, "Now you."

"You want me to find these items?" Viren said. "I can do that."

He strode out of the chamber feeling confident for the first time in a long while.

Ezran, Callum, Rayla, Zym, and Bait stood in a circle around Phoe-Phoe on the top of the cliff. Ezran crouched near her lolling head and stroked her iridescent feathers.

Tell me what's wrong, Ezran whispered. *Maybe we can help.* Then he buried his head in her soft feathers and listened.

Phoe-Phoe responded with a combination of chatter and trill punctuated with clicks of her tongue and beak—Ezran loved the rhythm and musicality of the way she communicated. When anyone spoke, whether a person or animal, Ezran always listened with his ears, but also with his heart. He could feel the great bird's exhaustion in his own bones. As he stroked Phoe-Phoe's feathers, Ezran's own breathing synchronized with the great bird's.

"Phoe-Phoe is okay," he said to everyone. "She's just tired. But she feels strong."

"Maybe she's carrying one too many passengers?" Rayla asked. Ezran caught her giving a meaningful look at Bait, who hurried over to Ezran and hid behind his leg.

"I'm just teasing, froggo," Rayla said.

Ezran shook his head. Phoe-Phoe wasn't just tired. She was getting too far from home.

"She gets her power from the Moon Nexus. The farther away we go, the harder it is to carry everyone."

"Wow, Ez, I can't believe you could understand all that," Callum said. He looked genuinely impressed. Ezran enjoyed impressing his big brother with his gift. It wasn't so long ago that Callum would ridicule him for communing with animals.

"You did such a good job getting us so far, Phoe-Phoe," Ezran said. She cooed pleasantly in response. "It's time for us to send you home."

Ezran gave her a soft pat on the head, and Phoe-Phoe took off with a majestic *whoosh*. She cawed as she reached her full wingspan and soared into the sky. A tiny feather floated down and gently landed on Bait's nose. It tickled, making him wriggle his nose. Then he sneezed.

"So. What do we do now?" Ezran asked.

"Well, Xadia's that way," Rayla said. She pointed across the wide bay visible from the cliff. "Across miles and miles of that blue fluid I both need to survive and hate more than anything in the world."

Ezran felt bad for Rayla and her fear of water, but he knew she could face the fear again. He was about to encourage her to cross the bay when Callum jumped in.

"You know what?" Callum said. "We'll just walk around it somehow. With our legs."

Ezran couldn't believe what he was hearing. But thankfully, Rayla shook her head no.

"That's sweet, Callum," she said. "But walking around is going to take too long. We need to get that former-egg-now-adorable-baby-dragon home to Xadia as fast as we can. We've got to go straight across."

"You mean over the water?" Ezran said. He wanted to make sure—sometimes the way Rayla spoke was confusing.

"Shh! Don't speak its name," she replied with a glint in her eye.

CHAPTER 14
THE RUTHLESS

After descending the cliff, Ezran, Callum, Rayla, Zym, and Bait arrived at some docks by the edge of the bay. There were boats and sailors as far as they could see. Callum thought Rayla looked a little greener than she had before, but traveling by sea was the only timely option.

The question was, who was going to help their ragtag gang? Callum tried to picture the scene.

"Hello, we're two human princes, one dragon prince, a Moonshadow elf, and an incredibly grumpy glow toad in need of a ride." No sailor in their right mind would take them on. Callum sighed and motioned for the gang to hide behind a stack of crates.

"Well, we need a boat. And . . . a captain who knows how to make it go," Ezran said.

"Right. Specifically, a captain who doesn't hate elves," Callum said, looking at Rayla.

"That won't be a problem—I can disguise myself as a human again," Rayla said. She clapped her hands together and grinned.

"Yes, that worked out incredibly well last time you tried it," Callum said. "Remember when you tried to 'borrow' a Sunforge blade and your disguise literally burned up?"

Rayla waved her hand at Callum to silence him. She pulled up the hood of her cloak, then she cleared her throat and adjusted her posture by slumping her shoulders.

"Hello again, fellow humans—human fellows," she said in a deep voice with a human accent.

"Rayla, come—"

"Ooh!" Ezran interrupted Callum. "You're going to love this, Zym. I'm a huge fan of 'Human Rayla.'"

Callum clamped his mouth shut.

Rayla puffed up her chest. "Let's go judge and criticize things other humans do . . . and then do the exact same things ourselves!"

Ezran laughed hysterically. "Do another one!" he shouted. Callum frowned.

"Sure thing, old buddy, old pal," Rayla said. "I am excited to rapidly eat a plate of unwholesome food in an excessive portion size!"

"Mmm! I'd eat a jelly tart the size of a dog," Ezran said.

"Human Rayla" was on a roll. "Look at me, I'm a human with all the things I need to make me happy . . . but then I compare myself to another human who has different things, and now I'm miserable!"

Callum was starting to think Rayla enjoyed offending humans just a little too much.

"Won't it be great to encounter other humans, and talk about which roads and pathways will take us somewhere slightly faster than other roads and pathways?" Rayla asked with mock seriousness. She started pointing this way and that and bending her elbows to demonstrate corners and turns. "You turn here, and you go around the bend like so, and then there's a little-known way to go, but trust me, all these little tricks will add up and save you nearly half a minute."

Ezran wiped tears of laughter from his face. "It is so true! We do love going slightly faster."

"Hey," Callum said. "Sometimes getting somewhere slightly faster is important. Like right now." He'd had just about enough of this act. "Ezran and I will find a sea captain. Rayla, you stay here and work on growing a fifth finger. That's the real secret of being a human: the pinko!" He raised a single pinkie in the air with greater pride than any human had ever had for their littlest finger.

"You got it, my smooth-skulled friend," Rayla said, giving Callum the thumbs-up sign.

Ezran was still applauding Rayla's performance as Callum hauled him off to the docks by the collar.

The sun was sitting low in the sky, and Rayla was pacing the docks. *Where were those princes? How hard could it be to find a sailor to help them? Zym was going to be a teenager by the time they got him*

to his mom. Then she heard voices, so she scurried back behind the crates to hide.

Rayla peeked through the holes in the crates and breathed a sigh of relief when she saw Ezran running toward her hiding place. He was grinning. Callum was not far behind.

"We found the perfect captain," Ezran said.

Rayla began adjusting her hood to better hide her horns. She stuffed her hands into her pockets.

"Don't worry," Callum said. He grabbed Rayla's hand and pulled her out from behind the crates. "Your horns are not going to be a problem with this guy."

"You're kidding," Rayla said. "Is he some kind of enlightened human who can really see the good in elves?" She could scarcely believe she wouldn't have to use any kind of disguise.

"Hmm . . . I'm not sure he can see the good in anyone, really," Callum said. "But that's part of what makes him uniquely qualified."

"You're being awfully cryptic," Rayla said. "Mysterious Callum is my least favorite kind of Callum."

"Well, the mystery is almost over," Callum said. "There's our captain." Callum pointed to the only person on the dock. It was a tall man, standing in profile, gazing out at the sea.

Rayla could see the captain's long red beard and wavy auburn locks tucked under a traditional black pirate's hat. He was wearing long brown gloves, a puffy white shirt, and a green coat and breeches. A patch covered his left eye, and a blue-and-red parrot was perched on his left shoulder. He looked like the captain out of one of the made-up seafaring stories Runaan used to tell her, where fearless sailors battled monsters ten times their size.

"We're back," Callum called to the captain.

The captain turned to face Ezran, Callum, Rayla, Zym, and Bait. Rayla gulped. Even in the most outlandish yarns Runaan had spun, she'd never heard of a captain who wore patches over *both* eyes. Rayla caught Callum looking at her, trying to stifle his laughter. Rayla stared at Callum in disbelief.

"You were gone for hours," she whispered. "This was the best you could come up with?"

"Greetings," the captain said. He turned to face Rayla. "The name's Captain Villads," he said, pronouncing the name *vee-lahss*. "The *D* is silent."

"There's a *D* in that name?" Rayla asked. She was going to give this so-called captain a tough time.

"Arr," Villads said.

"Wait, there's a silent *R*?" Rayla asked. If Callum wanted to be Mysterious Callum, she was going to be Befuddled Rayla.

"Narr," Villads said.

"Oh. Okay, so it's just the silent *D*, then," Rayla said. She glowed inwardly under Callum's glare.

"Aye," Villads said.

"Ahh, so there's a—"

"Ahem," Callum said, interrupting. "We need to get moving. This is our regular human friend, Rayla."

"Spelled like it sounds," Rayla said. *One final jab.* "And these are my . . . weird dogs . . . Zym and Bait," she added.

"Ahoy, Rayla. Ahoy, doggos," Villads said. "And this is me first mate, Berto." He pointed at the parrot.

Ezran seemed delighted. "Oh, 'Bird-O' is such a great name for a—"

"BERTO," the parrot said, interrupting Ezran. He sounded offended. "It's short for Roberto, not Ro-BIRD-o."

"Me ship's this way," Villads said. He walked down the pier to a rickety old ship. "Welcome to me water home, the *Ruthless*! Named after me dear wife, Ruth. Who sadly"—Captain Villads placed a hand over his heart and shook his head dramatically before continuing, a bit choked up—"doesn't enjoy sailing."

Rayla exchanged a look with Callum. He shrugged. Maybe Captain Villads was their best option because he was their only option.

"So, you said if the wind is on our side, we could make it across the bay pretty quickly?" Callum asked.

"Aye. Of course, there's a storm coming," Villads said, walking up the gangplank.

"A storm? Great," Rayla said. She felt a small wave of nausea.

"Wow, you can just tell a storm is coming?" Ezran asked, genuinely fascinated.

"Well, I can't see, as you know, but I rely on me other senses—"

"I told him!" the parrot suddenly interrupted, punctuating with a squawk. "I saw the storm and I told him."

Captain Villads turned to the bird. "And I heard you tell me! Hearing is one of my other senses, Berto. Either way, we'd best delay departin' for a few days to wait out the storm."

"A few days? Uh, we're on a tight schedule," Rayla said. "Isn't there anything we can do?"

Captain Villads paused to consider, and then brightened. "I suppose if we leave right now we could race across the bay and beat the storm . . ."

"Yes, let's do that," Rayla said. *Let's get this over with as fast as possible.*

"No problem," Villads said. "That should work just fine. Unless, of course, the storm catches us mid-bay and kills us all." He chuckled.

"Ha ha ha," Rayla said under her breath.

Ezran, Callum, Rayla, Zym, and Bait followed the captain up the gangplank and onto the *Ruthless.*

It took a few hours, but by late afternoon Viren had gathered all the items the Mirror Mage had requested. He thought that finding a spool of golden thread would be the most difficult acquisition, but the royal seamster seemed quite pleased that Viren was trying some sewing on his own and gave him what he needed. They even offered to give Viren free lessons any time.

And so Viren returned to the chamber. He held each item up to the mirror, seeking approval, which he knew he would get. The Mirror Mage looked over the spread and nodded. It was time to begin.

The Mirror Mage picked up the golden thread in his world. Moving with measured precision, he sewed a golden rune symbol into the purple silk. Viren copied his actions, though his work was neither as swift nor as elegant as the Mirror Mage's. Nonetheless, the mage nodded at him.

The Mirror Mage traced a glowing rune into the air before him—the same symbol he'd sewn into his purple cloth.

"I've never seen this rune before," Viren said.

The golden-threaded rune in the mirror began to glow and sparkle with all the colors of the night sky, as if thousands of tiny stars were twinkling in the magic symbol. A moment later, Viren watched the rune he had sewn begin to sparkle as well.

The Mirror Mage covered his geode with the glowing rune cloth—and Viren mimicked him. Then the Mirror Mage raised the small mallet and struck the geode through the cloth. He unwrapped the cloth to reveal it had split into two hemispheres, each forming a small bowl. The crystals inside seemed to sparkle and glow with the same magic that illuminated the rune moments ago.

Viren repeated the actions. He couldn't fathom where this experiment was going, but knew he was working with another powerful, gifted mage.

Finally, the Mirror Mage ground the pestle into the geode, creating a fine, twinkling powder out of the crystals in the rock bowl. He poured the sparkling powder into the goblet of water. The combination fizzed and burbled, producing an ethereal blue smoke. Then he drank from the goblet.

Viren copied the steps, but when he put the goblet to his lips, he hesitated.

"You expect me to drink this?" he asked. The elf in the mirror just stared at him.

Viren couldn't suppress his curious nature. He steeled himself and drank everything in the goblet. He wiped his mouth. "Surprisingly not terrible," he said. As if that mattered.

Finally, the mage picked up the gleaming knife and motioned to Viren to do the same. The Mirror Mage rolled up his sleeve, clenched his fist, and held the blade to his arm above the geode bowl. Then he paused, waiting for Viren.

Viren picked up the blade and considered whether he would cut himself for this stranger. Something felt wrong. Usually, doing magic made Viren feel powerful, but standing here, holding a blade to his own flesh at the behest of a mysterious stranger, he suddenly felt powerless.

"Why should I trust you?" Viren asked. "I don't even know who . . . I don't even know what you are." Viren lowered the knife. He was curious; he was never stupid. "I need time to think."

Some hours passed. Beneath a cloudless sky, the *Ruthless* cut through the bright blue waves. Everyone congregated on the deck to enjoy the view. Ezran, Rayla, Zym, and Bait sat near the bow, watching the horizon. At least for the moment, the sea was peaceful.

A pod of dolphins jumped out of the water almost soundlessly and swam beside the boat. Ezran and Zym hung over the rail to get a better look. Rayla was hanging over the rail as well, but she wasn't looking at the dolphins. She was losing the contents of her stomach.

Callum sat farther astern, watching Captain Villads adjust the ropes and sails. He was determined to pick up a few things about sailing. He didn't want to interrupt Captain Villads, but the captain was such an interesting figure Callum couldn't help staring at him. It was Captain Villads who spoke first.

"Ye might be wondering what happened to me eyes," he said.

"Well, I didn't want to be rude," Callum said. It was true though; he'd never seen a pirate, or anyone for that matter, wearing two eye patches.

"Me left eye was taken by a flock of mutinous seagulls," Villads said, almost wistfully, as if the seagulls had once been a band of loyal shipmen.

"Uh...wow," Callum said. It was hard to imagine being attacked by an entire flock. "And what about your right eye?"

"Don't know. Came at me from me left!"

Callum started to smile, but then stopped himself. He wasn't sure whether the captain was joking. Captain Villads certainly was an odd fellow.

Callum looked up at the wind vane and put his finger to the wind. He was no expert at sailing, but it seemed like the ship was moving perpendicular to the wind.

"Hey, wait. How are we going that way if the wind is coming from over there?" Callum asked.

"That's how you sail, me boy," Villads said.

"The wind doesn't push us where we want to go?" Callum asked.

"The sail is more like a wing, flying through the wind, pulling the boat against the water currents below us." Captain Villads moved the mainsail, and the boat swerved gently. "It's like shooting a willow melon seed from between your fingers."

He plucked a small seed from his coat pocket and squeezed it hard on both sides. The seed shot straight out of his fingers and plunked Callum on the nose.

Callum caught the seed and fed it to Berto. "I think I get it. Can I try?" he asked.

Captain Villads stepped aside, and Callum took hold of the wheel and mainsail. In less than a second, the boat swerved violently and the wind took Captain Villads's hat. The loose sail flapped feebly and Berto caught the hat. Captain Villads grabbed the wheel back.

"I'll take it from here," he said. "After you're in the elements long enough, you get a feel for where the wind is and how it's about to change. It's like a connection, deep in me bones."

"Hold on—you feel a connection to the wind? How did you get that?" Callum was suddenly very interested. Maybe a pirate feeling connected to the wind wasn't the same as a mage connecting to the Sky arcanum, but Callum knew he had something to learn from this unusual sailor.

"What, just because I'm blind and have narcolepsy, you thought I wouldn't have sailing sense?" Villads asked.

Oooops. Clearly, Callum had hit upon a sensitive spot. He'd just wanted to learn how a nonmagical being made the kind of connection Lujanne had been talking about. He tried to smooth things over. "No, that's not what I meant," Callum started to say. "Wait—narcolepsy? Did you say you had—" He looked at Captain Villads, who had suddenly fallen asleep at the wheel.

"Wake up! Wake up! Wake up! Wake—" Berto began to chirp.

Captain Villads bolted awake at the sound of the parrot's squawk. He gave Berto a light pat on the head.

"Huh?! What happened? The last thing I remember was talking about narcolepsy and then falling asleep," Villads said.

"Yeah. That's about right," Callum said. He decided to drop the whole connection to the wind discussion.

A soft clap of thunder sounded in the distance, and a few moments later, light raindrops started to fall. Everyone looked up at the quickly darkening clouds. Zym's eyes were wide with curiosity—he'd never seen rain before. He poked his head out from behind a crate to feel the droplets, and then quickly hid again. Ezran laughed as he watched Zym, but Callum's mind was spinning with all the possibilities of the oncoming rains.

"Storm's a-comin'," Villads said. "Seems as if we won't beat it after all."

"Hmm. Maybe the storm is good news, in a way. Maybe it's my chance . . ." Callum said. Maybe he could harness the storm for magic—even without the primal stone.

"Your chance to die," Berto squawked.

"I was going to say my chance to learn," Callum said. He was filled with anticipation and not in the mood to banter with a bird.

"To learn how to drown," Berto squawked again.

It was midday and sweltering beneath the sun. Amaya stood on the battlements of the Breach fortress. Tense but alert, she raised a spyglass to scan the horizon. Now she could see across the Breach into Xadia. She focused on a small area of the cliffs on the other side, where a jagged, tall formation of cooled lava rock jutted out.

Something was wrong. Amaya couldn't get the Sunfire knight out of her head. Where had the knight gone after Amaya had defeated her three warriors? Instinct told her that the knight wasn't the type to retreat to Xadia and call it a day. And yet, the search for the surviving knight had turned up nothing.

How much did the knight know? Had they stumbled upon the Breach crossing the natural caverns? Or had they known about the Breach and the secret outpost all along? Amaya slammed her spyglass shut and summoned a nearby soldier.

"Lieutenant Fen," Amaya signed. "Come over here." She beckoned him sharply.

"It's the top of the hour, General," Lieutenant Fen responded. Though he knew how to sign fluently, he always spoke aloud and relied on Amaya to read his lips. "The outpost should be signaling any moment now."

"It's late," she signed. Ever since Amaya's encounter with the Sunfire knight, she had insisted the outpost send a signal every hour on the hour. Up until now the communication had been timely.

"Yes, General, but respectfully, it's only two minutes late—"

"I saw elves on the Breach," Amaya signed.

"General Amaya, we've searched everywhere and there's been no sign of the elves," Lieutenant Fen answered. Though she saw nothing in his demeanor that was outwardly disrespectful,

Amaya could tell he was annoyed by her vigilance on this topic. "I think it's safe to conclude that the outpost on the Xadian side remains secret."

Then something caught Lieutenant Fen's eye. A steam jet burst out of part of the lava formation, followed by three brief steam jets.

"There! Look." Lieutenant Fen pointed. "The signal! The outpost is secure."

But Amaya remained unconvinced. She shook her head. "No, something's wrong," she signed.

"But . . . it's only three minutes late," Lieutenant Fen protested.

Three minutes is almost as bad as three hours, Amaya thought. She had to investigate. "Ready a scouting party," she signed. She'd noticed that the younger generation of soldiers tended to brush over the details. She'd have to train them better.

"Yes, General. I'll ready a party," Lieutenant Fen answered.

General Amaya led a small team of soldiers, including Lieutenant Fen, through the pass beneath the lavafalls at the Breach. She had crossed this passage dozens of times. She knew every twist and turn, every nook and cranny. But the path was so dangerous she never let down her guard.

Once on the Xadian side of the lava river, Amaya marched to a huge boulder. She touched a spot low on the boulder and it shifted ever so slightly, revealing a camouflaged gate that was only visible from one side. Through this gate, Amaya could cross into the mountain outpost. She didn't have to turn around to check—she knew her team was right behind her.

The inside of the outpost was dark and vacant, which was unusual, given that they'd just received the signal from this very spot. And yet, there was no sign of a struggle.

"I don't understand," Lieutenant Fen signed. "Why would the outpost be abandoned? They just sent the signal a few—"

Amaya held up her hand to silence Lieutenant Fen. Everyone froze, looked, listened. Now the squad knew something was off. They stood ready, hands drifting toward their weapons. Then a human soldier emerged from the darkness.

"Soldier! Your signal was late," Lieutenant Fen said. "What happened? Where is everyone?"

"Yes. My apologies, sir," the soldier answered Lieutenant Fen. But General Amaya noticed the soldier was looking at her. "The others went on patrol, and I missed my cue," he reported. "The next signal will happen exactly on the hour."

"Of course. Thank you, soldier," Lieutenant Fen said. He seemed satisfied with this explanation. He turned to Amaya. "Better safe than sorry, but it seems everything is under control."

To Amaya's mind, everything was not under control. The soldier looked shell-shocked. He was sweating profusely, and his hands were trembling.

The rest of the group had relaxed and begun to turn away, but Amaya stood still, squinting at the soldier. The young man tucked his hands tight against his chest and held her gaze. Then he tensely signed, "DANGER!"

Amaya bristled and scanned the darkness. And there it was—a glint of metal in the otherwise pitch-black outpost.

In an instant, Amaya had leaped in front of the soldier. She thrust out her shield and blocked an incoming arrow, saving his life. Then she looked around wildly.

Sunfire elves emerged from tunnels and crags in the rocky walls. The powerful Sunfire knight she'd encountered before was their leader.

Amaya knew there was no way she and her small team could fight them all off.

No matter, she thought. *I will go down trying.*

chapter 15
change of plans

As the afternoon wore on, the few raindrops wetting the upper deck of the *Ruthless* became a full-fledged storm. Gusty winds knocked the boat to and fro, and hard rain pellets pummeled the seafarers.

As the little ship rode huge swells up and down, Ezran, Callum, Rayla, Zym, and Bait watched lightning bolts crack over the water. Ezran glimpsed a nearby island in the middle of the bay and pointed it out. The island was a tempting place to stop . . . if Captain Villads could get control over the boat.

Ezran loved the wild movements, the wet wind in his hair, and the sense of adventure. But one look at Rayla and he knew she would never get her sea legs. Her face had turned an interesting shade of green.

"You're turning different colors. Is that your Moonshadow

form?" Ezran teased. Maybe he could take Rayla's mind off the bad stuff by reminding her how powerful she was.

"No, Ezran," Rayla said. "This is my rare glow toad impersonation. *Gruuuumpp.*"

Ezran wondered what Rayla had against Bait—the two of them seemed to have developed a rivalry almost from day one. Bait was staring back at Rayla judgmentally. Then he changed color to match Rayla's sickly green.

The boat heaved.

"Storm's too strong! Best we moor on the lee side of the island and wait till it calms," Villads said. He managed to sail through the slanting rain and point the boat in the right direction. It lurched toward the island. Callum stood at the helm near Captain Villads, clutching the railing.

"Berto, to the bow!" Villads shouted.

"Aye, aye, Captain," Berto said.

Berto flew to the bow and began shouting his own set of orders.

"Port, port!" Berto said.

Captain Villads moved to the left, and the ship made a sharp turn.

"Starboard, starboard!" Berto squawked. Captain Villads yanked the ship to the right. Ezran, Callum, Rayla, Zym, and Bait slid back and forth on the deck.

And then the boat was on top of the island. As they approached land, the mist cleared, revealing a rickety dock surrounded by large, jagged rocks. The dock was broken down and abandoned, but there was just enough space between the rocks for the ship to dock.

Ezran couldn't believe it—the ship slid right into the open

space on the dock. They'd managed to navigate numerous rocky obstacles with a blind captain.

"Current fast! Drop the sail!" Berto yelled.

Captain Villads untied a rope, and the front sail dropped. The boat stopped pivoting on its bow and swung in between the rocks, landing exactly parallel to the dock.

"Nailed it. *Squawk!*" Berto said. He flew a rope over to the shambles of a dock and looped it around the mooring point.

"Did he just say the word *squawk*?" Ezran asked. Ezran had tried to communicate with Berto in bird language, but Berto had ignored him. Ezran wondered if he had offended Berto earlier by mispronouncing his name.

"Never mind Berto," Villads said. "He's always thought of himself as more human than bird . . . if you can imagine such a thing."

"*Squawk* means squawk," Berto explained. "Same in human language as it is in bird!"

Ezran nodded. Somehow this explanation both made sense and made no sense at all.

"Anyway, since we didn't beat the storm, we'll just have to wait it out belowdecks," Villads said. He turned on his heel and nimbly skidded down the steps to the hatch.

"Hooray," Rayla said, pretending to celebrate. "We're wet and miserable and we saved no time at all." She really was very good at sarcasm, Ezran thought.

Rayla followed Captain Villads belowdecks, but Callum seemed content in the rain. He was staring at the island, his eyes glazed over.

"Hey, are you coming or what?" Rayla asked him.

"Yeah. I agree," Callum said thoughtlessly. He stood in place as the rain poured down his face.

"Uh-oh, I know that face. It's the dumb idea face," Rayla said.

"Rayla," Ezran said. It seemed like these two were always bickering. "Let's just everyone go down and dry off."

Callum half smiled. He ignored Rayla and Ezran. Several bolts of lightning struck the island, and Callum's eyes lit up. "Every time the lightning strikes . . . I can feel something," he said.

"Yeah, me too," Rayla said. "It feels good not to be struck by lightning." She gave Callum a toothy grin. Ezran noticed this was not technically sarcasm, but felt similar.

"No, I mean it feels like it did when I used the Fulminis spell," Callum said. When he had the primal stone and had successfully cast the lightning spell, there had been almost a tingling sensation throughout his whole body.

Zym jumped off Ezran's shoulder and ran to Callum. The little dragon was hopping up and down, nipping at Callum's outstretched fingers.

"Don't tell me you want to go out there?" Rayla made a face. "Please don't tell me that."

"Maybe if I'm brave enough to go into it, and face the storm . . . that's how I'll make the connection," Callum said.

"Come on, Zym," Ezran pleaded. He lunged after the little dragon, who seemed even more excited by the storm than Callum.

"Or," Rayla said, raising her pointer finger into the air, "the storm will blow you up until you're dead. Zap, pow, Callum dust."

Ezran laughed at Rayla's joke, but he stopped short when he saw Callum's face. Suddenly, Ezran wanted to get out of the way of the fight as much as the storm. Then Zym struggled against him, and Ezran realized—Zym was at home in a storm. He was literally in his element. Lightning flashes glinted in Zym's wide, innocent eyes.

"See? Zym gets it," Callum said. "He can feel it too. I'm going into it."

Ezran finally managed to scoop Zym up in his arms. "Actually, I think something *is* drawing Zym out there," Ezran said. He didn't look at Rayla. "It's like the storm is calling him. You really wanna go out there?" he asked the dragon.

"Oh no, no, no!" Rayla shouted. She smacked her hand on her forehead. "It's one thing for Callum to stupidly risk his own stupid human life, but I am not gonna let you risk the life of the future king of the dragons."

Zym looked at Ezran with puppy dog eyes and whined softly.

Ezran ignored Rayla and brought Zym over to Callum.

"He is a storm dragon—he'll be safe," Ezran said. He placed Zym in Callum's arms. "Take care of him, and take care of yourself."

"I will," Callum said.

"I was talking to Zym," Ezran said. Then he waved goodbye to his brother and the dragon. Everything would be okay.

As Callum and Zym disembarked from the *Ruthless*, Rayla shook her head. "If you die out there, I swear I'll kill you," Rayla called after them.

Callum just waved in response.

The sun was setting. Viren stood on King Harrow's old balcony, watching the orange beams wash over the kingdom, lost in his own thoughts. He wanted to learn more about the mysterious mage, but every cell in his pragmatic body told him there was nothing but danger to be found in the mirror.

As the sun finally dipped below the horizon, Viren took another sip of his afternoon cup of hot brown morning potion and turned the knife over in his hand. *Would he spill his own blood for this mystery mage?*

Ka-cawww!

Viren's head snapped up to the sky. Far above him, a large black crow flapped its heavy wings. It was headed toward the rookery, clutching a scroll. Viren jumped up and abandoned his hot brown morning potion, which admittedly was now lukewarm.

As he dashed off to the rookery, his staff in his hand, Viren could barely contain his hope that one of the other kingdoms had responded to his letter. *Would the other leaders suspect anything unusual? Or would the famous red seal protect Viren's message from scrutiny?*

Viren burst through the rookery doors, breathless. "Did something come for me?" he gasped.

The Crow Master looked surprised by Viren's harried entrance, but recovered quickly.

"Ah, yes, High Mage," he said. "Four messages, in fact." He turned to the shelf behind him to retrieve the scrolls.

Viren couldn't believe the oversight. This guy was truly an incompetent. "Four messages came for me and I was not informed?" he asked. He summoned his most withering stare.

"Actually, we searched the entire castle," the Crow Master said. "We couldn't find you anywhere. What, are you hiding out in some secret chamber somewhere?"

The Crow Master was joking, but he had guessed correctly.

Viren stared him down. "I was in the bathroom."

"Got it," the Crow Master said. "Sounds serious." He gave a little nod that struck Viren as way too familiar, so he ignored it.

The Crow Master started to sift through the messages, but Viren snatched them out of his hand. He skimmed the letters quickly, and a warm feeling flooded his body. It was exactly the response he needed. His plan was working, and Viren was bursting to share the news.

"The other four kingdoms have agreed to a summit of the Pentarchy," Viren told the Crow Master. Confiding in the Crow Master was beyond inappropriate, but this youth wouldn't know what he was talking about. Besides, he was Viren's only audience.

"Wow! That sounds important," the Crow Master said.

"Yes!" Viren shouted. He raised his staff in the air. "I will rally the kings and queens behind Katolis and finally destroy the Xadian threat! You, young man, are witnessing history."

"That's really great," the Crow Master said. "Yeah. Awesome." He picked some dirt out from underneath his fingernail. "Would you rate the service you received today as excellent?"

"Yes, yes, of course," Viren said. He had momentarily forgotten to whom he was speaking. "You can have the survey or what-have-you sent to my office."

Viren left the rookery with the scrolls tucked beneath his arm. This positive turn of events gave him the confidence to decide once and for all about the strange magic blood ritual and the Startouch elf. He walked purposefully to his secret study, knife in hand.

The Mirror Mage was seated in the same position Viren had left him in. His thin mouth cracked into a smirk when he saw Viren.

Viren stood in front of the mirror, holding the knife in front of him. Then he dropped the knife on the table.

The Mirror Mage stood up and pointed his own knife at his wrist again, as if Viren had misunderstood.

But Viren was never confused. He grabbed the heavy drapery he used to cover the mirror and threw it over the glass, ending communication with the elf . . . for now. His original plan was panning out; curious as he was about this elven mage on the other side of the looking glass, there was no reason to take any risks. He no longer needed to engage with this mysterious being.

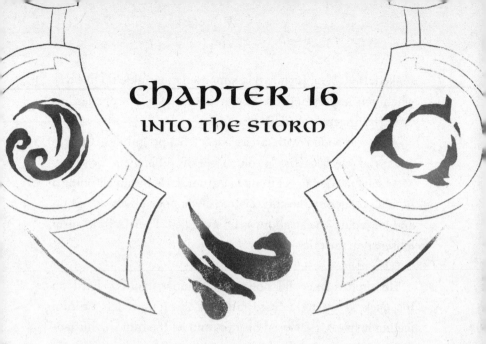

CHAPTER 16
INTO THE STORM

A hard rain swirled through the cloud-darkened skies, drenching Callum to the very bone. It wasn't that he was rethinking his decision to leave the relative safety of the *Ruthless* and face a brutal storm with a ten-pound baby dragon as his only protection . . . it was just that he'd lost some of his initial enthusiasm for the adventure.

Callum sat on a large, flat boulder with his legs crossed and eyes closed in search of a meditative state. Pebble-like raindrops hammered his cheeks, and Zym pranced across his lap like a puppy. Meditation was impossible.

Callum tried to focus himself and be present in the moment. Maybe if he spoke his thoughts and feelings aloud, he would gain some clarity. "Okay. It's wet. The wind is blowing," Callum said as a gust lashed at his face. "It's blowing a lot! I'm cold, I'm soaked. Hey, Zym, is your skin supposed to wrinkle up like this when you understand the Sky arcanum?" Callum opened his eyes. His fingers looked like prunes.

Zym responded with a cascade of happy gurgles. Callum made and released a fist. He didn't feel any different in the storm. Maybe he needed to get to higher ground. He began climbing a higher boulder up the cliff. Zym easily hopped up ahead of him and looked down at Callum as he struggled. Then Callum's grip loosened in the rain—

"Ooooomph."

He slipped and slid down the boulder, landing hard on his back. It wasn't a huge fall, but the impact left Callum feeling helpless. He closed his eyes and let the rain wet his face like tears he refused to wipe away.

Zym was watching Callum with concern. He crawled onto Callum's chest and spread his wings to shield him.

Callum held Zym up so they were face-to-face. He wished he could feel the magic again. He wished Zym could show him how.

"I don't know how I'm supposed to get this, Zym," he said. "You're a magical creature. Somehow, it's inside you. But I'm just a human. There's nothing inside me. I want this so much. When I could do magic, I finally felt like myself . . . and now I've lost that. I'm just trying to find my way back."

Zym squirmed in Callum's hands and looked toward the shore meaningfully. Callum followed Zym's intent gaze. An old wooden windmill sat atop another cliff that jutted out over the water. Bolts of lightning struck the area every few seconds. Something about the windmill seemed magnetic, as if it were attracting the power and energy of the storm to itself.

Callum curled his fingers into a spyglass shape and looked through the little window at the stormy scene. Blocking the rest of the world out with his hands made Callum feel as if he were staring at the primal stone again.

"That's where we need to go!" he shouted.

Zym was already running toward the distant windmill, which whirred and creaked in the heavy winds. As they drew closer, Callum realized the storm was worse on this part of the island. Tree branches crashed to the ground, and thunder rumbled.

Callum knew he had to reach the thin iron pole on the top of the windmill. Then lightning struck the pole, and Callum froze. The entire island was illuminated for a moment; a tiny speck on the enormous sea. Callum shuddered from the cold, but pressed on to the windmill.

When they reached a ladder at the windmill's base, Callum hoisted Zym onto his shoulders and started the slippery ascent. He could feel Zym's claws digging into his shoulders and the baby dragon's warm, fast breath on his neck. The danger didn't matter—all the secrets lay at the top of the windmill. Callum moved forward. This was the closest he'd ever felt to fearlessness.

When they finally reached the top of the windmill, Callum closed his eyes. *Okay, Callum. You can do this. You are right where you need to be. Now, connect to the Sky arcanum. Connect . . .*

Nothing happened.

Callum looked at the lightning rod. Then he reached out to touch the rod's cold, rusted surface. At the last moment, he winced and withdrew his hand. Up above, the storm swirled and flashes of lightning rattled the clouds.

"I have to do this," Callum said, more to himself than Zym. "I have to understand the Sky primal. Whatever the risk, it's the only way."

Callum lunged for the lightning rod. When he felt the cold metal in his fingers, he squeezed with everything he had, not caring that the rusted pole was cutting into his palm. Callum looked up at the sky. The thick, dark clouds roiled, and the sounds of thunder seemed to get closer and louder. His breath became faster and faster. He closed his eyes tight. What would it feel like? Would it surge through him, filling him with knowledge and power? Would it hurt, or even ... kill him?

"Come on, come on ..."

Wait. How stupid was he?! He couldn't risk his life to learn magic. He pulled his hand back. *That was close.*

Callum looked over his shoulder at Zym, who was staring at him with wide, round eyes. Callum immediately felt better. He knew his life was so much more important than any power he might gain. He wanted to cry and laugh at the same time, he felt so relieved. Was it possible the baby dragon was smiling at him?

CRASHHHHH!

A bolt of lightning struck Zym. The tiny dragon's expression froze as he tumbled off Callum's shoulders.

At a glance, General Amaya knew that the Sunfire elves outnumbered her troops. The only practical option was escape.

But they had been surrounded so quickly that there was no longer a clear path to retreat, so Amaya intended to create her own path. She braced herself and lifted her massive shield. With her head lowered beneath the shield, she charged through a line of elven warriors. She could feel the onslaught of elves falling against her shield, and she knew that any moment might be her last. But if her troops could escape through the path she was forging, it would be a worthwhile sacrifice.

Just as Amaya sensed that the route was clearing and her troops came up beside her, she came face-to-face with the Sunfire knight.

The knight wielded her glowing Sunforge blade, unstoppable by human weapons. She strutted toward General Amaya, knocking out a few of Amaya's soldiers on the way. But Amaya knew that she was the elf's real target. The Sunfire knight was sizing her up, circling her, determining just how difficult a battle this would be.

The Sunfire knight smiled. Amaya recoiled at her confidence. Then she sheathed her own sword and put her shield on her back. Both were useless now.

Amaya raised her unarmed hands and gestured to the Sunfire knight. Even though the knight probably didn't understand sign language, Amaya was pretty sure her meaning was clear: *Bring it.*

The Sunfire knight rushed at her, swinging her searing-hot blade. Light on her toes, Amaya ducked and dodged. It was a risky, dangerous dance, and Amaya focused all her energy on her nimble feet.

Finally, Amaya managed to grab the elf's sword hand for an

instant, just long enough to grapple her to the ground. They rolled and wrestled in a contest of strength to gain control of the magical weapon. In a sudden move, Amaya flipped her opponent, and the blade flew far across the outpost. Amaya waved at her troops to flee. The Sunfire knight roared with fury.

Amaya did a double take. Was the knight's skin ... changing color? It darkened and crackled with molten fiery lines. Amaya knew that some elves had inherent magical abilities, but she had never seen this one before.

The knight seemed to draw upon the intense heat energy of the lava for a fearsome burst of strength.

As if to prove her new power, she struck the cavern wall with one fist, causing the rock to crack and break. Then she charged Amaya.

Amaya thought fast. She could fight this elf now and likely lose her life. Or she could sacrifice the mountain fortress and retreat. Amaya had too much left to fight for—she wouldn't sacrifice her life for the fortress. She backpedaled and joined her retreating troops.

Moments later, Amaya and her troops had slipped through the gate. As it slammed behind them, Amaya looked back wearily. The mountain fortress was lost.

Callum scooped Zym up in his arms and brought him close to his face. The baby dragon's eyes were closed, but he was breathing steadily.

SOOBBBB.

Callum wished he could expel all his self-hatred with a single sob. *What a stupid thing to do. Risk his own life—well, who cares? But to risk the baby dragon's?* He hobbled down the boulders to the shoreline and turned toward the *Ruthless*. The weather had started to clear, and a few rays of light pierced the evening clouds. Callum could see Rayla and Ezran standing on the ship. Both had their hands shielding their eyes, like they were trying to see out into the distance. As Callum hurried toward them, he could see Rayla pointing in his direction. *They could see him!*

Callum looked down at Zym. Rayla had been right, of course. She was going to rub it in his face for sure. And he deserved it. The only thing to do was take ownership of his actions—to admit how foolish he'd been. Callum lifted his head up as he approached the boat.

"Callum!" Ezran yelled from the boat. "Hey, where's Zym?"

Callum didn't answer. He heard Rayla whispering. It was hard to make out exactly what she was saying to Ezran, but the words *stupid* and *idiot* were unmistakable. Before Callum knew what was going on, Rayla and Ezran were scrambling along the shore to meet him.

"Callum! What happened?" Rayla shouted.

"We went into the heart of the storm, and Zym . . . he got struck by lightning," Callum said. He choked back another sob.

Rayla gasped.

"But I think he's okay," Callum said a little sheepishly. He revealed Zym, bundled in his arms. The baby dragon squinted and cocked his head to one side. Then he smiled.

HIC! Little lightning sparks crackled out of Zym's mouth as he hiccuped.

"I'm so relieved," Ezran said. He scooped up Zym and hugged him.

"I'm really, really sorry," Callum said. "I feel stupid. You were right." He looked Rayla directly in the eye.

"Callum . . ." she said. She reached her hand out and placed it on his shoulder.

"I could have gotten Zym killed. I put us both in danger. And worst of all, when we were right there, in the center of the storm? I wanted to understand magic so badly I almost risked my own life. But in the end, I didn't have the guts . . ."

"Good," Rayla said. "That's good." She hugged Callum hard.

Callum gulped. Rayla's thin, strong arms wrapped around him meant everything. He smiled and hugged her back.

CHAPTER 17
SUMMIT OF THE PENTARCHY

It was daytime on the top deck of the *Ruthless*, and for all Callum knew, they'd been on the boat for months. The passage of time seemed to stop on the wide-open water, with no landmarks to tell them if or how far they were progressing.

Captain Villads tilted his head back and sniffed.

"Ah yes, the smell of land . . ."

"Woo-hoo," Ezran yelled.

"Oh, sweet land," Rayla cried.

"Finally," Callum said.

"Let him finish," Berto squawked.

"The faint, distant smell of land, that is," Villads said.

"There it is," Berto squawked.

"I'd say about a full day of sailing ahead until we reach the shore," Villads said.

A day could have been a year as far as Callum was concerned. Ezran and Zym walked to the railing to resume counting clouds, while Rayla dropped to a seated position on the deck. She was clutching her stomach again.

"Hmm. Nothing really fun to do," Callum said. "Guess I'll go downstairs and draw a picture of myself having fun." He walked to the hatch leading belowdecks and descended the stairs, shutting the hatch behind him softly. Then he pulled out the letter from King Harrow. The last letter he would ever get from his stepdad.

Callum traced the red wax seal with his finger and picked at the edges. He realized his hands were shaking, and he put the letter down next to him. He closed his eyes and took a long, slow inhale. Then he grabbed the letter in his fist.

Bait was tired of sunning himself on the deck of the *Ruthless* and decided to see what Ezran and Zym were up to. Last he'd heard, they were going to count clouds, which sounded awfully dull. But Bait was lonely.

When he found them, Ezran and Zym had fallen asleep curled next to each other. Bait assumed out of boredom.

Bait didn't mind the little blue dragon, especially since Zym treated him with the utmost respect, but if he was going to be honest, he was a little jealous of all the time Ezran had been spending with Zym. No, he was a *lot* jealous.

Bait decided he could go for a snooze too. He tried to nuzzle himself into the Zym and Ezran cuddle. But every time he got comfortable, the pair would change positions, squeezing him out.

Finally, Bait gave up. He felt dejected and especially grumpy. So he turned around and headed to the hatch belowdecks. The steps down the hatch were intimidating. Bait didn't think his little froggy legs could manage them gracefully. So, he began jumping down, step by step.

THUD.

THUD.

THUD.

This method of descent proved effective, but it was stoking Bait's appetite. He hoped he'd find a tart or cake down in the hatch. Even a stale biscuit would do.

"Hey, can't a guy get a couple of minutes of below-deck privacy around here?" an angry voice yelled.

Bait fell down the next two stairs.

THUD. THUD. He was almost at the bottom now.

"I'm serious, leave me alone—"

Why was Callum shouting at him? Bait looked up at his friend. Callum was sitting on a bench by himself, swinging his legs. *Didn't he want some company? Why didn't anyone want to play?*

Bait felt all the glow go out of him. He was pretty sure he was changing colors. This was so embarrassing. Now Callum would know he was sad. Bait turned around and began to climb back up the stairs.

"Hey, wait," Callum said. "Why don't you join me down here? I could use a little extra light."

Bait turned around once more. Callum wasn't kidding—belowdecks was overly dark.

Bait's entire body brightened. Callum needed him. He headed over and jumped up on the bench with a THUD.

The promising responses from the four other human kingdoms set Viren in motion. Each and every ruler had expressed their desire to hear more about the Xadian threat. They had agreed to a summit of the Pentarchy: a special meeting of the leaders of the five kingdoms.

The first summit of the Pentarchy had been held centuries ago, and it had brought an end to the Mage Wars and created the modern order of the five human kingdoms. These summits were held at a neutral location at the top of Allhaven Hill, in a round temple. Though the hill was technically located in Duren, a former king of Duren had declared this lone hill to be neutral territory many generations ago. According to legend, when someone asked the king if this hill was now a "no-man's-land," the wise king smiled and said, "Quite the contrary, it belongs to *all* humanity."

They all want to meet with you. They think of you as the leader of Katolis.

Viren could barely wait for the meeting. These leaders had only seen him on the sidelines. But he knew all about them. There was King Ahling, the affable monarch of Neolandia, whose sole purpose was to enjoy his life. King Ahling was known across the kingdoms for his love of food, music, and wines. He was not known for his wisdom in any of the kingdoms.

Then there was Queen Fareeda of Evenere. The stately queen stood as tall as her male counterparts and wore her dark red hair piled into a tower above her head. She was the friendliest of the bunch, in Viren's opinion, but also the most cautious.

King Florian of Del Bar would be putty in Viren's hands. The high mage had never heard of King Florian having an original thought.

And then, of course, there would be the regent of Duren, who made decisions for the child queen Aanya until she came of age. The regent was bound by certain constraints that would work in Viren's favor. As long as they all believed the setup—that Viren was now regent of Katolis—he would have a unified group of kingdoms to work with.

Viren traveled with very little. His sole aim was to convince the other leaders of the dire circumstances humans were in and rally them together against the elves. To that end, he carried with him a large, enchanted scroll to make his presentation. His sorcery would terrify and unite the kingdoms.

Viren and the Crownguard rode through the night for the meeting. Just after sunrise, they reached the base of the hill.

A guard standing in front of a massive stone arch held up his hand to prevent Viren from continuing.

"Halt!" the guard cried.

Viren pulled his horse to slow.

"Dismount, disarm, and proceed alone to the meeting point," the guard said. He pushed a large wooden box in Viren's direction. Viren tried to push the box aside, but the guard pushed it back. "For your weapons, sir," he said.

For once, can't these imbeciles treat me appropriately? Maybe when I save them all from Xadia I'll be greeted with greater respect.

"I suppose 'Welcome, Lord Viren' would have been too much to ask," Viren said. He would keep his baser thoughts to himself.

"You'll be officially welcomed when you are disarmed," the guard said in a monotone.

Viren dismounted, carrying the huge rolled scroll and his staff. He arched one eyebrow at the wooden box and handed the staff directly to the guard. The guard tossed the staff into a pile with all the other weapons.

"Welcome," he grunted.

"How gracious," Viren said.

The guard gestured to a path that ascended a mossy green hill. Viren looked in front of him and trudged up alone, carrying nothing but his scroll. It was a beautiful walk up to the grand rotunda at the summit. Though the monarchs referred to it as the "gazebo," it was no quaint wooden structure but rather a stately building, made of fine marble with a soaring dome.

When Viren reached the great doors, he sighed with satisfaction. This was the place where the leaders of the five human kingdoms had been meeting for centuries. And now Viren was a part of this legacy. Despite disagreements among the kingdoms, when the leaders visited this place of peace and beauty, they often put aside their differences in an attempt at resolution.

Three of the monarchs were already there.

"You're the fourth to arrive," King Ahling announced. His portly body nearly enveloped his throne. He stroked his graying beard and mustache slowly, but Viren could tell the king was smiling under all that facial hair. Whatever he lacked in intellect, King Ahling was a good-humored soul.

"May I say on behalf of Neolandia and all the other kingdoms . . . we were deeply saddened to hear of King Harrow's passing," King Ahling added.

Viren placed a hand over his heart. It struck him to hear someone else speak of the king's death. Somehow, the tragedy seemed that much more real. "Thank you, King Ahling. That means a lot," Viren said.

"But," King Ahling said, "we were reassured when we received the scroll informing us that you would be the regent of Katolis until the young King Ezran comes of age."

Viren kept his gaze steady. It seemed the other rulers had not doubted his lie. They accepted at face value not only that Ezran was alive, but that Viren had been made regent. *And why wouldn't they accept it? In a more rational world, it would be true, and the council would have entrusted me with the leadership of Katolis.*

Still, Viren knew he couldn't let any false movements or words betray his secret. He bowed to the other leaders. "It is humbling to be trusted with the boy's education and training, as well as decisions of state," Viren said. "And speaking of regents—it seems we are only waiting on the regent of Duren?" Viren asked.

The other leaders nodded and started to murmur. Duren had always had a reputation for timeliness.

"I apologize for my lateness," a child's voice said. A short, slim figure stood in the enormous doorway. The figure walked into the room briskly with her head held high. Her blond hair was piled on top of her head in a neat bun, and her long white dress was cut sensibly—pleated neatly for horseback riding.

Viren stared. This was the eleven-year-old queen, Aanya.

"Queen Aanya," Queen Fareeda said warmly.

"Aanya of Duren—how you've grown," King Ahling said. "Welcome."

Viren smiled at Aanya as she took her place in the circle. "We are here to discuss some rather weighty matters," Viren said. "Will your regent be joining us soon?" Aanya had been queen since she was orphaned as a baby. Until now, Viren had only seen her appear with an older adviser, her regent.

"I speak for myself now," the queen said with stark confidence. "And for my people."

Viren hesitated, looking around at the other leaders for signs of concern. Not finding any, he decided to say something himself. "This is a very serious situation. I intend no offense, but these issues require an adult perspective."

Expecting to intimidate Aanya as he did his own children, Viren blanched when the barely adolescent queen looked him directly in the eye.

"It seems I am a crown without an adult, and you're an adult without a crown," Queen Aanya said. "Let's just begin." She walked over to the throne for Duren and sat stiffly.

Viren thought he heard a chuckle from across the room, but decided to let it slide. "Very well," he said. He paused, gazing around the room and making eye contact with each leader. "I called us here today . . . because I am afraid. I am scared. Terrified!"

Viren walked to the center of the room, carrying his enormous scroll. With a grandiose gesture, he unfurled a map of Xadia and the five kingdoms that ran the length of the rotunda floor. Viren sprinkled magic dust over the map, a powder derived from dried Xadian moon-night mushrooms. The map immediately appeared to come to life, becoming three-dimensional. Whether the powder affected the map itself or distorted the perception of the viewers was unclear, but the important thing was that it would bring out the visual and emotional impact of the disturbing history lesson Viren was about to commence.

"After centuries of fighting among ourselves, the five human kingdoms finally found a balance—an era of peace." Viren looked around and observed the other leaders nodding. "But a new threat has arisen to challenge all humanity: a threat from Xadia." Viren waved his hand over the map again, and blue winds arose from the parchment, whipping through the rotunda. The walls of the chamber suddenly faded to black, and apparitions of Moonshadow elves appeared on the walls. The apparitions were ominous—dark black shadows with glowing red eyes.

King Ahling screamed. Queen Fareeda fanned her face with her hands. And King Florian jumped out of his throne.

The effect on his audience was exactly what Viren had intended.

"On the night of the full moon," he continued, "the Dragon Queen sent assassins, Moonshadow elves, over the border. They murdered King Harrow."

The terrifying apparitions started to move across the floor, brandishing their weapons. As they approached the human leaders, some gasped in fright at the illusions.

"Now Sunfire elves are gathering near the border," Viren said. At once, the walls became red apparitions of fiery Sunfire elves moving like waves of flame.

"An invasion is imminent. Even worse, there are reports of shadows in the clouds. We think dragons are flying high above the towns of Katolis." Viren closed his eyes. "When I close my eyes, I see fire raining down, death and destruction everywhere."

In a final dramatic flourish, Viren swept his hand over the map to create the illusion of a swelling, uncontrollable inferno.

"It won't stop in Katolis," Viren said. "They will spread their wrath to all the human kingdoms soon enough."

At this point the entire map had been consumed by the blazing hellfire. The other leaders strained backward in their chairs to get away from the fake flames. Except, of course, for King Florian, who had backed up against the rotunda walls long before.

"The time to stop Xadia is now!" Viren shouted. He swept his arm in the air and closed his fist. In an instant, he'd extinguished the fire effect, and the other leaders relaxed. "We must stand together to protect our common humanity. I call on you to join me, to join Katolis: fight beside one another to drive back this threat."

Viren looked around. He knew his performance had shocked the others. King Ahling sat with his mouth agape. The other monarchs appeared equally awed—although Queen Aanya's reaction was inscrutable.

Viren looked around the room, waiting for the supportive reactions he expected to receive.

"Lord Viren," King Ahling said. "The people of Neolandia understand the common humanity that binds us. If the other kingdoms agree to act in unity, we will commit to this alliance."

"Yes," Queen Fareeda said. "In unity, you will have our support as well."

"King Florian?" Viren asked.

King Florian looked to the others, then back to Viren. "If we are all agreed—then the kingdom of Del Bar will join you," he said.

"Very well." Viren smiled. "And Queen Aanya. What say you?"

Queen Aanya said nothing.

Viren's smile wavered. As the silence continued, it turned into a frown. Could it be, he'd traveled so far, taken so many risks, all to have his plans thwarted by a little girl?

Finally, she spoke.

"I am undecided," Queen Aanya said.

"Undecided?!" Viren couldn't believe that his magical presentation had failed to convince. What could she possibly be worried about?

"Yes, it means I've yet to make up my mind," Queen Aanya said.

Viren pressed his lips together lest he say something he would regret. He addressed everyone but the young queen. "This is why we need an adult," he said. "A leader who can make strong choices for their kingdom. Everyone else here was capable of making a decision."

"I won't send my armies to face unknown danger based on a

two-minute speech," Queen Aanya said. "I may be a child, but apparently, I'm the least impulsive of us all. Besides, I hardly call 'we'll do what everyone else does' a decision."

"She's got a fair point," King Ahling said. He chuckled.

Though he had never considered the monarch of Neolandia a genius, how King Ahling could laugh at a time like this was beyond Viren's comprehension. He collected himself once again and approached Queen Aanya—more calmly.

"Perhaps I was rash in my words. I apologize. You are a young queen, but evidently far wiser than your years." Viren bowed deeply.

But the tiny blond wisp of a leader did not take to buttering up.

"As a child ruler, I have had to survive adults trying to usurp my throne, coups, conspiracies, and assassination attempts," she said. "But sometimes it's not the hard threats, but the soft threats, that are the worst. Sweet words can be more dangerous than hidden daggers."

Viren seethed.

"My nineteen-year-old doesn't know half the words you just said," King Ahling said. He seemed to be amused by his own child's failings. "And he still fights back about eating his vegetables."

Viren ignored King Ahling. If Queen Aanya was truly undecided, he believed he could convince her to join him with another incredible story, one that the young queen would find considerably more personal. "Queen Aanya, would you allow me to share a story with you? A story of a time when our kingdoms worked together to achieve something . . . miraculous?"

She nodded.

"Nine years ago, my oldest friend, Prince Harrow, became the King of Katolis," Viren began. "I remember the coronation as if it were only yesterday." Viren closed his eyes to visualize the coronation.

chapter 18
champion of love
and justice

Viren gazed over the cheering crowd and then back at his friend, the crown prince. Prince Harrow was kneeling on the grand balcony in front of the people. His head was bowed, and the low dusky sunlight shone on his jet-black dreadlocks. As the high cleric placed the crown on Harrow's head, Viren breathed with excitement and clapped for the young monarchs.

The new king stood and grabbed Queen Sarai's hand, then turned to face the crowd.

"I want to make a difference!" Harrow shouted to the crowd.

Viren believed that Harrow would do just that. He had the support of his wonderful wife. Viren watched as Sarai brushed a lock of hair from King Harrow's face and cupped his chin in her hand. "You will," she told her husband. "You'll be a champion of love and justice. And I'll be fighting by your side."

Viren was proud to be the high mage to King Harrow. Though he had served the previous king, Viren had known the prince—*the new king, rather*—since they were teens. He knew Harrow to be humble, approachable, friendly, and funny. He seemed to truly care. Viren admired how Harrow paid attention to people no matter who they were, and showed them respect and kindness.

Katolis was on the brink of great things. Viren could feel it.

The energy of newness and possibility was still in the air days later, when the royal family posed for their first portraits together in the throne room. King Harrow was so giddy he could barely stand still. The artist was at his wit's end trying to paint the king.

"Are we done yet?" Harrow asked through a frozen smile. "It looks pretty done to me."

"Baby Ezran and little Callum have more patience for their portraits than you, My King," Viren said.

"I don't doubt that," King Harrow said. "Can I move now?"

The painter shrugged. He was mostly finished.

"Phew," King Harrow said. Everyone relaxed their portrait faces.

"Hold on, you're not free yet," Viren said. "The king must pose for one more."

"Ah, my official portrait," King Harrow said. "For the history books and whatnot."

"You don't care to impress the history books?" Viren asked. He would love to have his portrait passed down from generation to generation in venerable tomes.

King Harrow beckoned toward Viren. "Why don't you join me, Viren?" he said.

"But . . . this is your official portrait as king," Viren said. It wouldn't be right for him to stand with King Harrow . . . as much as he wanted to.

"Yes. And you should stand next to me—as I know you will stand by me through anything," King Harrow said.

Viren nodded and walked silently to stand next to the king. He stood up straight as a rod, looked directly in front of him, and was careful not to move a muscle for the entire session.

Queen Sarai did not consider herself an idealist as her husband did—rather, she called herself an "optimistic realist." Even so, her realism was in no way complacent or accepting of the status quo. She wanted to do things differently—to change the world.

The evening after the coronation, when many new monarchs would have been celebrating, she wound down from the day in her chambers with baby Ezran and her husband. Queen Sarai had been circling the room with a tired, fussing baby when Harrow entered, holding something behind his back.

"I brought you a surprise," he said.

Queen Sarai smiled. Harrow was always doing little things like that—showing up with something small but sweet and unexpected. This time, he pulled out an entire tray of jelly tarts and placed it on the bed.

"Jelly tarts in bed?" Queen Sarai asked. It seemed indulgent, even for royalty.

"We are the king and queen now. We can do whatever we want," Harrow replied mischievously.

Queen Sarai laughed at the absurdity of doing whatever she wanted. She'd never believed that was the role of a monarch.

King Harrow gazed at her and the baby, but then his gaze seemed to drift. He suddenly seemed far away—his body was present, but his mind was somewhere else.

"What are you thinking about?" Sarai asked.

"Baby Ezran is a lucky boy," he said. "Born a prince, as I was. But there are so many in our kingdom who were born with less."

Queen Sarai placed Ezran on the bed in his swaddle and reached over for King Harrow's shoulder.

"What troubles you?" she asked.

"Why do I deserve this? What did I do, except being born . . . with everything?" Harrow asked.

"You are humble and grateful and kind," Queen Sarai said.

"Sarai, my father told me that above all, I must be a just king. The night he died, Lady Justice came to me in a dream."

"I'm generally not in favor of strange women coming to you in dreams, but this time, I'll make an exception," Queen Sarai said with a smile.

Harrow stood and walked over toward the fire. He stared into the flames as he spoke.

"Lady Justice said that justice was more than fair decisions and fair consequences—true justice was a fair system. Then she laid before me her scales, her sword, and her blindfold, and told me to choose."

Queen Sarai knew immediately which item her husband

had chosen—even in his dream. "You chose the blindfold," she said.

He nodded. "I did. She said the blindfold gives us a way to test the system." Harrow covered his own eyes with his hand. "She said that I should use it to imagine I had not been born yet—and that I did not know if I would be born rich or poor, what color my skin would be, what culture or practices my family would have. That a fair system should be fair no matter the accident of my birth. That the rights and laws and opportunities within the system should stand to protect and empower everyone."

He uncovered his eyes and looked at the queen searchingly.

Queen Sarai stood up and softly approached her thoughtful husband. "You're especially inspiring when you say things like that . . . with jelly smeared on your nose," she said, smiling.

"What?" Harrow flushed with embarrassment as he put his hand to his nose. He'd been pouring his heart out with a nose covered in red jam. So, Queen Sarai did the only thing she could think of—she licked the jelly off his nose.

"Gross," King Harrow said.

"Quite the contrary. Delicious!" The queen laughed.

It wasn't long after Harrow took the throne that the queens of Duren came to visit Katolis. Duren was in trouble, and the queens needed help. They were elegant and formal. When they entered Harrow's throne room, they stood side by side and immediately knelt.

King Harrow couldn't accept this display of humility.

"No, please—you don't have to kneel," he said, standing up from his throne.

But they remained on their knees.

"We are here to humble ourselves, and beg for your help," Queen Annika said. Her cropped, snow-white hair was tucked behind her golden crown and her hair partially covered her sad eyes.

"The kingdom of Duren has been suffering from a terrible famine for nearly seven years," Queen Neha added. She looked up at the king and brushed a long, braided lock away from her face. Her pale blue makeup highlighted the sincerity of her dark brown features. "Our food and resources are almost gone. This winter, we will run out of food, and a hundred thousand people will die." She closed her eyes as if she couldn't bear to contemplate the casualties.

The queens were both pale and wan. King Harrow knew that Duren had struggled, but he was unaware of the severity. He couldn't bear to think of others starving while the people of Katolis had plenty.

Harrow leaped out of his throne, eager to help.

"We will come to your aid," he said. "The kingdom of Katolis will share all that it has with the people of Duren."

The queens seemed to breathe easier almost immediately. Their faces shone with relief and gratitude. Queen Neha touched Queen Annika's arm and looked at her with tears in her eyes.

At last, Harrow felt that he could do some significant good in the world. But before he could put plans in place, he felt someone tugging on the sleeve of his robe like a small child. Viren.

"What is it, Viren?" King Harrow asked. He shook the high mage's hand from his sleeve.

"King Harrow, if you'll excuse me," Viren said. "Before you dig yourself into a deeper hole, we must consult."

"Very well," the king said. He excused himself and followed Viren into his study.

"Well?" the king said. "What's your concern?"

"My King—with respect . . . you spoke too soon," Viren said. "Katolis has barely enough food to sustain its own people through the winter—there is not a handful of grain to spare."

"Viren, I cannot turn my back on people in need," King Harrow said. The struggles that plagued the kingdom of Duren were a perfect example of the inequality of life. Just because a family was born in Duren and not Katolis, they would starve to death this winter? This situation made no sense.

"If you share with Duren, one hundred thousand people may still die—but half of them will be from our own kingdom," Viren said.

"Then it seems we have no choice," King Harrow said.

"Exactly. I'm sure they will understand . . ."

Harrow smiled. No one ever understood a refusal of help. "Viren, we will share whatever we have with them. And we will share in their suffering."

The high mage could barely conceal his shock and disgust at this course of action. But he said nothing.

Later that day, Harrow returned to the king's tower. He stood on the balcony, musing over the commitment he had made. *Was it a foolhardy promise? Was Viren correct? What if he'd condemned his own people to a winter of starvation and death?*

The king was about to send for Viren when the high mage walked out onto the balcony weighed down by a tower of scrolls and books. "I have been doing research!" Viren announced gleefully. "I've spent the past few hours poring over ancient texts and maps in the archives. I may have found something that could save lives. A creative solution!"

"Well, go on. Tell me," King Harrow said eagerly.

"Behold," Viren said. And with an entirely unnecessary flourish, he opened his fist and revealed what appeared to be a dark gray mass of granite.

"Viren, it's a rock," King Harrow said. "I mean, it's a great rock, don't get me wrong."

"This 'rock' is, in fact, a rare relic from Xadia," Viren said, holding it up at eye level so he could admire it. "It's a very small piece of a very big monster, a rocky giant who lives high in the mountains: a magma titan."

He tossed the rock to King Harrow, who turned it over in his hands. "It's very warm," the king said.

"Yes," Viren replied. "The titan lives close to the border of Xadia. If we can hunt this monster, and slay it, I can use the heart of the titan in a powerful spell that will warm the land and allow us to magically grow an incredible bounty."

"Enough to feed two kingdoms?" King Harrow asked.

"Enough to feed ten kingdoms," Viren said.

It was all so tempting. By hunting this titan, everyone would have enough food without human sacrifice. At the same time, it went against the principles Harrow and Sarai had agreed on.

Hard work and unity in hardship. Peace. Justice. Besides, Harrow wasn't interested in killing. Even if it was just a monster. What's more, the mission was sure to be risky.

"Crossing the border is dangerous," King Harrow said. "From dawn to dusk, the king of the dragons soars high above the continent and can see a thousand miles—he guards Xadia jealously. He has always spotted human invaders within minutes. You know all this."

But Viren had thought out all the angles.

"That's why this must be a night mission," he said. "We will enter Xadia at dark, and be out again before sunrise."

Harrow considered this approach, thinking of every little thing that could possibly go wrong. "Even if we somehow succeed, and return with the heart of this titan . . . the spell . . . are you certain it will work?" he asked.

Viren nodded slowly.

Unfortunately, it seemed like killing the titan was the only chance to save a hundred thousand lives. But Harrow could not commit to this mission without consulting his queen.

It was midday, the sun was bright, and Queen Sarai had just jabbed King Harrow in the side with a wooden spear. "It's a mistake, Harrow," she said. "I don't like this plan one bit."

Harrow stepped back as she shoved the spear deep into his rib cage.

"Sarai, we're just sparring," he said with a gasp. "Take it easy. Anyway, why do you have such a problem with Viren's magma titan plan? We kill one monster to save a hundred thousand people."

Queen Sarai wondered why Harrow would bother to get her opinion if he was so sure Viren's plan was solid.

"You keep calling it a monster," she said. She pressed her shoulder against his, staring him down.

"Yes, it's a giant beast made of rock and magma," he said. "I call that a monster."

"Is it intelligent?" Queen Sarai asked. She twirled around, spun her spear, and disarmed Harrow. His spear flew into the air and clattered to the courtyard grounds—well out of his reach.

"What?" he asked. "What do you mean, 'Is it intelligent?'" He had his arms up to block the incoming jabs.

"Does it think? Does it feel?" she asked. *Jab. Jab.* He had no response. "Does it have a family?" Harrow was backing up, trying to create enough distance between himself and Sarai to grab his sword from his waist.

"I sincerely doubt it has a family," he said. He yanked out the sword and whipped it up in front of his face.

"Well, then, is it the last of its kind?" she asked.

"Why does any of that matter?" he asked.

Queen Sarai believed Harrow had always been too easily swayed by Viren's creative solutions. Dark magic was always just a little too easy. "I know it seems like this will solve things," she said. "But could it possibly cause more problems?"

"Like what? And anyway, what choice do we have?" Harrow asked. He rushed at Sarai with a high inside attack and pushed her back on the defensive. The king's swordsmanship was excellent.

"You said you want to build a better world, to really change things—but that's going to take decades of hard work." Queen Sarai was pacing the courtyard now. Harrow was spent. She would finish him off in minutes. "There's a special kind of courage that you need for consistency and perseverance," she said. "There's no monster you can slay to solve all your problems. There's no shortcut."

Queen Sarai wanted the best for the kingdom of Duren, but she wanted to solve problems the way she and Harrow had planned in their long, late-night discussions. Those plans had never included dark magic. She raised her spear and turned to face her husband.

"This is going to be a very slippery slope!" she yelled. Then she charged, overwhelming him with blows, and forced Harrow onto the ground.

"Harrow, please tell me you won't do this," she said.

But he didn't respond.

Later that day, once King Harrow had bathed and recovered from sparring with Sarai, he sent for the queens of Duren to meet him and Lord Viren in the throne room. He'd had a few hours to reflect on what Sarai had said—and why he had even been motivated to get her opinion in the first place. He no longer wanted to use dark magic to help.

"My Queens," Harrow said, "Katolis will do everything we can to help the people of Duren. We will share all the grain that we—"

"No—King Harrow, we must decline your offer," Queen Neha interrupted.

"What?" he asked. He passed a hand through his thick hair in shock. *Why would they refuse any help at all? That was certain death for their people.*

Queen Neha looked at Queen Annika, who nodded solemnly. She wiped a tear from her cheek. "We have learned that Katolis barely has enough food for its own people. We cannot accept such a sacrifice," she said.

King Harrow could barely speak. He could hazard a guess as to who told the queens about Katolis's mediocre grain supply. He was certain the queens had been forced into this moral dilemma.

"Very well," he said. There was no use arguing, but he hated to feel so powerless. He sank back into his throne.

"The people of Duren are strong," Viren said. "We know you will face the hardship of the coming winter with bravery and grace."

The queens bowed and turned to exit. But King Harrow couldn't bear it—couldn't bear to let them go back to their people empty-handed.

"No, stop," he said, standing up from the throne. He looked at Viren and nodded. "I can't let you leave like this. There may be a way to help everyone—the people of both our kingdoms."

He knew his decision would disappoint Queen Sarai, and that weighed heavily on him. But the thought of so many innocent people starving to death outweighed his sense of right and wrong.

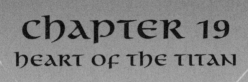

CHAPTER 19
HEART OF THE TITAN

King Harrow knew there was no time to lose if they were going to kill the magma titan. By early evening, he had assembled the party at the gates of the kingdom. Viren and Queens Neha and Annika were there, as well as Sarai's sister, General Amaya, who would lead many troops on horseback. The mission was dangerous and Harrow's heart was heavy, but he was there, ready to lead.

"We will enter Xadia through the Breach," King Harrow said loudly. "There we can pick up supplies and—"

But before he could finish, Queen Sarai galloped up to the group. She was dressed in full battle armor. The creases on King Harrow's face softened. This mission suddenly seemed doable.

"Queen Sarai," Harrow said. He couldn't understand her change of heart.

"Yes, Harrow, I'm here," she said. "I disagree with this choice—but I stand by you anyway."

Harrow's heart melted. He didn't deserve this wonderful woman. As the castle gates opened and everyone galloped off, Harrow grabbed Sarai's wrist to keep her back with him for a moment alone.

"Thank you," he said. Queen Sarai had never looked as beautiful as at that moment. He couldn't even begin to express himself.

"I think this was in our marriage vows, right?" Queen Sarai asked. She grabbed King Harrow's hand in her own and smiled at him. "Something about keeping you alive when you're acting like a brave idiot?

"Come on," she said. There was a monster to slay and a kingdom to save.

Harrow's confidence in the mission soared as they traveled to the Xadian border. Sometimes he felt like Sarai was the source of his strength and energy. He couldn't imagine facing this world without her.

With Queen Sarai by his side, he was part of a bold adventure—a union of two human kingdoms bound to each other against the threats from the mystical world across the Breach.

As the group approached the Breach, Harrow and Sarai could see the river of lava swirling ominously, oozing and sizzling with red-hot magma. Harrow swiftly guided the group through the rocky, unstable terrain, drawing on his years of training when he was crown prince.

Once all had crossed safely, they sought shelter in the secret fortress that Katolis had built on the Xadian side of the Breach. There they prepared themselves with the large armaments they would need to hunt the magma titan.

King Harrow turned to address the brave adventurers.

"The king of the dragons patrols the skies of Xadia from dawn until dusk. They say Thunder can see a thousand miles, so every minute we spend in Xadia in the light of day is a minute we risk attracting his devastating wrath. So, we cannot enter Xadia until sundown—and we must return with the heart of the titan before the first moments of the sun's rise."

Queen Neha eyed the three giant crossbows mounted on wheels. She seemed unsure. "Will these ballistas be able to take down a magma titan? Can they pierce its rocky armor?" she asked.

King Harrow looked at the ballistas. Though these were mighty by human scale, if Viren was right about the magma titan, it would dwarf the humans' weaponry.

But Harrow believed that when a cause is righteous, providence guides the hand of the humble and courageous. He looked at Queen Neha. "If our aim is true, we will prevail," he said.

Viren made sure that not a single person left the secret fortress before the skies were fully dark. Thunder took his patrols seriously—their only chance was in these few hours of darkness while the great dragon slept.

As the soldiers and queens began their rapid battle preparations, Viren lingered behind—weapons and warfare were not his areas of expertise. But locating the magma titan—that was a task for him alone. For miles around, there was nothing but boulders. There was no time to waste just looking for the titan.

Viren unpacked the items he needed for the location spell.

He lit a small fire and crushed the small rock from the titan—the piece of the monster that he'd tucked away in his secret office—with a mortar and pestle. Next, he opened a glass jar of glowing wisps that could only be acquired from a very special grotto. Then he mixed the dust from the rock with the powder from the fire's ashes. With a flick of his fingers, he incinerated the mixture.

Viren could feel everyone's eyes on him. "Ecnesse ruoy esuf," he chanted in a deep, mystical voice. He felt the familiar dark magic energy take over his body—his eyes and fingers glowed with power.

He pressed his glowing hands around the jar of wisps. The wisps absorbed the energy and turned bright purple. Viren lifted the jar skyward and chanted again: "Natit amgam eht kees."

When he opened the jar, the super-charged wisps shot out, arcing across the sky in search of the magma titan. Viren consulted his magic map, where a glowing purple line drew itself, showing the way to a craggy area.

"This way!" Viren yelled.

He started off for the titan, but stumbled a bit. The spell had weakened him temporarily. And all at once, he knew he was in the biggest battle of his life. This place held both the promise of salvation and the threat of destruction.

But what Viren found wasn't anything like what he had expected. His map led them to the glowing wisps, which fluttered frantically near a deep chasm. The wisps drifted from the chasm toward what appeared to be an unusual pile of rocks. There was no monster.

Had the spell failed? Viren approached the pile of rocks. On closer inspection, he realized the pile of rocks *was* the magma titan. *Of course, the spell had worked.* But the monster was prone, completely still, lying on its back. It looked long dead.

Queen Neha panicked. "It's dead," she said. "What do we do now?"

"Don't sound so disappointed, Queen Neha," Viren said. "If it's dead, we don't need to kill it. We just . . . open it up and take what we need."

"You mean its heart," she said.

"Yes," Viren said.

Queen Neha wasted no time climbing up onto the chest of the monster. General Amaya joined her, lugging a huge warhammer. Queen Neha positioned a giant chisel in the center of the monster's chest.

Everyone watched breathlessly as they prepared to cut into it. Each time Amaya swung the hammer, it connected with a *thwack*. But for all her power, the chisel made only small dents in the magma titan. The work was steady, but too slow for Viren, who knew only too well how limited the time was.

Then there was one hard hammer slam that sounded different than the rest. Fissures appeared in the monster's chest. Progress at last!

No sooner had they cracked the beast open than something stirred from deep within the dormant giant. Great rumbling noises shook the ground as the magma titan began to glow from within. The cracks in its body lit up, radiating with life.

What had looked like death was only a deep sleep. As the monster awoke, its body glowed with magma energy. Viren watched in horror as it rose—a beast as tall as one hundred humans standing on one another's shoulders.

Then the monster let out an earsplitting roar. The ground shook and Viren shuddered, his heart suddenly heavy with fear and guilt. *There's no way they'll be able to defeat this monster. This doomed mission was all my idea.*

As the battle began, King Harrow and the queens Sarai, Neha, and Annika showed tremendous bravery. Viren felt sick knowing they could never conquer this beast.

When the magma titan stirred from its slumber and rose to its full height, Queen Sarai didn't flinch. She knew there was danger on every side. The titan towered over a steep chasm. One misstep, or one vicious blow from the titan, meant the humans would plunge into the abyss—forever.

So Queen Sarai faced the titan head-on and started hurling spears at its body—but they merely bounced off the rocky creature. It was chaos, and she could only focus on what was right in front of her. All around her, soldiers were being crushed and trampled.

"Fire the ballistas!" Sarai yelled at the soldiers. The ballistas were stronger than any spear or sword—perhaps there was a chance.

"Aim for the cracks between the rocky plates!" Queen Neha shouted. "We can chain it down."

They attached two bolts to chains and fired them off. Both hit their mark and lodged into the sides of the titan. Temporarily, the creature was under control. But the magma titan easily removed one of the bolts by its chain, swung it overhead, and tossed it away. The other it simply crushed in its hot, fiery hands.

Amaya and Sarai stayed close to each other on horseback, braving the terrain nearest to the giant. The two were so close they could communicate without speech, even without signs. Silently, they agreed to draw the titan's attention toward them and began to coordinate an attack.

Harrow stayed with the queens of Duren and the ballistas.

"Take aim at the center! Fire right where we first cracked into it," King Harrow shouted.

The soldiers fired another bolt, which successfully harpooned the center of the titan's torso, its long chain still connected to the heavy ballista from which it had been fired.

"Now what?" Queen Neha asked.

"Push," Harrow said. "Push it over the edge of the chasm!"

Brilliant! Queen Sarai watched the soldiers push the ballista off the ledge and into the chasm. The chained bolt was wedged into the giant's rocky armor. When the ballista plummeted off the ledge and into the chasm, the chain grew taut and tore the rocky plate in the center of the titan's chest right off.

Queen Sarai pointed at the enormous gap in the monster's

rocky armor. She winked at Amaya. But before they could execute their unspoken plan, the titan swung its arm out in anger, spraying loose magma in an arc. A stray blast of the searing-hot liquid rock grazed Amaya's face and sent her flying off her horse.

Amaya stood up, fierce and defiant, despite the deep, burning gash in her cheek.

It was clear the titan wanted to crush her sister. Sarai didn't have time to think. She charged the monster on foot. At the very last moment, Amaya lifted her shield up as a platform for Sarai, who used it as a springboard and leaped off the shield, plunging her spear deep into the exposed hole at the center of the titan's torso.

The titan roared in pain. Its mammoth body shook like the beginning of an avalanche. It rocked back and forth on its heels and then fell to its knees, stunned. It hacked and coughed up lava.

For a moment, it looked like the monster might get to its feet again, but then it fell down. It was dead.

Everyone was silent.

A few moments later, the rocky armor crumbled away. Lava flowed from the dead titan, revealing the prize they had risked everything to attain: the titan's heart. It was a stunning crystal, the size of a boulder. It was magnificent, clear and bright and captivating. It seemed to pulse with light.

Viren approached the heart with great care and knelt beside it.

"The legend was true," he said, incredulous. "The heart of the titan—it radiates with life and magic." He spoke with a sense of awe shared by the humans around him.

"So . . . do you think you can . . . use it?" Harrow asked.

"Yes," Viren said. The hard edge was back in his voice. "We can save them all!"

Everyone cheered, and the queens of Duren embraced. "Our people . . . they'll be fed," Queen Neha said.

Sarai signed to Amaya, "You did it—we did it."

But Amaya didn't respond. She was standing nearby but she was facing away. She looked unsteady.

"Sister!" Sarai cried out and rushed to her. "Amaya!"

Amaya turned around when she sensed Sarai's presence. Blood poured from her forehead and cheek and swam in her eyes.

Sarai folded her wounded sister into her arms and stroked her head. She examined the wounds while Amaya caught her breath.

"How does it look?" Amaya signed to Sarai.

Sarai could tell her sister was terrified. She laid her down, then signed, "Not great. But you should see the other guy."

Amaya smiled.

Queen Neha, Queen Annika, and a few soldiers secured the giant gemstone-heart onto beams so it could be carried back to Katolis. Viren stood near Harrow, whispering. There was a familiar, scheming look on his face. Sarai strained to hear what he was saying.

"Time is short. There's barely an hour until sunrise," he said. "We can't risk the wrath of the Dragon King. We must take the heart and hurry back."

"Yes, of course," Harrow said. "We'll move as fast we can."

Then Viren glanced at Amaya and lowered his voice even

further. "The wounded must be left behind," he whispered. "We can't afford to slow down . . ."

Amaya was watching Viren closely. She was reading his lips. She turned to her sister and signed, "He doesn't have to whisper . . . I'm deaf."

"Hey, Viren," Sarai said. "I get it—you think it would be safer to leave the wounded behind. Did you forget Amaya can read lips?"

Viren looked . . . he looked . . . embarrassed.

Sarai smiled. "But Amaya says she'll be okay even if you leave. She just needs a little rest and then she can make it back."

"We won't leave you here alone," Harrow promised Amaya.

Viren, however, said nothing.

"I'll stay with Amaya," Sarai said. "We'll make it home together. Everyone else should take the heart back. Completing this mission is what matters most."

Viren turned to Harrow. "They agree. Time is of the essence."

"No," Harrow said. "We leave no one behind. We do not leave our wounded."

"You're risking everything—trading the lives of many for the lives of a few," Viren said.

"It's principle," Harrow responded firmly.

"It's foolishness! You're hiding behind your idealism, but you're being selfish and you know it. You wouldn't do this if it wasn't your wife's sister."

Viren wouldn't even look at Sarai and Amaya as he spoke. In that moment, Sarai hated him viscerally . . . but she also agreed with him.

"I've made my decision, and it is final," Harrow said.

Viren marched across Xadia beneath the purple predawn sky. He was furious.

A few soldiers were carrying Amaya and another wounded warrior; all others walked beside their horses. On top of the beautiful crystal heart, these burdens were slowing them down. As a result, they were moving half-speed at best. Viren feared they wouldn't make it back to the Breach before sunrise.

He saw the pinking dawn in the sky and picked up the pace. They were near the border, but still on the Xadian side of the Breach. The sun rose on the horizon, its first new day beams beating on Viren's neck like the hot doom he knew was coming.

"There's the entrance—we've almost made it," Harrow called out from up front, doing his best to encourage everyone.

"Faster," Sarai said. "All our strength now."

Viren increased his speed and hoped the others would do the same. Maybe, if they all made one last push, they would all get out alive.

Minutes passed, and the humans drew closer and closer to the border. Their safe escape was in sight. Perhaps they would make it after all.

Then suddenly the heat evaporated and the morning light disappeared. Viren felt a chill as a shadow covered the sun.

"Thunder," Harrow whispered.

The storm had come. The king of the dragons arrived in a burst of lightning. With a great booming crash, he landed just behind the humans.

Everyone scrambled up the mountainside toward the entrance to the Breach as the roaring dragon approached. But their organized march soon collapsed into fear. Viren knew they should have left the wounded behind.

"We'll never make it," Queen Neha said.

From her stretcher, General Amaya signed rapidly to Queen Sarai. She reached for her shield, which the queen kept away from her.

King Harrow turned to the others. "We have to hold off the dragon as long as possible so those carrying the heart can make it back," he said. He looked back at the enormous, angry dragon. "Even if our lives buy only a minute . . ."

Harrow drew his sword, ready to go back toward Xadia.

"We'll slow him down," Queen Sarai said. She was ready to die alongside her husband. But as soon as they started to move, Queen Annika put her hand up.

"Stop," she said. She looked at Queen Neha. "This is our day to sacrifice," she said.

Queen Neha nodded. "You get the titan's heart to safety," she said. "Save all our people."

Queen Neha mounted her horse. Queen Annika grabbed Harrow's hand and pressed something into his palm, closing his fingers around it. She'd given him the ring she'd been wearing on her hand. It was a gold band with a large oval sapphire. Then she climbed onto her own horse.

The queens charged down the mountainside, knowing their fate.

Finally, Viren thought. *At least the queens of Duren could think rationally.* He watched as they rode off to fight Thunder. He admired their courage and nobility.

But Viren couldn't escape the fact that all this fighting, bloodshed, and sacrifice had stemmed from his idea. He closed his eyes and gathered his thoughts. The only chance the queens would have would be with magic. Was he really ready to give his own life for thousands of regular citizens? People he didn't know and would never meet? But on the other hand, he would be remembered forever as a hero.

"I can help," Viren said to Harrow. Without waiting for his response, he turned back down the mountain. Even if he couldn't save the queens, he could buy them some time, ensuring the safety of the others.

Viren pulled his primal stone from his cloak and traced an advanced rune in the sky.

"Aspiro frigis!" he yelled into the stormy chaos. And with all the air in his lungs, he blew a freezing blast at Thunder.

It worked. The spell generated enormous icicles around the Dragon King's head, freezing him in place.

The queens didn't waste a moment of Thunder's vulnerability.

"For Aanya!" Queen Neha shouted as she charged the frozen behemoth.

They galloped at full speed toward Thunder, rushing directly at his huge face. His massive eye stared down his human attackers, but he remained immobilized by the ice. The queens drew closer and closer. They raised their swords, prepared to strike the vulnerable eye of the great Dragon King.

But the ice wouldn't hold any longer. Thunder's whole body

crackled with electricity. His power shattered the ice, blowing fragments in every direction.

With his head finally free, Thunder whipped around. The queens' horses were terrified. They were now way too close to the very angry king of the dragons.

Thunder brought his massive tail crashing down where the queens stood. The impact was like an earthquake. It knocked Viren off his feet. With ice and debris flying around him, he lay still on the ground, listening to Thunder's deafening roar.

King Harrow tried not to think about Viren, who had stayed behind to face the dragon. He focused on getting the titan's heart out of Xadia. As they neared the Breach, he realized that they were going to make it after all.

"They bought us enough time. We've made it," Harrow said to Sarai.

His relief was palpable. They had finished the mission and would feed all the hungry people.

But Queen Sarai wasn't looking at the Breach—she was looking back. Harrow turned and followed her gaze. It was Viren. He was sprawled on the ground, injured.

"Without Viren to perform the spell, the titan's heart is worthless, and this was all for nothing," Sarai said.

Harrow knew she was right. But what could he do about it? Maybe they could figure out a way to use the heart back at Katolis.

Sarai had stopped moving toward the border.

"Sarai, what are you doing?" Harrow asked. He felt dread growing where seconds before there had been relief.

Queen Sarai mounted her horse.

"I'll see you on the other side," she said as she galloped toward Viren and Thunder.

But King Harrow never saw Queen Sarai again.

Viren was dazed and injured. He knew the queens were dead—there was no way they could have survived the attack from that dragon tail. *I must be doomed.* He knew Thunder was out for blood, but he couldn't see the dragon for all the dust.

And then, Viren saw a figure charging toward him on horseback. He thought he might be seeing things that weren't there, but the figure grew closer and closer until there was no mistaking it.

It was Queen Sarai. She'd come back to rescue him. She slowed her horse and reached her hand down to Viren. He grasped it. With surprising strength, she hoisted him onto her horse.

"Thank you," Viren said. He owed her. When they got back to Katolis, Viren would be more considerate of Sarai, he promised himself.

"Don't thank me yet," she said.

The horse galloped back toward the border. But by then, Thunder had them in his line of sight. With a single beat of his wings, the dragon was airborne, blowing blasts of lightning breath.

Thunder's aim was imperfect, and Queen Sarai was a

champion rider. Viren felt the horse dodge and weave through blasts, leaping over obstacles.

Thunder became angrier and angrier, and the lightning blasts became wilder and more desperate. But Sarai's path remained relentless, precise, and agile. Viren began to believe they might evade the dragon after all.

Then the furious barrage of lightning blasts stopped. Had the Dragon King given up? Viren was afraid to look back.

But the dragon had simply paused to gather his senses and take aim.

BOOM! An enormous blast lifted the horse off its feet, throwing the queen and her high mage through the air.

Viren landed hard and far away, with the wind knocked out of him. As the dust settled, he coughed violently and scanned the ground for Queen Sarai. When he spotted her, Viren's stomach churned.

Sarai was quite still, lying on the ground, covered in dirt and ash. But she was breathing. Viren forgot his own injuries and ran to her.

"Come on," he said, tugging at her arm. "We have to run."

She opened her eyes. Viren shook her. She was so strong; he knew she would get up. But she just shook her head and said nothing.

Viren was with Queen Sarai as she took her last breath. In one hand, he held her fingers, squeezing them to give her a sense of human presence as she passed. In the other hand, he held the empty jar that had once contained the wisps—soon it would contain something even rarer.

CHAPTER 20
LIFE AND GROWING UP

King Harrow returned to Katolis safely, but his life was never the same. The land of Xadia had stolen his most precious loved one, and he felt that all the strength had been sapped out of him.

The king tried to console himself with the notion that Queen Sarai's ultimate sacrifice had changed the world.

The heart of the titan worked exactly as Viren had promised. It yielded its incredible life force. King Harrow witnessed barren, fallow fields transformed into verdant abundance. A hundred thousand lives were saved. Families celebrated their life and health and gave thanks to three incredible heroes. Three queens—three mothers—became legends.

After returning to Katolis, King Harrow spent a day locked in his chambers, avoiding Prince Callum. Telling the young prince that his mother had died would take strength, and he had none left. The only person he was willing to see was Viren.

"It should have been me," Viren said. He was sitting on a chair with his head in his hands. King Harrow leaned over the hearth.

"No, it should have been me," King Harrow said. "Queen Sarai sacrificed herself for a plan she never believed in." He pulled the crown off his head. He didn't care about being king anymore. It meant nothing without Sarai by his side.

"Exactly!" Viren said. "It was my plan, and, therefore, my fault. You can't blame yourself."

"No," King Harrow said. "You see, she didn't believe in the plan . . . she believed in me." The king's voice cracked. Tears rolled from his eyes into the crackling fire. He began to sob.

Viren said nothing for a long time. Finally, he spoke. "I'm so sorry," he said.

Then a guard opened the door without knocking. "Your Highness," she said, "he's waiting for you now. The boy is confused and he insists he will only speak with you." The guard was referring to Callum.

"Okay," King Harrow said.

The king wiped the tears from his eyes. He had to tell Callum, and he had to be strong for him. Harrow imagined Sarai's love filling him up with the strength he needed. The king corrected his posture. He followed the guard to the throne room.

"Are you ready?" a guard asked.

"No," Harrow said. *He'd never felt so completely unprepared. How could he face Callum?* "But you may open the doors."

When he saw small Callum standing alone in the great throne

room, King Harrow's heart nearly split in two. But he kept moving forward. When he reached Callum, the king knelt to his level.

"Callum," he said. "I want to talk to you about life. And growing up. And how sometimes there are changes ... you don't expect."

CHAPTER 21
LIKE A RIVER

Queen Aanya had vowed to remain stoic as she listened to Lord Viren recount the story of her mothers and their deaths. She knew Lord Viren was trying to win her over for his own purposes, but despite herself, the queen was welling up. She clutched the pendant on her neck and released it almost by reflex. She always kept her mother's ring inside. The pendant was shaped like a closed red flower. When Queen Aanya touched its latch, the flower opened, revealing the sapphire ring Queen Annika left with King Harrow so many years ago.

"I'm sorry you were never able to know them," Viren said. "Your mothers."

Queen Aanya didn't like Viren and she didn't trust his condolences, but his story had given her a little more insight into her mothers, and for that she was grateful.

"Thank you for sharing this story, Lord Viren," she said. "I feel lucky to have heard so many beautiful stories. This is how I've gotten to know my mothers." Aanya touched the latch on the pendant, which closed around the ring.

"They were very brave and very strong, and wise," Viren said. He looked down at the ground, remembering. "I know it is not my place to say—but I am sure they would have been very proud of you."

Aanya smiled. Lord Viren was right—it was not his place to say such a thing. And yet she was affected. She wiped tears away from her cheeks. "It may seem strange to miss someone I've never known," she said. "But I miss them so much."

Viren nodded kindly, and Aanya wondered if there wasn't some good in him. After all, he had returned to help her mothers on that fateful day.

"Queen Aanya," he said. "Knowing what you know now, can you see why I believe that if your mothers were here today . . . they would choose to join us, and fight by our side?"

Queen Aanya stared at Viren. She touched the latch on the pendant and looked at the ring once more. "I think you are right, Lord Viren. Perhaps my mothers would join Katolis in this fight." The thin smile spreading on Viren's face reassured Queen Aanya that the decision she was about to make was the right one. "But I will not join you."

"What?" Viren asked.

Aanya couldn't help feeling a small victory at Viren's baffled expression. She could sense the eyes of the other monarchs on her, and she knew she had them in her pocket.

"We owe Katolis a great debt, there is no doubt," she said. She rose from her throne and walked around the rotunda, her hands clasped behind her back. "We received so much kindness and courage and sacrifice. But I cannot repay a debt of a hundred thousand whose lives were saved . . . by sending a million men and women to die in violence."

"Did you not listen?" Viren asked. He was almost shouting. "Did you not—King Ahling! Help me talk some sense into her."

But Queen Aanya knew King Ahling. He would only act in unison. He seemed intimidated by Viren, but not so much that he would go against the grain.

"Viren, we sympathize with the plight of Katolis, but I'm afraid we can no longer—"

"Coward!" Viren yelled at King Ahling.

Aanya couldn't help thinking Viren might be right about that.

Then Viren turned to the other monarchs: "Traitors! Each of you standing here today, you betray—humanity."

"Lord Viren, I'm sorry . . ." King Ahling started to say. He was the type of person who couldn't stand it when anyone was angry with him. He reached out to put a hand on Viren's arm, but Viren glared at him until he drew it away again.

"Save. Your. Empty. Apology," Viren spat. "There is danger coming. They'll be on your side of the border soon. You'll all pay the price for ignoring my warnings."

Queen Aanya watched as Viren exited the gazebo in a haze of fury. She could almost see the steam coming out of his ears. She felt a little sorry for the aging mage, but a new time was upon them. As a young ruler, she had the opportunity to correct the course of violence that her parents had been a part of. And she hoped to do just that.

Rayla wondered if Captain Villads really could smell land nearby, hours or a day away, or whatever his crazy parrot told them to believe.

They'd been sailing on the *Ruthless* for days now and it seemed that everyone else had grown their sea legs. Rayla gripped the edge of the boat tightly, focused on keeping her breakfast inside her stomach.

Despite her best efforts to ignore Captain Villads, he continued to make small talk as he steered the ship. Rayla felt rude not responding.

"So, Rayla . . . that's an unusual name, isn't it?" Villads asked.

"Oh yeah, uh, my human parents had an unusual taste in names . . . Villads with a silent *D*," Rayla said. She made no effort to conceal the sarcasm in her voice.

"'Tis fair," Villads said with a shrug. "So, what do you do for a living?"

"I'm an assassin," Rayla said. She twirled one blade in the air. People deserved shocking answers when they asked boring questions.

Villads laughed heartily, but when Rayla didn't join in, the laughter quickly petered out.

"Oh. You're not joking," he said.

"Well, I'm supposed to be an assassin," Rayla said. She shrugged. "But I've never actually, you know . . . killed anyone."

"Well, maybe someday," Villads said cheerfully. "Never give up on yer dreams. I'm a blind, narcoleptic pirate, and I still sail the seven seas. Or is it eight seas? How many seas are there these days?"

"Thanks for the encouragement," Rayla said. "But the truth is, I'm not sure being an assassin is my dream after all." She turned to look out at the water.

"Ohhhhh," Captain Villads said. "So, then, what is your dream?"

"I wish I knew," Rayla said.

Suddenly, the ship rolled over a big wave. Rayla gripped the railing and clenched her jaw. "But I'd settle for getting off this stupid boat and standing on some firm ground."

"I'm a crazy old man, but let me share some wisdom wi' ye," Villads said. "That is, if you think you can stomach it."

"STOMACH-IT!" Berto squawked. "Good one, Captain!"

"Why not," Rayla said through her teeth. Her eyes shot daggers at the parrot. "I love wisdom. Bring it on."

"Life," Captain Villads said, "is like a river." He removed his hands from the wheel to make wavelike motions.

Rayla sighed and sat down on the deck in despair. "Oh great. That's exactly what I was afraid of."

"You can't see too far ahead," the captain said. "I can't see at all, as I might have mentioned."

"You mentioned!" Berto squawked.

Captain Villads left the wheel to sit down next to Rayla. "You don't know where the river of life will bend and turn. You don't know where it will go at all."

"How is this supposed to be helpful?" Rayla asked. The advice was depressing her. She already felt that she'd failed at her calling. "You know that wheel is spinning around on its own?" She pointed at the out-of-control captain's wheel.

"That's all I'm saying, Rayla," Villads said. "Don't try to control where the river goes. There's just one thing you can know and control—yourself."

Rayla thought about that. She liked the way it sounded. Things hadn't worked for her when she tried to control Runaan or the mission. But she was pleased with herself for following her heart rather than killing Ezran. Following her instincts had brought her to the egg, Zym, and a whole bunch of new and valuable friendships.

"Look at yourself," Villads said. "Who are you, Rayla? What do you stand for? Once you know that, then wherever the river takes you—you'll be right where you were always meant to be."

Rayla felt chills run up and down her arms. She knew what she wasn't—an assassin—and coming to terms with that fact was difficult. She hadn't looked at the other side of things—now she had the opportunity to decide what she *was*.

Rayla stood up, suddenly energized.

"Villads, that's amazing. When you started talking, I was sure you were going to spout some complete nonsense, but what you said . . . it's beautiful." Rayla turned to Captain Villads, beaming, but he was fast asleep on the deck.

"I'll tell him later!" Berto squawked over the snoring captain.

CHAPTER 22
LAST WORDS

I've had King Harrow's letter for a few days now, but I just can't bring myself to open it," Callum told Bait. He was bouncing one leg nervously, wondering if he should return to the upper deck and forget about the letter altogether.

Bait jumped on his nervous leg.

"Sorry," Callum said. He stopped the nervous tapping.

"I know it sounds crazy, Bait, but it's like right now there are words he hasn't said to me—and they're all right in here, waiting to come to life. But once I read it . . . once I read the last word? Then he'll really be gone. Forever."

It was such a strange sensation—holding on to these unread words. But Callum knew he was just fooling himself. His stepdad was dead even if Callum never read the letter.

Was Bait looking at him sympathetically, or was Callum

imagining things? Bait put a foot on Callum's hand.

Callum took a deep breath. He was as ready as he'd ever be.

"Okay. Here we go. Thank you, Bait." He placed his finger on the thick wax seal and loosened it.

As he read, Callum could hear the king's warm, strong voice.

Dear Callum,

Over the years, there may have been moments when I let there be a distance between us. Because I am your stepfather, I was trying to give you the space I thought you needed to love your real father, even though he had passed away. Now I wonder if I should have held you closer. I wonder if showing you how much I loved you would have been okay, and would not have disrespected your relationship with him.

Callum, I know I am not your birth father. But in my eyes and in my heart, you are my son. I see myself in you. I am proud of you. I love you unconditionally.

As I write this, the sun is setting, while Moonshadow assassins prepare to end my life. A few months ago, I took my revenge on Xadia for your mother's death. Tonight, it is their turn. I may not have long. So, I am forced to ask myself: What can I pass on to my sons in the short time I have left? In this letter, I will share with you a lie, a wish, and a secret . . .

Callum put the letter down for a moment to take a breath. He wiped the tears falling from his face. "This isn't easy," he said to Bait, who looked up at him with big, understanding eyes. Then Bait looked back at the letter.

"Wait—you can't read, can you?" Callum asked.

When I am gone, your brother, Ezran, will become king—and you will be his partner, his defender, and his closest adviser. Soon you will both face a lie—the great lie of history.

Advisers and scholars will tell you that history is a narrative of strength. They will recount stories of the rise and fall of nations and empires, and they will be stories of armies and battles and decisive victories. But this isn't true strength—it's merely power.

I now believe true strength is found in vulnerability. In forgiveness. In love.

There is a beautiful upside-down truth, which is that these moments of purest strength appear as weakness to those who don't know better. For a long time, I didn't know better.

I ask you and your brother to reject history as a narrative of strength, and instead have faith that it can be a narrative of love.

Callum read these words with surprise. He had believed the "lie" of history—and the lie had tormented him because he wasn't good at remembering battle names or at swordsmanship. He wasn't muscular like Soren or brave like his mother, Queen Sarai. He was just Callum. But reading his stepfather's words, he started to think that there was a source of strength inside him. He knew how to love.

The last time I saw your mother, she said, "I'll see you on the other side." I don't know what lies on the other side. But I do know I will be watching over you and your brother always.

I have tried to be selfless as a king—but as a father, I have a selfish wish. And that is for you and Ezran to be...FREE. Reject the chains of history. Do not let the past define your future, as I did. Free yourself from the past. Learn from it, understand it, then let it go. Create a brighter future from your own hearts and imaginations.

And finally, you must be wondering about the SECRET I promised to share. Well, good news—the secret is hidden in the Banther Lodge, where you are right now! How's that for planning?! Right now, go upstairs to the game room. There I have hidden an unusual cube with rune symbols on each side.

After the initial feeling of hopelessness that the journey had taken him far from the Banther Lodge, Callum realized his stepdad was writing to him about the rune cube Rayla had rescued. He'd always known that cube was important. Maybe now Rayla would start listening to him... and maybe now he would find out how he could use the mysterious cube.

Callum opened his bag and pulled the cube out. Then he continued to read the letter.

This cube is an ancient relic that has been passed down through the ages. It belonged to an elven wizard in Xadia, the Archmage Aaravos—a master of all six primal sources. It is hidden in a box of keys because it is known as the "Key of Aaravos," and legends say it unlocks something of great power in Xadia. Perhaps it will be you, Callum, who discovers the key's secrets.

Well, so much for a detailed explanation of how to use the cube, Callum thought. Still, he held the cube aloft and looked at it with new wonder. Even Bait seemed to look at the cube with new respect.

As he looked back to finish the letter, Callum noticed something a bit odd. There were ink spots on the passage he had just read about the cube. The Archmage *ink spot*. The Key of *ink spot*. Callum was sure he remembered reading the name... Aaravos? He must have smudged the letter somehow.

P.S.: One last extra-super-secret bonus secret. Did you know that Bait—our most sour friend—secretly loves belly rubs?

Callum looked at Bait, and Bait eyed him with suspicion. Ever so slowly, Callum moved his hand toward the rounded, yellow belly and gave Bait a tentative scritch. Bait's eyes rolled back, and he flopped on his back happily like a puppy.

Callum rubbed his gold and teal belly.

"Aw, who's a tubby lumpa grump?" he said playfully. "Come on, Bait. Let's go find Ez." He scooped up Bait and hustled upstairs, walking right past Rayla and the captain, who seemed deep in conversation.

"Stand up," Callum said to Ezran.

"Huh?" Ezran said. He was just waking up from his nap, and he rubbed his eyes. Then he stood up.

Callum wrapped his arms around his little brother, hugging him tight.

"What's that for?" Ezran asked.

"You're my brother. And you mean everything to me," Callum said.

"Is this a trick?" Ezran said.

"No." Callum suppressed a laugh. *Maybe he should say kind things to Ezran a little more often.* "It's not a trick, Ez. I just love you," Callum said.

"Well, I love you too," Ezran said. "So, are we there yet? Are we close?"

"We are close! I smell land," Villads said, who had also

woken. He took a couple of deep sniffs of the air.

Callum's eyes followed the direction of the captain's nose . . . and there it was. In the near distance, he could make out the shore and mountains.

Callum was about to break out in a cheer when a large shadow fell over the deck.

"Hey, what was that?" Rayla asked. "A shadow?"

"You're asking the wrong pirate," Villads said.

"There's something up there," Rayla said. "Look."

Callum looked up at the sky just as the silhouette of a dragon passed above the clouds. He inhaled sharply: There were dragons in Katolis!

chapter 23
facing the threat

Callum couldn't believe it was time to say goodbye to Captain Villads. He could barely believe they'd survived the trip with Captain Villads, come to think of it. But there they were, on the other side of the bay and all in one piece.

"Well, thank you for everything," Callum said.

"Aye, well, I do what I can to help out the young folks," Villads said.

"Where will you go now?" Ezran asked.

"Oh, probably turn back and spend a bit of time on shore myself. Would be nice to see me beautiful wife, Ruth. Sure has been a long time since I laid eyes on her."

Callum and Rayla exchanged a look.

"He means metaphorically!" Berto squawked.

"Good luck to you, kids," Villads said. "And Callum, one last piece of advice. Always remember the wisdom of the wind. You cannot see it or hold it. You've just got to feel it." Captain Villads sucked in some sea air and then exhaled directly into Callum's face.

Callum scrunched up his nose in disgust. "Ugh, why do people always feel the need to blow on me when they're making a point?"

"Oh, don't take everything so personally," Rayla said. "Come on, we've got to find a place to stay before it gets dark out."

"Lead the way," Callum said.

"I think there might be caves up in those mountains behind you," Rayla said.

"This way?" Callum asked. He pointed over his right shoulder.

"No, that way," Rayla said.

As Callum turned to look, Rayla blew on the left side of his face.

A few hours later, Ezran, Rayla, Zym, and Bait were sleeping peacefully in the warm cave Rayla had found for them. But Callum was awake obsessing over the Key of Aaravos. What could he achieve with it?

Eventually, Callum left the cave to go play with the rune cube undisturbed. He rolled the cube like a die and attempted a few spells. For a while, nothing worked. Then the cube lit up! Callum jumped with excitement. Then he saw that Bait had snuck out of the cave; the cube was just detecting the glow toad's Sun primal energy.

Callum sat back down. He whispered "Fulminis" and closed

his eyes. Maybe if he thought hard enough, he could invoke magic and light up the cube on his own. But when he looked down, the cube was dark and Bait was frowning.

"Ugh. Nothing. What do you think this thing is anyway?" Callum asked Bait. "He said it was a key—but a key to what?"

Bait didn't respond.

Callum rolled the cube a few more times, noticing that the marks it was leaving in the dirt were all pointing in the exact same direction. Was he accidentally creating the pattern by rolling the cube the same way, or did it mean something?

Callum's thought was interrupted by a rustling sound, and he jolted to attention . . . but it was just Rayla. She emerged from the brush with her arms crossed.

"Are you practicing magic, or are you losing to Bait at a game of rollycubes?" she asked.

Callum decided to ignore the sarcasm. "Oh—sorry I woke you up. I was trying to practice magic."

Rayla's expression was dubious, and Callum felt like he had to convince her. "Actually, I think I'm getting close," he said. "There's so much swirling around in my head, but I need a way to bring it all together." Callum didn't care if he sounded foolish. He believed he would figure out primal magic.

"Like some kind of breakthrough?" Rayla asked.

"Yeah! But . . . it's not happening," Callum said.

Rayla sat down next to him. "Well, I've learned some wisdom recently," she said. "Half the moon is dark, the other half is light, and . . . life is like a river! Put it all together and you have . . ." Rayla trailed off.

"Moon river?" Callum asked. Rayla was talking nonsense.

"Yeah, wisdom is stupid," she agreed.

Callum noticed that the cube's Moon rune glowed when it got near Rayla. He felt a pang of jealousy. "Hey, wait—what about you, Rayla? You were born with the Moon arcanum."

"I . . . suppose so," Rayla said.

"So . . . when you do cool Moon powers, you're connecting to the moon, right?" Callum asked. "What does that feel like?" If he could just understand what magical creatures felt, maybe he would be able to perform real magic, without a primal stone or killing an innocent creature.

"Uh, I don't really think about it," Rayla said, shrugging. "I just stand in the light of the full moon, and then there's a feeling like . . ." Rayla stopped talking and looked at the moon. Her eyes began to glow. "It's like *shwa-wa-wawa-wa*." Rayla swept her arms in undulating motions. "And then there's a sort of . . . *TING!*" Rayla shot up into a standing position. "And then: *bfshhwowww*. Moonshadow powers!" She struck a triumphant pose, head thrown back, arms reaching toward the sky.

Callum stared at her. He was feeling less and less confident about ever doing magic again.

"Does that help?" Rayla asked.

"Not at all," Callum said with a smile. "But I enjoyed it!"

Rayla sat back down and Callum tried to explain himself. "I have to be a mage again," he said. "We saw a dragon in the clouds. Things will only get tougher once we get into Xadia."

But Rayla just shrugged again.

"And crossing the border, that's going to be crazy dangerous," Callum said.

"Well . . . maybe not," Rayla said.

Callum wondered what she was talking about. The only entrance to Xadia he knew of was the Breach. "There's a river of lava! *One does not simply walk into Xadia*," he said.

"Actually, one does simply walk into Xadia," Rayla said. "There's a secret path—the Moonstone Path. It'll be safe and easy, even for you, magic or no magic. It would be tricky for a human to find, but luckily you've got a smart, capable elf to lead the way."

Callum felt reassured but glum at the same time. "You are smart and capable. I just don't want to be useless," he said.

Rayla stood up. Callum sensed she was frustrated with him. "Stop doing that human thing where you worry about things that are all in your head," she said. "Come get some rest."

"You're right." He sighed. "Let's go back to sleep."

They walked back to the cave together with Bait lagging behind. Callum felt a cold breeze blow. He looked up just in time to see a dark shadow passing high above their heads.

Soren and Claudia had barely slept since they'd captured Corvus. They'd trudged along on horseback, their prisoner tied up and marching behind them. It took a few days, but they'd followed one of Claudia's magic maps and eventually arrived at a border town. Several soldiers were patrolling the streets, although it was the wee hours of the morning. They barely noticed Soren, Claudia, and Corvus.

Soren, for one, was sick and tired of their prisoner, who kept trying to escape.

"Hey, Claudia, now that we're at a town, we can ditch Corvus in jail or something and be done with him, right?" Among other things, Corvus was slowing them down.

"We're so far off Callum and Ezran's trail now," she said. "Do you think we can catch up with them?"

Was Claudia ignoring him? Soren didn't feel all that confident about catching up with the princes, but he'd learned in times like these to appear bold and overly confident.

"Of course, we can catch up," he said. He rolled his eyes at her. "We promised Dad."

"You know, I could help you track them," Corvus said. He held his bound wrists up to Soren. "If you untied me, that is."

"Oh no, no, no, no! If I untie you, you're just going to try and escape. Again," Soren said.

That incident had been one of Soren's more embarrassing moments. Corvus was an expert tracker—was it so ridiculous of Soren to hope the guy could help with their mission? Claudia seemed to think so when she returned from the bathroom to find Corvus untied and running full speed through the forest. She'd performed another one of those snake-turning-into-chain spells to get him back, and she hadn't been happy about it.

"No, not this time," Corvus said. He opened his eyes very wide. "This time will be different. I promise."

The guy had an honest aura about him, Soren had to say. He tilted his head and considered untying Corvus.

"What are you thinking?!" Claudia yelled from her horse.

Soren immediately reconsidered.

"Hey! You're just trying to trick me." Soren whipped around to glare at Corvus. "Fool me once, shame on you. Fool me twice, shame on me. Fool me three times . . . back to you again!"

"That's not how it goes," Corvus said.

Soren stared at Corvus and shook his head. "Shame. On. You." Then he hurried over to a group of soldiers.

"Yoooo-hoooo, yoooo-hoooo. We're looking for a town jail," Soren said. He waved his hand in front of one soldier's face. "We've got a horrible traitor to lock up for, uh, traitorous words and deeds. Standard traitor stuff."

Why wasn't the soldier paying attention to him? Soren flashed his crownguard insignia. "Uh, excuse me? Crownguard here." He tapped the insignia, but the soldiers all kept their eyes on the sky.

Claudia frowned. "Something's . . . weird," she said.

"I know! No one's listening to me," Soren said, still pounding his insignia.

"What?" Claudia asked.

Even his sister didn't have time for him. What good was being part of the Crownguard if no one took him seriously? Soren pouted.

"AHHHHHHHH!!"

Soren looked up. A soldier was screaming and pointing at the sky. "It's back!"

Soren snapped to attention and turned his gaze to the sky. A huge shadow was passing above the clouds. He heard a low rumble, and then it appeared: A dragon—huge, magnificent, and powerful—broke through the clouds at full speed. It dipped low over the town, flapped its rust-colored wings, then rose again. It was circling the town.

"Is that—?" Claudia stammered.

"A dragon?!" Soren finished for her. For once it was his sister asking the stupid questions. "You'd better believe it."

Claudia didn't say anything. Even Corvus wasn't smirking anymore.

Soren tapped one of the soldiers on the back. "What's going on here, soldier?" he asked.

"It's the third night it's flown over us," the soldier said. Soren could tell he was a high-ranking soldier from his uniform, but the man's face and lips trembled as he spoke. *What was wrong with these townspeople? They would just watch as a dragon intimidated them? They didn't ask for help or take action?* Soren could barely believe the cowardice. He could show these people, and Corvus and Claudia, what he was made of.

"What? And you haven't shot it down yet? What are those ballistas for?" Soren asked the soldier. Three ballistas stood ready on the town-wall ramparts.

"Well, it hasn't attacked us," another soldier responded.

"So? We're in a war against Xadia!" Soren shouted. "That dragon is the enemy. I'm taking command here. Crownguard, I might have mentioned." This was his chance to prove himself. If Soren could knock out the dragon and save the town, everyone would start listening to him.

The high-ranking soldier nodded. "Follow the Crownguard!" he shouted at his troops.

Soren ran to the wall and scrambled up to the top of the tower.

He would act fast and decisively. This dragon wasn't scared—it wasn't expecting a battle. Soren would catch it completely off guard.

A bunch of soldiers followed him. Claudia and Corvus were not far behind.

"Hold on, Soren!" Corvus yelled after him. "Please think this through. The dragon isn't attacking. It's just trying to intimidate us."

"Well, then, I'll just have to show it that humans won't be intimidated," Soren said. As if he would consider advice from a prisoner.

Soren leaped onto the ballista, turning it hard and taking aim at the dragon as it circled high above.

"Soren—please. Don't start a fight you can't finish," Corvus said. He was almost begging.

For a moment, Soren hesitated. He gazed up at the dragon. Even from such a great distance, Soren thought the dragon had spotted him. It seemed to hold his gaze. It swooped low over Soren's head and snarled.

Soren wound the chains around the ballista as tight as he could. He felt fierce and unbeatable. He fired.

Soren's aim was spot on. The bolt streaked across the sky . . . but at the last second, the dragon dodged the bolt and swept back up into the clouds. The bolt fell back to the earth, taking out a portion of the town wall.

Everyone on the ground fell into a tense silence, waiting to see if the dragon would return. But Soren was sure that it had left for good. "Heh. See?" Soren said. "Scared it off. Dragon problem solv—"

But a furious roar from a reinvigorated dragon above interrupted his bragging.

The dragon swooped down for a second pass, but Soren was ready. He orchestrated the release of three ballista bolts. The soldiers aimed well, and the bolts arced toward the dragon.

Despite its size, the dragon was nimble and managed to dodge all three bolts. In response, it opened its jaws and sprayed a wave of fire toward the ramparts. Soren and Claudia and the soldiers dove for cover.

When Soren opened his eyes, he saw that the dragon had incinerated two of their ballistas. Soren backed away from the last ballista.

The first lights of dawn were scattered around the burning town. Villagers ran in every direction, some so scared they ran toward the fire. Screams pierced Soren's ears from every angle.

He had only been trying to help, but Soren knew he was in over his head. He turned and looked at Corvus, who was on his knees with his wrists bound together. Soren drew his sword and lifted it above his head.

"Soren! What are you doing?" Claudia asked, trying to get between Soren and Corvus.

SLASH! Soren brought down his blade, slicing through the ropes around Corvus's wrists.

"I don't understand," Corvus said. He rubbed his wrists.

"These people need help," Soren said. "Get as many as you can to safety."

Corvus nodded slightly at Soren, searching his eyes.

Soren nodded back. He wanted to say something, to wish Corvus luck, but no words came.

"Don't get yourself killed," Corvus said. Then he rushed into the chaos to help.

"I think I really messed up this time, Clauds," Soren said. "I don't know how to stop it."

"Don't say that yet," Claudia said. "I have an idea."

She dug around in her bag and yanked out a tiny velvet box. When she flipped open the top, Soren peeked inside. He immediately wished he hadn't looked. The things his sister carried around with her.

"What *is* that, Claudia?" he asked.

"It's the eye of a griffin," she said. Claudia didn't seem grossed out at all. "With this, I can enchant a ballista bolt to never miss its target—no matter what!"

"So, you just carry a griffin eyeball around with you? Who does that?" Soren asked.

"How about, 'Thank you for carrying a griffin's eye with you, Claudia'?" she said. "How about, 'You're so prepared, you're the best'?"

Soren stared at her. He managed to muster a reluctant "Thank you, Claudia."

But that was enough for his sister, who smiled and rushed off to the last ballista. She slipped the griffin eye out of the box and gently closed her hand around it. When she opened her hand, it was bursting with searing magical purple energy. Her eyes glowed the same color.

Soren shuddered. No matter how many times his sister or

father did dark magic, he could never get used to the glowy-purple-eyes-thing.

Claudia held her hand to the tip of the ballista bolt, and the energy ignited around its deadly point, charging the bolt with magic. She started to chant: "Kram ruoy dnif tlob rekeestraeh."

Soren angled the ballista to face the dragon, who had turned back around to the scorched town. As the dragon neared, Claudia took careful aim and fired. The bolt streaked through the sky, trailed by a magical tracer.

The dragon twirled elegantly in the air to elude the ballista. Soren couldn't believe his eyes—Claudia's magic had failed.

But just as Soren was giving up hope, the enchanted ballista appeared to grow wings. It changed directions to follow the dragon.

Confused, the dragon panicked and banked to the left. At the last second, it dodged the bolt. But then the enchanted bolt made another impossibly sharp turn. This time, it hit the dragon deep beneath its wing.

CHAPTER 24
CRASHING DRAGON

"GAAAAHHHRRRR!"

Rayla, Callum, Ezran, Zym, and Bait woke up to an earth-shaking rumble.

"Oh no. I know that sound," Rayla said. "That's not a good sound." Rayla's assassin training immediately kicked in and she leaped up, ready for anything. She ran out of the cave and everyone followed behind. Night was just ending, and the first pink rays of sun were peeking up above the horizon.

"Ezran, it's not safe out here!" Rayla shouted. "Go back in the cave with Zym. Protect him."

Zym looked up at Rayla with his wide, round eyes.

"Don't worry, little dragon," Rayla said.

"Bait will stay inside with Zym," Ezran said.

"Fine." That grumpy toad would make a good-enough

babysitter. At least he wouldn't be outside giving her dirty looks. She watched as Zym followed Bait back into the cave like an obedient puppy.

From the top of the overlook, Rayla could see the nearby town. The entire village was burning. Flames licked at dozens of buildings, some of which were so damaged they were beginning to crumble. The dragon circled high above. If Rayla knew anything about dragons, this one was preparing to attack.

"What's it doing here?" Callum asked her. "Why is it attacking that town?"

Rayla shook her head, stunned. "I don't know," she said.

"Are we too late?" Callum asked. "Has the Dragon Queen declared all-out war?"

Before Rayla could answer, she saw blood dripping down from underneath the dragon's wing. The dragon roared again in agony.

Tears sprang to Rayla's eyes. Even though it seemed to be attacking the town, she couldn't bear to see the great creature suffer a devastating injury.

"They hit it," she said.

Ezran clutched his side—there was a sharp pain in his rib cage. The dragon lurched in the air as it struggled to escape from the village. *Please get away, please get away.*

Ezran stared at the dragon and hoped with all his energy that it would escape. He felt the dragon's fear and its pain. He reached his hand out into the sky. Although the dragon was still flapping its wings, Ezran knew the animal was going to crash. Its pain was too great. Then he felt his own body slam to the ground.

"Get down! Get down!" Rayla was yelling.

The dragon's wings could no longer support the weight of its body. It nosedived into the forest, passing right over their heads. Branches snapped off the trees as it plummeted down, and a huge wind followed in its wake.

BOOM.

The dragon crashed, and the earth shook. A shock wave of dust rushed up into the air like a volcanic eruption.

Ezran got onto his feet and started to run before the dust had even settled. *Please be okay, please be okay*, Ezran thought as his feet pounded across the forest floor. He skidded down the hillside and into the clearing where the dragon had gone down.

Ezran froze. There was a crater in the earth surrounding the enormous creature. The ground beneath the dragon smoldered, but the injured animal remained still and silent.

"Wait up, Ez!" Callum yelled. "You can't just take off without us!"

Ezran turned. His brother was out of breath from trying to keep up with him. Rayla was right behind him.

"Is it dead?" Callum asked.

Ezran wasn't sure. He approached the dragon cautiously until he was directly in front of it. As he did so, a calm came over him, as it always did when he approached an injured creature. Ezran reached out his hand and placed it softly on the dragon's face. Something stirred beneath his hand.

Very slowly, the dragon opened one yellow eye. Ezran knew

the dragon didn't trust him, but she didn't seem angry at him either. She was waiting for a cue. Ezran did his best to reassure her.

"You're in pain," Ezran said. "Don't worry—we can help you." He leaned in and placed his head on the dragon's forehead. *Where are you hurt?* He listened, his heart beating in time with the dragon's.

When he had his answer, he stepped back and turned to the others.

"It's there, beneath her wing," Ezran told Rayla and Callum.

Rayla approached the wing cautiously and tried to lift it, but it was too heavy. "Come on. Help me," she said to Callum.

As Callum and Rayla worked together to lift the dragon's limp, injured wing, Ezran continued to soothe her. He just had to keep her calm long enough for them to remove the bolt. Ezran knew the dragon was listening to him. He could feel her head nestle further into his arm.

Out of the corner of his eye, Ezran saw Rayla extract the bolt. The dragon groaned and shuddered. Then she slumped in Ezran's arms, and her eye drifted shut. She didn't say anything else to Ezran.

Ezran was trying to think of what else he could do to help the dragon when he heard horses approaching. He didn't know exactly who to expect, but Ezran knew they weren't safe in this clearing. He placed his hand on the dragon one last time to say goodbye. Then he locked eyes with Callum and they started running back toward the cave. But Rayla had drawn her weapons and wasn't following.

"What are you doing?" Callum called.

"The humans are coming—we have to protect her." Rayla sounded desperate.

"We can't fight them, Rayla," Callum said.

"I can't just leave her," Rayla replied.

Ezran hated to leave an injured animal too, but Callum was right. "Even if we could fight them off, we have to get back to Zym," he said to Rayla.

"We did what we could—come on," Callum said.

Callum and Ezran hurried to leave. Rayla lingered a moment longer, then folded her weapons and followed the princes.

When Ezran looked back to make sure Rayla was behind them, he spotted Soren and Claudia approaching in the distance, followed by several human soldiers. From the frozen look on Callum's face, Ezran could tell he had seen them too.

"Come on," Ezran whispered, tugging on Callum's arm.

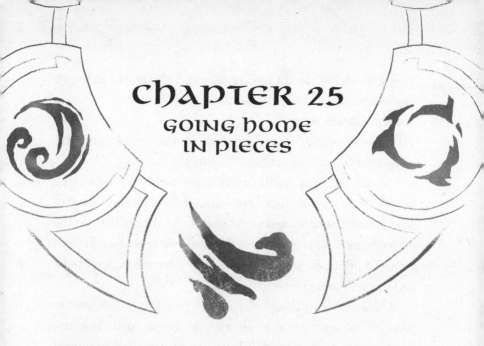

CHAPTER 25
GOING HOME
IN PIECES

By the light of dawn, Claudia led the way to the fallen dragon. It was easy enough to guess where she had landed, considering the massive debris and destruction she had left in her wake.

Soon enough, Claudia, Soren, and a handful of troops arrived at the spot in the forest where the dragon lay, apparently dead. Claudia thought Soren was looking a little bit pompous, considering she'd done all the hard work.

"I always thought it'd be you who took down a dragon, not me," she said.

"Huh?" Soren wasn't really paying attention.

"I mean, wasn't this one of your life goals? Slaying a dragon?" Claudia asked, making sure to keep a completely straight face.

Soren's expression flattened in irritation as he moved ahead.

They approached the unmoving dragon. Soren stared at her for a moment, then kicked her jaw with his foot.

Crass, Claudia thought.

"I think it's dead," Soren said. "But we can't be too sure." He turned to the gathered soldiers. "Secure the dragon!"

The soldiers had no difficulty tying down the unmoving dragon with several thick ropes and chains. Claudia jumped down from her horse and stood back to let the soldiers do the manual labor. As she watched them, a little ball of excitement gathered in her chest. She grabbed her dark magic spell book and started flipping through it.

"There's so many things we can do with a dragon," she said to Soren. "There's even a whole chapter about spells that use dragon snot—it's some seriously powerful goo!" Claudia flipped a few more pages. "Oh, and I hope it has gross waxy ears! Dragon earwax is the key ingredient for plenty of magical candles." She put the book down at the base of a tree next to her satchel. "We don't have the Dragon Prince, but do you think if we brought this whole dragon home, Dad would—?"

"It's something," Soren said. "But it does weigh about, I don't know, a million tons. How are we going to move it?"

Claudia smiled. "In pieces."

Rayla, Callum, and Ezran arrived back at the cave with Ezran leading the way.

"Zym! Zym, are you okay?" he called out.

Rayla let out a sigh of relief when Zym scampered up to Ezran immediately, wagging his tail. But she still felt like a complete failure. While Callum and Ezran cooed over Zym and an especially grumpy Bait, Rayla stayed a few feet back.

"I should have done something," she said. How could she have left that dragon at the mercy of the humans?

"Rayla, you're always the one who reminds us that the only thing that matters is getting Zym back to Xadia," Callum said. "Why are you hesitating now?"

That was unfair. She wasn't hesitating. Zym did have to get to his mother. At the same time, she felt physically compelled to help that poor dragon. But could Callum even understand that both were true?

"I'm not hesitating," Rayla said. "This is different—every fiber in my body is telling me this is wrong. That dragon is defenseless. And I just left her there."

Callum shook his head. "Our mission is Zym. He is the most important dragon in the world. He is the dragon we swore to protect."

Rayla looked off in the direction of the fallen dragon. Callum didn't understand.

Why was Rayla being so distant? It had been two hours. She was still staring silently in the direction of the dragon with her lips set in a thin line.

"I don't get it, Rayla," Callum said. He felt irritated with her. They had done their best. "Why are you so worried about a dragon that just set fire to a town?"

"I've been thinking about something someone once told me," Rayla said. "About how when one person hurts another, then that person hurts them back—it becomes a cycle that never ends."

"Who told you that?" Callum asked.

"You did," she said.

"Oh," Callum said. Now that she mentioned it, he did vaguely recall using that logic to convince Rayla not to kill him or Ezran.

"But Callum, to break that cycle, someone must take a stand when no one else will," Rayla said.

And then suddenly, Callum got it. Breaking the cycle of violence was the whole point of his stepfather's letter. It was what he wanted Callum to do. Callum looked at his feet. It was a tall order, to stand up when nobody else would. But he owed it to his stepfather—and to Rayla. "You're right," he said. "If we're really going to change things, we can't just watch while humans and Xadia keep hurting each other."

"That's right," Rayla said.

"But how do I take a stand?" Callum asked. "Believe me, I want to go down there with you and be the hero who stops all the fighting and saves the day, but I can't do that. I can't do anything."

Rayla squeezed his arm. "It's okay, Callum. I'm not asking you to come with me. Protecting that dragon doesn't just feel like the right thing to do—it feels like the right thing for ME to do. It's where I'm meant to be." She stared into the distance.

Callum was suddenly struck by an intense wave of gratitude. He'd never met anyone as brave as Rayla. How did he get so lucky as to be her friend?

"I'm going back down there," Rayla said. "If I don't come

back, you and Ezran can get Zym to Xadia. I believe in you."

Callum blushed. No one had ever said those words to him before, or at least not that he remembered.

"Thanks, Ray—"

But by the time Callum looked up, Rayla was gone.

The sun was beginning to rise over the uneven towers of Katolis Castle when Viren and his troops returned from the failed summit of the Pentarchy. Viren dismounted slowly, still in a daze of disbelief at the decision the other kingdoms had made. He felt defeated; a worn-down husk of a man battling alone to save humanity. What he wouldn't give to have his wife, Lissa, here with him now.

Where did that thought come from? he wondered. He hadn't seen Lissa in years. For the past decade, all Viren needed to get him through the day was dark magic and a few cups of hot brown morning potion.

"How dare you?" a sharp, angry voice shouted from the courtyard gate.

Lissa's here! It was the first thought that ran through Viren's head. Almost immediately, he laughed at his own foolishness. It was Opeli. *Of course,* Viren thought. *I must now deal with the person in Katolis who reviles me the most.* He looked up and tried to acknowledge Opeli, but noting the horror on her face, he quickly looked away again.

Opeli was clutching a scroll bearing one of the other kingdoms' seals.

"I've been to the Crow Master," she said. "You used King Harrow's seal to summon the Pentarchy—and then you lied to them!" There was venom in her voice . . . and truth in her words. "You called yourself regent of Katolis. You committed treason, Viren. And for what?"

Viren paused. There was no use in denying it. He'd thought his lie would work out for the best. He'd believed the end would justify the means. He'd been wrong. "For nothing," he said, shrugging. He turned to walk toward the castle.

"You'll be removed from the council for this—and you'll be lucky if that's all!" Opeli shouted after him.

Viren trudged down the spiral staircase to his dark-magic chamber. He stared at the ground as he walked.

"Welcome back. I hope you had a pleasant trip," Gren said. He struggled to stand up in all his shackles.

Viren froze in his tracks and stared at Gren for a long moment. He'd almost forgotten about his remaining prisoner. As bad a situation as he was in, there was no arguing . . . Gren's plight was worse.

"How can you possibly remain so cheerful in your dire circumstances?" Viren asked. He truly wanted to understand.

The prisoner appeared to consider the question carefully. "Well, I think about it like this: Why see myself as chained down, when I can be chained . . . up?" With chained hands, he gave Viren two thumbs-ups.

"I admire your tenacity," Viren said. He shook his head. When all was said and done, he had no desire to be so optimistic. Optimism was a foolhardy approach to life. A positive bias is still a bias, and Viren knew he would always rather see the stone-cold truth. Optimists could be magnetic and charismatic, no doubt—but they tended to miss things in their need to always turn to the light. Their optimism left them vulnerable to anything lurking in the shadows of reality, which they refused to gaze upon.

Viren entered the dungeon chamber and closed the door behind him. The stone walls provided no insulation, and he shivered in the dank darkness. The mirror remained covered, and the spell ingredients and tools lay untouched on the nearby table.

Viren surveyed them, focusing on the long, sharp dagger. He reached for the cover on the mirror, then paused, repulsed by the decision he was about to make. He clenched his fist in determination.

"I have nothing left to lose," he said.

Viren yanked the cover off the mirror—but the Mirror Mage was nowhere to be seen. The room on the other side was empty. Viren sighed, frustrated, and sat down to wait.

CHAPTER 26
YOUR KIND
OF MAGIC

Hood up, eyes narrowed, Rayla retraced their steps
through the forest to find the fallen dragon. It wasn't
long before she spotted her.

Rayla hid behind a few bushes and watched as human
soldiers patrolled the area. Soren was standing watch over the
injured animal, whose bright red wings were tied to the ground
with stakes and chains.

Rayla knew she was absurdly outnumbered. She didn't care.
She drew her weapons. It didn't matter what happened to her.
Live or die, that dragon was going home.

Rayla snuck up on one soldier from behind a boulder and
took him down without a sound. With utmost stealth, she
began disarming and incapacitating soldiers one by one, and
she cut the ropes binding the dragon as she went.

Soon she'd moved toward the metal chains holding the dragon down. She was considering how best to break them when suddenly Soren stepped in front of her. He had a group of cronies behind him. They all brandished their swords.

"Oh. This guy again," Rayla said. "Of course."

"A dead dragon and a dead elf all in one day," the big doofus said. "Everything's coming up Soren."

Rayla barely had time to blink before Soren charged her with his sword. She dodged and weaved, but he seemed determined to hack off at least one of her limbs.

Once again, Rayla was surprised by Soren's strength, which seemed close to her own. She'd never given humans much credit in the way of strength.

When he shoved her to the ground, she rolled as far away from him as she could get, only to find herself surrounded by troops who slowly and deliberately closed in on her. She backflipped onto the dragon's back while fighting off two of the soldiers. She hacked at the chains with her blades, but barely made a dent.

"So, chains are made of metal," Soren said. "Kinda hard to cut."

That idiot and his taunting ways. "I'm not backing down," Rayla said.

Rayla knew she could have taken any one or three or even five of the soldiers no problem. But ten or twelve, with more coming every moment? It was just too many. And she was already tired. She got to her feet and pulled up her blades.

This is it. I'm going down fighting.

Callum was sketching intensely outside the mountain cave. He was drawing a picture of Rayla—a powerful, heroic figure. He still couldn't believe she had left. His palms were sweating and his chest felt tight. What if she didn't come back? Could he and Ezran and Bait really manage to get Zym to Xadia?

"What are you doing?" Ezran asked, leaning over his shoulder.

"I'm just drawing," he said. Callum didn't want to be rude, but Ezran was annoying him.

"You seem upset," Ezran said.

"Yep. I draw when I'm upset," Callum replied. He didn't need Ezran hovering over him, stating the obvious.

Callum gritted his teeth, and his pencil snapped. His sketchbook slipped off his lap. When it landed, it fell open to another page. Callum found himself staring at a sketch of Claudia in the Moon Temple, holding her dark magic spell book. All the feelings from that night came rushing back to him— Claudia's beauty, her love of ancient ruins, and her honesty about his father's death. Then he remembered her betrayal. The way Claudia used dark magic to try to capture him and Ezran and Zym.

For a moment, fury seized Callum. He was about to tear the drawing in half when he had an idea. He traced his finger over the outline of Claudia's dark magic spell book. *Maybe...* He scooped up the sketchbook and slammed it shut.

"Maybe there is something I can do," Callum said. "Ezran, you stay here. Protect Bait and Zym. Don't worry. I'll be back soon—with Rayla."

The forest was a big blur of green and brown to Callum as he raced toward the dragon. Thoughts whirred through his mind. Could he really bring himself to go through with his plan? What if he didn't succeed? What if he compromised his beliefs and it ended up being all for nothing?

Callum reached the crash site in time to see Rayla fighting Soren with one blade while fending off several soldiers with the other. He ducked behind a bush. Claudia was there—she was standing away from the dragon, her back to Callum. Claudia's white horse stood between them, tied to a tree. Her magic satchel lay near the horse's front hooves.

Callum stayed hidden, still torn over what he should do.

As the fight continued, Rayla became increasingly outnumbered. She jumped onto the dragon's back and climbed to where two chains intersected to pin the dragon down. She was surrounded, but it looked like she might free the dragon. Callum watched as Rayla swung at the chains, but her blade bounced off with a clang, sparks flying. She reeled back and tried again. Nothing happened. She was in trouble. Callum inched toward Claudia's horse.

Rayla was breathing hard, and Callum could tell she was exhausted. Her eyes darted around looking for an escape.

"Oh no." Callum gulped when he saw Claudia approaching Rayla and the dragon.

"I'm not backing down," Rayla shouted.

"Try not to kill her, Soren," Claudia said. "She can lead us to Ezran and Callum."

I think that's my cue. Callum was out of time. He sprinted to the tree behind Claudia and grabbed her bag. *There it was. The dark magic spell book.* Callum flipped through the book as fast as he could.

"She doesn't have to lead you anywhere, Claudia," Callum said. "I'm right here."

Claudia turned around, and for a second, Callum thought she looked genuinely pleased to see him.

"Callum," she said. "You're safe." She started to walk toward him.

But Callum wasn't going to be fooled by her again. He'd found a spell that would do the trick. Maybe it wasn't the best spell out there, but that didn't matter. Callum clenched his hand around an embalmed snake's rattle he'd grabbed from Claudia's satchel.

"What are you doing?" Claudia asked. She froze.

"Your kind of magic," Callum said softly.

Claudia approached Callum slowly, with her hands up. "You don't want to do this, Callum. It's really dangerous unless someone shows you how."

"You already did," Callum said as he crushed the rattle and chanted: "Dnibnu leets gnirehtils."

Callum felt an immediate jolt through his body. His stomach surged up into his throat, and for a moment, he thought he was going to vomit. But the nausea passed, and a tingling sensation spread from Callum's gut up through his chest and arms and head. The world around him melted into a dizzying array of colors. Though he could see Rayla, Soren, and Claudia staring at him, they seemed like paper-thin figments of his imagination.

Callum watched with wonder as purple streaks of energy arced from his fingertips directly toward the chains that bound the dragon. The creature would be free in moments. Callum's heart thumped with the power of the magic flowing through him.

Callum had reversed the spell Claudia used on him (or thought she had) up on the Cursed Caldera. The spell transformed the links of the giant chain into snakes. Within seconds, the snakes slithered off the dragon and attacked the surrounding soldiers.

The dragon and Rayla were free! Callum had done it!

But the dark magic energy evaporated almost immediately. His heartbeat slowed down, and his glowing vision faded. Where moments before he felt filled with magical energy, he suddenly felt empty and hollow inside. His arms and legs felt . . . unmanageable. They were like long strands of spaghetti attached to his torso.

Callum swayed and stumbled and then fell backward. His eyes felt like someone was poking hot sticks into them. *I should probably rest my eyes*, Callum thought. *Just for a moment.*

Soren watched the step-prince transform the chains into snakes. *Wow*, he thought. *Callum can actually do magic. Too bad his little stunt wasn't going to save the dragon or the elf.*

"Congratulations!" he yelled. "That was impressive. Really. You did everything you could to save a monster that torched a town of innocent people."

But Callum didn't respond. He wasn't looking so good—lying there on the ground with that creepy dark magic stare in his eyes.

Soren turned to the dragon, which wasn't moving even though she was free. So she actually was dead after all.

"Come on, come on, get up! You're free!" the elf yelled. She was pounding her fists on the dragon, but it still didn't budge.

Soren walked toward Rayla, smiling. It had started to rain—pour actually—but Soren didn't care. He was going to have a little fun with the elf. "Your dead dragon is free," he yelled.

"Wow. That dragon is so super dead," he continued as he walked closer and closer.

Why was the elf looking at him like that? Soren looked down at the dragon just in time to see one of the dragon's yellow eyes blink open. An instant later, the dragon pushed herself up to her full height.

"Run!" Soren shouted to Claudia.

Claudia and the soldiers scattered to safety, but Soren stayed put. He had stood up to this dragon only hours before and brought her down. He would do it again.

Soren flinched a little at the dragon's red leather scales, her hot fiery breath, and huge quivering nostrils, but he knew he would face her. The dragon made eye contact with Soren and trampled toward him with bared teeth. Soren bared his own teeth and drew his sword. Then he let out a battle cry and lunged at the dragon, swinging his sword at her neck.

Much to Soren's surprise, the sword made contact. It hit the dragon's horn and chipped a piece off. The dragon roared in fury, lunging and snapping at Soren. Soren dodged once, smirking. *He was smaller, but all he had to do was win one small exchange at a time, literally chipping away at the dragon.*

But it was all over before the next exchange even began. Before Soren realized what was happening, the dragon swung her massive tail, slamming into him and sending him flying. He smashed into a boulder with a crunching sound and slid to the ground.

When Soren opened his eyes, he was on his back, looking up at the dark gray sky. Rain poured down on his face and into his open mouth. He tried to roll away from the downpour, but something was wrong. His body didn't seem to be listening to his brain. Maybe he was pinned down beneath something?

He went to wipe the water out of his eyes to get a better look, but when he tried to move his hand to his face, nothing happened. Then he saw the dragon. She was coming right at him.

Soren opened his mouth to scream—he didn't care what anyone thought of him. These moments, his last few on earth, belonged to him, and he was going to spend them screaming as loudly as his lungs would allow.

Then the most unexpected thing happened. The dragon stopped in her tracks and turned away from Soren. Soren struggled to crane his neck to see what had distracted the dragon.

It was that little dragon puppy! Zym! He was standing at the big dragon's feet, looking up at her. Soren had never been so happy to see a baby anything in his life. The enormous dragon seemed totally mesmerized by Zym. She stood still, the flames she'd intended for Soren still burning in her mouth.

Zym shrank down to the dirt with his ears pinned back.

"Zym!" called Ezran.

What was the crown runt doing here? Soren watched from the ground as the young prince came running into the clearing and wrapped his arms around the baby dragon.

The huge dragon just stared. Then she beat her wings, kicked up a cloud of dust, and took off into the sky.

I'm saved, Soren thought. *Time to get up.* Soren tried to roll onto his side once more, but once again, nothing happened. Then he tried to lift his feet, but they didn't respond to his commands either. He tried reaching for his sword—still nothing.

Finally, he managed to lift up his head. There was his sister. Claudia was running after Ezran and Zym. It looked like she was going to capture them. Soren didn't care. He needed her.

"Claudia," he tried to yell, but his voice was weak and it came out as a whisper.

Claudia didn't seem to hear him. She reached her hand out toward the baby dragon, and her snake bracelet started to glow.

"That little dragon's coming with me," she said as she marched toward Ezran.

"Help," Soren gasped.

"Leets gnirehtils . . ." Claudia started to chant.

Soren closed his eyes and gathered as much oxygen as he could into his lungs. "CLAUDIA! Help me!" he screamed.

Claudia halted. Her gaze turned to Soren—finally. Her eyes faded back to normal, and she rushed to his side.

"Soren! I'm here," Claudia said, kneeling beside him.

Soren turned his eyes to look at Claudia, but he didn't have the energy to say anything else.

"Come on, get up. We have to get you some help," she said.

Soren just shook his head.

CHAPTER 27
DARK
CONSEQUENCES

Hours later, the doorknob in the mirror room finally turned, and the mysterious mage entered the parlor. Viren stood at attention, but it took a moment for the figure to notice him. He squinted and approached the mirror.

Viren lifted the dagger in response. "I am ready," he said. But he thought, *I am desperate.*

The stranger smiled faintly and bowed to Viren from his waist. Together, they resumed the spell. Viren held the dagger with one hand, the other hand clenched in a fist. With a quick, sure hand he pricked himself and let his blood drip slowly into the geode. Initially it appeared as if the droplets were falling into a pool of sparkling, magical energy. Soon the sparkling magic and blood appeared to swirl and spiral within the geode.

When it finished, there was a strange sparkling blood mixture. He wondered if he was supposed to drink it?

Viren lifted the geode toward his lips as if to ask the figure in the mirror, but the mage on the other side shook his head. Then Viren watched in astonishment as the mage lifted his own geode to his own mouth. As he drank, the liquid within Viren's geode disappeared. The mage closed his eyes and smiled with a satisfied look on his face. Viren waited seconds, maybe minutes, as the figure on the other side remained still.

Then Viren noticed the mage was struggling with something in his mouth. Whatever was in there was squirming and writhing. Viren stepped back from the mirror as the mage allowed his lips to part in a round O. A large, purple caterpillar dropped from his tongue into his geode. The caterpillar crawled in circles around the geode's edge, slowly disappearing into a magical haze at the bottom. Moments later, what appeared to be the same caterpillar crawled out of the geode on Viren's side of the mirror.

Viren stood perfectly still, his breath tight and controlled. He would betray no fear. The caterpillar crawled up his arm, onto his shoulder, and then onto his neck. Viren felt himself flinch, but remained as still as possible. Finally, the caterpillar nestled behind his ear. Its tiny legs scraped along Viren's scalp and caused terrible itching. It took tremendous willpower for Viren not to rip it out. Then Viren felt a warm breath on his neck and heard a gentle whisper:

"Speak."

Viren whipped his head around—he'd heard the voice clearly,

but he couldn't place its source. He looked back and forth around the chamber.

"Wh-wh . . . I . . ." he started to say.

The caterpillar's tiny legs curled and clutched at Viren's ear. The voice came again, more urgently, almost pleading:

"Speak, so I may hear you," the voice said.

Viren realized that the voice in his ear, the one coming from the caterpillar, belonged to the Mirror Mage. The caterpillar wrapped around his ear acted as a conduit to the world in the mirror.

"Who are you?" Viren asked.

"Ahh. So long have I waited for the sound of another voice," he said. "But my name would mean nothing to you."

Viren scowled. He was never one to appreciate a cryptic response.

"Well, then, tell me: Where are you?" he asked.

The Mirror Mage seemed to consider the question. He looked around for a moment. "I don't know," he said.

"Don't lie to me," Viren said.

"I'm not lying. I never lie," the mage said.

Nobody "never" lies, Viren thought. He began to pace. This mage could not be trusted. Perhaps if he offered information, he would receive some in return. "I found this mirror in the lair of the Dragon King," he said. "This mirror meant something to him—*you* meant something to him."

"Perhaps," the mage said. "Tell me what you need, and I will help you."

"I need your name," Viren said.

The elf in the mirror pulled the hood of his cloak from his head, revealing his white hair and horns. Astral tattoos sparkled all over his face. He looked Viren in the eye and spoke slowly in a deep voice: "Aaravos. My name is Aaravos. Now, how may I serve you?"

This response satisfied Viren for the time being. He grabbed a nearby glass jar and pulled on the caterpillar. It detached from his ear with a loud *thuck* as the suction released. Viren dropped the creature into the jar and sealed it inside. He would return to it later.

The rain poured down in thickets as Rayla and Ezran ushered the weakened Callum back to the camp in the mountain cave. Zym scrambled ahead, leading the way.

Rayla wasn't surprised to see that dark magic had made Callum ill. Blackish rings circled his eyes, and he was speaking incoherently. He stumbled as he walked, but Rayla and Ezran held him up as best they could.

"Come on, Callum," Rayla said. "We've gotta keep moving— we're so close to the border." She was so mad at this stupid idiot for using dark magic. It was just fine with her if he suffered for the rest of their journey. She had no plan to slow their pace. "We could be in Xadia in just a few hours," she added.

"I know we're close, Rayla," Ezran said, "but Callum's not doing well."

Obviously, Callum was not doing well. He was putting most of his weight on Rayla as they trudged up the mountain. But Rayla wasn't about to sacrifice the mission. "Well, that's his own fault for messing with dark magic," she said. But a pang of guilt struck Rayla as soon as she uttered the words. She was worried about the stupid idiot.

"Yes, you're right, you're so right," Callum said in a singsong voice. He staggered as he spoke. "Right as . . . rain! And this rain is just a big, wet . . . rain blanket. We must move onward."

But as he tried to raise a finger and urge everyone onward, Callum tripped and fell in the mud. Rayla pulled him up.

"I'm okay," Callum said, brushing Rayla off. "I just need to rest my eyes while we walk." Callum closed his eyes and smiled.

Sleepwalking was not a solution. It didn't matter how close they were to Xadia.

"Let's get him inside," Rayla said to Ezran.

Once again, Claudia had had the baby dragon within reach, and once again, he had escaped her grasp. But she couldn't dwell on losing the dragon again. The only thing that mattered to Claudia right now was helping her brother.

As rain poured down, she knelt by Soren's side and brushed some of the matted hair from his face. He was lying still, slumped against the rock where that awful dragon had thrown him. Claudia had never seen a sorrier sight. She put one hand on Soren's shoulder and turned his face to get a better look at the gash on his cheek.

"I don't feel anything," Soren said.

Maybe Soren was overreacting. He sometimes had a flair for

the dramatic. Claudia grabbed some skin on his hand and pinched it as hard as she could.

"Can you feel it when I do this?" she asked.

"No," Soren said. "What are you doing?"

"I'm pinching you, Soren," Claudia said. He really wasn't faking. Not even a little.

"Well, that's just rude," Soren said. "Way to make a guy feel worse when he's down."

Claudia rummaged through her satchel. There had to be a way to fix this. "Hold on, I'll have you back on your feet in no time," she said. She pulled out a purple daisy-like flower from her bag and started yanking off its petals. She placed one petal into each of Soren's ears.

"So, this spell uses a flower?" Soren asked.

"Just close your eyes," Claudia said. She placed more petals over his eyes.

"At least it's not gross," Soren said.

"And the last step has just a tad of grasshopper goop…" Claudia said, pulling out a vial of pale green liquid.

"Ohhh, do we really have to use that?" Soren started to say. But Claudia muffled his protests by shoving the goop into Soren's mouth. He was easy to manage in this injured state. She sprinkled a green dust over Soren and chanted: "Sbmil eseht ot efil gnirb"

It was an uncommon spell, but Claudia believed it would fix Soren right up. Dark magic filled her body, and she looked up to the sky. Then she channeled all the energy into her fingertips. The magic cascaded over Soren's body in an arc of glittering sparkles. The petals evaporated. Claudia and Soren watched the sparkly effects.

"Well, that was super pretty," Soren said. "But I still can't move."

Claudia sat silent—momentarily stunned. "You can't move?" she asked. "Are you sure?" Claudia couldn't remember the last time dark magic had failed her. *Had it ever failed her?* Maybe she'd chanted the wrong words . . . but no, she was positive she'd said them correctly.

"Yeah, pretty sure," Soren said.

"That should have worked. Hold on, I must have something that will work." In a panic, Claudia started tearing items out of her bag. There were glass vials filled with every color liquid imaginable and all kinds of animal parts. There was the other eyeball of the griffin, three hairs from a three-toed river-rabbit, greenfish droppings. And not a single item that she could use in this situation.

"Ughhh. That's all I have for healing," she said.

Soren didn't look that worried; in fact, he looked like he didn't care anymore.

Claudia glared at the nearby soldiers. They were staring at the ground and shuffling their feet. "Don't just stand there!" she barked. "Help me get him back to town. We need to find a doctor."

After Viren returned from his journey to the summit, Opeli decided to hold an emergency council meeting. She did not appreciate all the secrecy that seemed to follow Viren wherever he went. She was going to put a stop to him. It's what King Harrow would have wanted—she was sure of it.

Opeli remembered the time almost five years ago when King Harrow had suggested removing most of the guards from around the castle. He'd wanted the citizens to feel that it was "their castle too." Opeli laughed a bit to herself when she remembered that crazy idea of his. But she remembered looking around at the council members, all nodding their agreement to what would surely have resulted in an overthrow of the kingdom. Opeli told King Harrow exactly what she thought of this idea. He frowned and stared at her. She thought it was the end of her career.

And then he'd said, "It is clear to me that you serve no king."

Opeli remembered quaking in her robes, sure she was about to be demoted . . . or worse.

"The only power you serve is the truth. And that's why I'm making you head of this council. You were the only person with the courage to stand up to the king. That's exactly the kind of leadership we need."

It was a position she had held on to for five years.

A few hours ago, she'd called the current meeting. She hoped to confront Viren in the open, with many people around. But the high mage was conspicuously absent from his usual haunts. His disappearance was a telling sign of a guilty conscience, in Opeli's opinion. Or at least a sign of fear. He had to be found. It was time to begin the meeting.

"Ahem," Opeli began. "We must find the high mage."

The council members looked around, waiting for her to continue.

"It's come to my attention that Lord Viren has committed treason." She let that sink in. "He appropriated King Harrow's seal and sent letters to the other kingdoms. He pretended to be regent of Katolis. As regent, he gathered a summit of the five kingdoms and tried to unite them in war against Xadia."

Opeli looked around the room. Most of the council members were nodding in agreement. It was inexcusable to steal King Harrow's seal. Not to mention the disrespect. But one council member was shaking his head.

"What is it, Salir?" Opeli asked.

"I guess I just don't think what Viren did should be considered treason," he said.

"Explain yourself," Opeli barked at him. She'd never liked Salir—he was always looking for shortcuts. But she let him speak.

"Look at the situation we're in," Salir said. He addressed himself to all the council members. "Our king was assassinated by Moonshadow elves. Prince Ezran, the presumptive king, has gone missing. No one knows if he is still alive. And even if we do find him alive, Ezran is a child. The kingdom of Katolis is effectively paralyzed—it is a ship without a rudder. I agree, Viren's means were not highly ethical, but he was trying to protect Katolis."

"Have you quite finished?" Opeli asked. She didn't like the way the other council members had started murmuring. *Did they think Salir was right?*

"I agree with Salir. Katolis is in need of protection," she said. "But we must go about strengthening the kingdom in the most transparent way possible. We must find the princes and appoint an appropriate regent if that is necessary. That is how we will win the hearts and minds of the other kingdoms. Viren's lies and treachery reflect poorly on our entire kingdom."

Opeli could see she had won back her council.

She turned to a guard captain. "Take two men and search for Lord Viren. Search everywhere. He is in this castle. And when you do find him, be ready for anything. Do not underestimate him."

Time was passing at a strange rate for Callum. It felt like forever since they'd left the dragon. But when Callum realized they were back in the cave, protected from the downpour, it felt like no time had passed at all. He had some vague sense that Rayla and Ezran were busying themselves around the cave, but he couldn't tell what they were trying to achieve. Callum felt nauseous.

"I'm so uncomfortable," he moaned. He could really use some sympathy right now. Maybe a cool hand on his forehead and a comforting voice in his ear.

"Uncomfortable with your choice to use dark magic, perhaps?" someone shouted in the distance. *Why were people so mean?* Callum wondered.

"Rayla!" Ezran shouted. His brother's voice was awfully harsh too, Callum thought. But then he could feel Ezran's presence over him, adjusting blankets and stroking his arm. "Is that any better?" Ezran asked.

"Soo uncomfortable," Callum repeated. And then Ezran disappeared completely, and Callum found himself alone in a room with no windows. What had happened to the cave? Why was he suddenly on a stage? Did he have to give a speech? Callum had terrible stage fright and he was sure he had forgotten something very important.

A bright light hit Callum in the eyes, and he squinted. There was a spotlight on him, coming from somewhere high above. He looked down. He was lying on a bed of thousands of golden keys.

CHAPTER 28
IN DARKNESS

Callum was on a stage, but there was no one in the audience. This bed of keys was a horrible resting place. Sharp pieces of metal poked into Callum's back. He sat up, reached down, and grabbed a few of the keys. They were light as air. He watched the keys flow off his hand and into space. Gravity played by different rules in this place. He heard an irritating buzz somewhere beneath him. There was some large, glowing object hidden among the keys. Callum gasped.

"Something's down there," he said.

Callum reached around until his fingers latched onto a glowing rune cube. It was similar to the Key of Aaravos, but it wasn't quite the same. One of the sides glowed red.

Callum turned the cube frantically to see which primal was

glowing. How could any of the primals glow in this dark place? But none of the primal runes were on this cube. Sky, Moon, Earth, Sun, Ocean, and Stars had all been replaced with a single rune symbol Callum had seen only once before—on Claudia's spell book. The rune's red glow burned Callum's eyes.

Something about this cube tied his stomach in knots. It wasn't natural. A vision flickered in front of his face. Dozens of dead animals in a field. A dead butterfly. A dead deer. A dead unicorn. Cackling laughter.

"Nooooo!" Callum yelled.

He chucked the cube away from him with all his might. The glowing rune was dark magic. It represented death.

About fifty feet away, a cloaked figure stood in another spotlight. It reached its hand up and, in a single, swift motion, it caught the flying cube.

Callum lifted himself from the bed of keys and slowly walked toward the cloaked figure. He could hear his own footsteps echoing as he walked. He slowed his pace when he neared the figure, nervous to get too close.

"Who are you?" Callum asked.

But he received no response.

Callum held his breath as the cloaked figure began to turn around. Slowly, the shadowy figure pulled down the hood of his cloak, and Callum found he was looking at himself. He was alarmed at first, but his nerves calmed when the cloaked version spoke to him kindly.

"Callum, don't be frightened," Cloaked Callum said.

"I'm not frightened, just confused," Callum said. He scratched the back of his head.

"Of course, you're frightened," Cloaked Callum said. "You tried dark magic for the first time. No one expects that to be easy."

"But that's the thing," Callum said, looking away. "It was easy. It was too easy. Even though I know it's wrong." Callum shrugged. He couldn't believe how much simpler it had been to unchain the trapped dragon than connect to the Sky arcanum.

"But is it really so wrong?" Cloaked Callum asked.

"Yes," Callum said. He believed it with all his heart.

"Is it though?" Cloaked Callum asked. He twirled the dark magic rune cube.

"Yes."

"Is it?"

"YES!!" Callum yelled at himself. He crossed his arms in anger.

"Callum, look at me," Cloaked Callum said. "You're looking at yourself. You need to accept your destiny."

"I can't accept that dark magic is my destiny," Callum said. He shook his head vigorously.

"You're a human," Cloaked Callum said. "You weren't born with an arcanum to do primal magic, but you were born to do magic. The kind of magic humans can do." Cloaked Callum held the rune cube out to Callum. All six sides were glowing with the dark magic rune. "You can have unlimited power. And you can choose what to do with that power. You can make a real difference in the world. All you need to do now is accept that your destiny is already written." Cloaked Callum held the glowing cube out to Callum again, urging him to take it. "Accept your destiny."

Maybe he was right? Maybe Callum could make a difference in the world using dark magic. After all, Callum had saved Rayla and freed the dragon with dark magic. Those were good deeds, weren't they? And he never would have been able to do it with primal magic. He'd tried so hard to connect to the Sky arcanum. It just wasn't working.

Callum slowly reached toward the cube. But before he touched it, a different voice interrupted him.

"Callum. You are free."

Callum whipped his head around. It was his stepfather speaking. King Harrow was sitting on his throne, wearing the clothes Callum had last seen him in. But he was covered in chains that were strapped across his ankles, waist, and chest.

"You are free from both the past and the future," King Harrow said. "Nothing is written in stone. Fate is a lie. You are free."

Suddenly, Cloaked Callum was standing between King Harrow and Callum. He was shaking his head knowingly. "Look inside yourself, Callum. Dark magic is your destiny. You can't deny it."

Callum looked back and forth between the mirror image of himself and his stepfather. His stepfather had wanted to change the world ... and look what had happened. He'd ended up trapped in the age-old cycle of violence.

Callum reached out to take the rune cube. As his fingers drew closer to the dark magic cube, he expected that the moment he grasped it he would feel some sense of relief, simply accepting his destiny and his power. But an instant before his fingers touched the cube, he glimpsed something he knew was the horrifying truth. Cloaked Callum's face suddenly distorted and became gaunt, with dark pits in the places where his eyes should have been. The hand that was holding the cube changed before his eyes. The skin shrank and tightened until it appeared as if only bones held the object. Cloaked Callum opened his mouth wide to laugh, revealing a set of rotting teeth.

Callum dropped his hand. His eyes narrowed, and he backed away from the rune cube. "No," he said. "I get to choose who I want to be."

"Your destiny is already written," Cloaked Callum said, a little more loudly this time. He shoved the cube in Callum's face.

But Callum's resolve was firm now. He regained control. "No . . . destiny is a book you write yourself!"

The declaration seemed to strike Cloaked Callum like a dozen daggers. The glow of the dark magic cube faded and he dropped it. An abyss appeared out of nowhere to swallow it up. Then Cloaked Callum shattered into thousands of tiny pieces, crumbled, and disappeared.

Callum breathed out a sigh of relief. He took a moment to compose himself, and then turned to King Harrow. "That was horrifying," Callum said.

King Harrow shrugged. "It's your dream, kid."

Chapter 29
King Ezran

E zran watched Callum tossing and turning all night in a feverish sweat. He was very worried. At one point, Callum rolled over, sat up, looked Ezran in the eye, and shouted, "Who are you?!" Then he crumpled to the cave floor.

This was one of the creepiest parts of the journey so far. Ezran was scared for his brother. *Would Callum ever be himself again?*

Everything felt a little more hopeful in the morning light. Then Ezran heard a soft but distinct rustle coming from outside the cave. Someone—or something—was stalking them.

He looked at Rayla. *What should we do?*

She put her finger to her lips and drew her weapons.

"Who's there? Show yourself or I'll greet you with my pointy friends!" Rayla shouted.

Ezran peeked out from around the cave opening. He saw a

tall, strong man with a weapon attached to a chain. The man had dark skin and jet-black curly hair. *Did he know this man? He seemed familiar.*

"You," Rayla said. She stopped to size the man up. Rayla seemed to know him too.

Then the man saw Ezran. He placed his weapons on the ground and raised both his hands.

"I'm not here to fight," he said to Ezran. "General Amaya—I mean, your aunt Amaya—sent me. My name is Corvus." He walked slowly toward Ezran, who nodded at Rayla to let her know to stand down. She narrowed her eyes, but let Corvus pass.

Corvus paused when he got near Ezran. A strange quiet hung in that pause, and somehow Ezran felt that this moment was a cusp, though he didn't know what was coming next.

Then Corvus dropped to one knee and bowed.

"I am here to serve the king," he said.

Ezran stood frozen and confused. *What is he doing? My father is the king.*

"King Ezran," Corvus said.

"But I'm not the king. I'm just a prince," Ezran said, even though the realization was starting to set in. "My dad is king."

Corvus was silent. Ezran started to panic. "Wait, that's not what you're saying? He isn't . . ." Ezran inhaled deeply and looked over at Rayla, who was tearing up.

Why was she crying? It couldn't be that his father was dead.

Rayla had known. Maybe she'd known all along.

"No. No, no, no!!" Ezran shouted. He didn't care if he sounded like a two-year-old.

"Ezran. It's going to be okay," Rayla started to say.

That was about the dumbest thing anyone could possibly say, Ezran thought. Nothing was ever going to be okay again.

"You knew," Ezran said. He felt like a dumb little kid. "Oh, I'm an idiot. I should have figured it out." He slapped his forehead. "When we met you, you had two of those assassin ribbon things. And then one came off that night." *His father had been dead this entire time.*

Rayla nodded. "That's right. That must have been when he fell," she said.

"Fell," Ezran said. He felt his face tighten in anguish. She didn't even have the guts to say the words.

"Yes," Rayla said. She made no attempt to hold back her tears.

"Fell?" Ezran repeated. Now his face felt hot with anger. "He didn't fall, Rayla! He didn't trip and land on the ground. He got killed." Then he looked over at his brother, writhing on the cave floor. "Callum. Does he know yet?"

"He knows," Rayla said.

Ezran shook his head, still in disbelief. Everyone had known about his dad, and they'd all been keeping it from him. Did they think he couldn't handle his father's death? He was king now—he was going to have to handle a lot of serious problems.

"I'm going for a walk," Ezran said. He had to get away from Rayla.

As he stomped out of the cave Corvus stood up, in his way.

"I can't let you go alone," Corvus said.

Ezran stared Corvus down. Corvus couldn't tell him what to do. No one could anymore. "If I am the king, then you must let me go," he said.

Corvus immediately backed down. But Rayla jumped in front of Ezran.

"You're not my king," Rayla said. "But you are my friend, and I'm coming with you."

"Rayla, please. Just let me go be alone. Please."

For the first time Ezran could remember, Rayla backed off.

Zym trotted off to follow Ezran. Ezran didn't have the heart to yell at him. But Bait nudged Zym gently and brought him back to the cave by the scruff of his neck.

Claudia sat slumped over in the hospital waiting room. The first hospital they found was in the tiny border town, and the waiting room did nothing to inspire confidence. Some of the wooden beams were rotting, the floors were covered in mud and grime, and the patients all looked miserable. But the waiting room was next to Soren's room, so Claudia could watch the doctor examining Soren in his bed.

When the doctor finished looking at Soren, she walked directly to Claudia. Claudia jumped up—it had to be good news. She couldn't accept anything less.

"Well? How long will it take for him to get better?" Claudia asked.

The doctor's bland expression didn't change. "He's not going to get better," she said.

"What?" Claudia asked. This couldn't be happening. Maybe this doctor was a total incompetent.

"He won't die," the doctor said in the same matter-of-fact tone.

"He's lucky to have survived a direct attack from a dragon. But he's never going to walk again."

Claudia sat down. Poor Soren. His physical strength was everything to him. How would he ever cope with this injury?

"I haven't told him yet," the doctor said.

"Don't," Claudia said softly. "I'll tell him. He should hear it from me."

Claudia smoothed back her hair and took a deep breath. Then she walked into Soren's room.

The sick room was filled with brilliant sunlight. The contrast between the beautiful weather and the news she had to deliver made Claudia's task seem that much more depressing. When Claudia saw Soren's big strong neck in a splint, she almost started to cry.

Stop it. She had to be strong for him.

"Hey, Sor-sor," Claudia said. She sat at his bedside and rubbed his arm. "All the people in town are talking about you. About how you faced the dragon and saved the town. Everyone's calling you a hero."

"Saved them from a problem I caused, maybe," Soren said. "Is that what heroes do?"

He sounded so depressed. So down on himself. Claudia wondered if this was the right time to tell him that his injury was permanent. She brushed those thoughts away. Soren had to know the truth.

"So. I talked to the doctor," Claudia said. "And I guess they did some test." She paused.

"I already know," Soren said.

"You know what?" she asked.

"I can't move. I can't walk," Soren said. "And it's not going to get better." He looked away, out a window.

Claudia followed his gaze. Outside, some kids were running by, laughing and playing.

"I don't want you to pity me, Claudia," Soren said. "It's for the best. I'm glad I can't move."

"What are you talking about?" Claudia asked. "Soren, why would you say that?"

"Remember when I was eating all those jelly tarts before we left?" Soren asked. Claudia nodded. "It was because Dad gave me a secret mission that was really stressing me out."

"He did?" Claudia asked. This was surprising. Their father usually entrusted the secret missions to her alone.

"I was confused, and I didn't want to do it," Soren said. "But I do want Dad to love me and be proud of me." Soren sucked in his breath.

"He is proud of you no matter what," Claudia said. She put a hand on Soren's cheek. She knew she was her dad's favorite, but it was just because she was more like their father than Soren was. Claudia knew that deep down, Viren loved his son. Deep, deep down.

"And Dad is so smart, so I figured there must be a good reason for the mission," Soren said.

"Soren. What exactly did Dad ask you to do?"

Soren stared at the ceiling. "You know what, don't worry about it, Clauds," he said. "It's not important now."

"What are you getting at, Soren?" Claudia asked. "You

know you can trust me. Whatever it is, it can't be that bad."

Soren nodded. "Dad told me to kill the princes."

Claudia's face darkened with disbelief. Had she heard him right?

"Kill the princes?" Claudia repeated. She was glad she'd gotten the story out of him, but now she had to tell him he was wrong.

Soren nodded.

Claudia felt bad for her brother. Clearly, he believed those had been his instructions. "No, no, that can't be right," Claudia said, shaking her head. "You must have misunderstood."

"It doesn't matter if you don't believe me," Soren said. "Now I can't do anything terrible to the princes, because now I can't do anything."

Was it possible? Her father was capable of a great many things, but ordering the execution of King Harrow's sons? Claudia didn't want to believe it. At the same time, Soren did seem relieved that he couldn't walk. And that was just impossible to understand . . . unless he was telling the truth.

CHAPTER 30
DRAGON SMASH BOY

Viren snuck over to the castle library. After his encounter with Opeli, he had a feeling that the council would soon force him to face consequences. If he was going to utilize his mysterious new friend in some way, he was going to have to act fast.

As he turned a corner, two guards walked by, and Viren flattened himself against the wall. Yes, it was happening already—Opeli probably had the entire Crownguard on the hunt for the "treacherous" high mage. Viren strode through the stacks of the library, pulling out books and scrolls. Anything with even the slightest relevance he piled into his arms. He dumped the enormous stack on a table and began to pore over the tomes.

"Let's see here. Aaravos...Aaravos...there!" His finger

came to rest on the word *Aaravos*, but before he could read anything, all the text surrounding the name blacked out before his eyes, as if black ink had been spilled and was soaking into the paper. Somehow the name *Aaravos* and everything associated with it was being magically redacted.

"What? What's going on here?" He unfurled another scroll, and his finger alighted on the name *Aaravos* again. But immediately the words and passages turned to black blobs. "What is happening!" Viren hollered. Never in his life had he witnessed anything like this.

"Shhhh! You are in a library."

Viren turned. The librarian was giving him a warning glare.

Viren looked around. There was no one else in the library. "Yes, I'm quite aware I'm in a—"

"SHHHHHHH!!" She shook her head disapprovingly.

The library was useless anyway. Viren slammed a couple of books shut for good measure and glowered at the librarian on his way out.

He hustled back through the hallways to his office, altering his usual path slightly to avoid an encounter with several more guards. Once in his office, he proceeded down to his secret chamber without delay. He closed the door behind him and stood before the mirror.

"What's going on, Aaravos? Every time I found a mention of you in an ancient scroll or tome, the entire passage disappeared as soon as I looked. What game are you playing?" he demanded.

Viren waited for an answer. Aaravos was reading a book. He seemed highly engrossed and was not paying Viren much mind.

Unhurriedly, Aaravos placed the book down and walked over to face Viren. He nodded his head at the glass jar with the caterpillar in it, and tapped his ear.

Viren had momentarily forgotten their appalling means of communication. He yanked the top off the jar and stuck the caterpillar onto his own ear.

"Why should I trust you?" Viren asked softly. He was regaining his equilibrium.

"You shouldn't," Aaravos said. "Yet."

This might be the first bit of honesty the mystery mage had uttered. But Viren remained wary. "I should end this right now," Viren said. "Throw the mirror into a river and cut you off forever." The thought of destroying the mirror made Viren's heart rate fall a little. Even so, he hoped Aaravos would panic at the thought.

The elf remained unnervingly calm.

"You won't," Aaravos said. "You are too curious. Hungry for knowledge and power. Both things I can provide."

Viren thought for a moment. He hated how well Aaravos could read him.

"Allow me to earn your trust," Aaravos suggested.

"How would that work exactly?" Viren asked. But Aaravos had his attention.

"Search your heart," Aaravos said. "There's something that you want very badly. But—something or someone stands in your way."

Viren contemplated the suggestion. What he wanted most of all was to unite the five kingdoms against Xadia. But that union seemed like wishful thinking now. Opeli had probably already sent crows to tell the other kingdoms of his treachery. He wondered if Aaravos could help him out of this unfortunate situation.

"I am having a problem getting some people to listen to me," Viren said. "They refuse to hear the importance of what I am saying."

"Who are these people?" Aaravos asked.

"They are kings and queens—the leaders of the other four human kingdoms . . ." Viren replied. He sat down in his chair. Just thinking of their stubborn attitudes made him furious all over again.

"Then we will have to get their attention," Aaravos said with a smile.

Claudia was pacing the hospital room. She couldn't believe Soren's attitude. Initially, he'd seemed devastated by his prognosis, but his frame of mind had improved. In fact, he seemed to be in good spirits.

"It's okay, Clauds," Soren said. "I'm relieved, actually. I'm free to do what I want, with no expectations from Dad, or anyone."

"So, what are you going to do with this newfound freedom?" Claudia asked. Soren was lying flat on a bed, and presumably would for the rest of his life. He did not look free to her.

"I've been thinking about that for the last ten minutes," Soren said. "I've decided I'm going to reinvent myself."

What could her brother possibly want to do for his second career? Now he'd piqued Claudia's interest.

"I'm going to be a poet, Claudia!"

"AHAHAHAHAHAHAH." It was a relief to laugh. Then Claudia looked at Soren. He wasn't even smiling. "You're not joking?" she asked.

"I'm going to be a poet, and people will come to hear my poems. They'll come visit me, and we'll drink some kind of soothing tea. And then I'll say my latest poems to them."

"Soren, are you sure?" Claudia asked. It was hard to imagine this plan working out well.

"I already have my first poem. It's a haiku," Soren said. "Just tell me when you're ready."

"Uh. Okay. Ready," Claudia said. She plastered a fake smile across her face.

Before Soren delivered his poem, he took a long, easy breath, and his expression became more placid than Claudia had ever seen. Soren recited:

Dragon smash boy
Say the good words now
They light the hearts of other people

Claudia stared back at him. She counted the syllables on her fingers.

"Do you like it?" Soren asked. "I'm inspiring, right?"

"No, Soren. No. That was a terrible poem. And it . . . it's not even a haiku!"

"How can it not be a haiku?" Soren retorted.

"It has the wrong number of syllables," Claudia answered.

"Maybe I'm innovating on the form!" Soren shot back.

"But the whole point of a haiku is that when you count—"

"Well, I'm rebelling against the tyranny of the haiku!"

Claudia thought she might cry. Soren could not live out his days as a poet. He would be the joke of Katolis. She had to do something.

She opened one cupboard and tossed aside its contents. There had to be something in here that could heal her brother. She threw open another cabinet and did the same. Bandages and medicine crashed to the floor, but she didn't care.

"I can't leave you like this," she said to Soren, or maybe to herself. "There must be a solution."

She opened several drawers and then slammed them shut. She didn't even know what she was looking for, but she knew she had to find *something*.

"Dragon smash boy," she muttered. *More like "dragon smash bozo."*

She *had* to fix this. HOW would she fix this?!

The doctor and a nurse entered the room as gauze and tonics flew from the shelves.

"You need to calm down," the doctor said to Claudia.

"No, I don't, you need to . . . calm up!" she shouted. "You need to help him!" Tears were streaming down her face.

The doctor and nurse each grabbed one of Claudia's arms. "This is a hospital, miss; we're going to have to assist you out of here."

As they marched her out of the room, Claudia only became more upset. Didn't they understand that this was her brother?

Her sword-spinning, muscle-bound, crown-guard brother? She often teased him about all that physical bravado, but the reality was, it was all Soren had. Claudia would never have wished *this* on him. It would be like telling her she couldn't do magic.

"He can't be like this—he can't even count syllables!" she wailed.

The doctor and nurse escorted Claudia through the waiting room and kicked her out of the hospital. She fell with a thump onto the town street. The door slammed shut behind her with a decisive *BANG*.

From an open window, Claudia thought she could hear her brother working on another poem.

> *Oh, how I miss*
> *My dark-magic sis*
> *I drank too much water*
> *And now I must . . . use the bathroom*
> *Nurse!*

Corvus paced back and forth outside the mountain cave, furious with himself. It had been hours, and the young king had still not returned.

"The king is missing," Corvus told Rayla, Zym, and Bait.

"He's not 'missing,' he just went for a walk," Rayla said.

"And he hasn't returned, and we don't know where he is," Corvus said.

"Right," Rayla said.

"That is the *definition* of missing," Corvus said. He was willing to tolerate this elf who had apparently befriended King Ezran, but he wasn't going to let her redefine words.

Rayla counted on her fingers, putting things together. "Yeah. Yeah, you're right, he's missing."

"You shouldn't have let him go," Corvus said. "We need to find him."

"Aren't you a tracker?" Rayla asked. "Isn't this your whole job?"

"Yes," Corvus said. He was a terrific tracker. He hadn't wanted to encroach on the young king's mourning, but now King Ezran had been gone too long. Corvus would show the elf exactly what he could do. "I shall bring the king back safely. You have my word."

Corvus picked up where he'd left off, tracking Ezran through the woods. He noted broken twigs, trails of mud, and the king's tiny footprints.

"You're making this easy for me, young king," he said. Corvus's mood brightened as he followed the footprints. But very suddenly, they ended. Where the footprints ought to have been, Corvus saw giant animal prints instead. Judging from the size and shape, the prints could only belong to a banther, an enormous deadly beast that was larger than a bear and faster than a panther. Corvus's heart fell. "Oh no! This can't be happening," he said. He turned around and took off running back to the cave.

Corvus paused at the entrance of the cave to catch his breath. He swallowed. He really did not want to give Rayla bad news about Ezran. He was emotionally drained and not up for a fight.

But he peeked into the cave and beckoned to Rayla to come out so he could speak with her.

"What's wrong?" Rayla asked. "What happened, did you lose his trail?"

"No. It's worse than that," Corvus said.

"What do you mean?" Rayla asked.

"King Ezran's trail *ends*," Corvus said. "Very clearly and very badly. His footprints are replaced by banther tracks. The king has been eaten by a banther."

"HAHAHAHAHA." Rayla was laughing so hard tears were streaming down her face. "Great job; you've lost the King of Katolis."

"This isn't funny," Corvus said, scratching his beard. He'd been prepared for Rayla to pull her blades on him. She was certainly unpredictable. "Why are you laughing?"

"Your king happens to be a very special boy. He can talk to animals," Rayla said. "So, if there are banther tracks, it means Ezran caught a ride on the banther, not *inside* the banther."

Still laughing, Rayla turned her back on Corvus and returned to Callum's side.

Corvus chafed. Once again, the elf had gotten the better of him. On the other hand, at least the king was safe.

CHAPTER 31
CHANGES YOU
DON'T EXPECT

GRRRRRRRR.

    The banther growled as he and Ezran emerged out of a tunnel into the light of an alley. There was a shadow at the end of the street.

Ezran listened closely. The shadow seemed to be chanting something. "There is no synonym for cinnamon, there is no synonym for cinnamon." The voice grew louder as the shadow approached them. Ezran laughed to himself.

"It's okay," Ezran whispered to the banther. He was sitting on top of the enormous beast. He placed one small hand on the top of its head. "It's just Claudia."

"Ezran?!" Claudia gasped.

"Hi, Claudia," Ezran said. "I guess you weren't expecting to see me here." Ezran wasn't quite sure what to say to Claudia.

He liked her, he missed her, but he didn't really trust her anymore.

Ezran decided to remain sitting atop the enormous black banther. Claudia looked a little bit intimidated, and this was okay with him. Ezran kept his hands buried deep in the animal's bristly fur. This banther had a warm heart and a love of children, but based on its ferocious appearance, Ezran doubted Claudia would pick up on those qualities. And the banther didn't warm to Claudia either. It immediately growled at her, and she kept her distance.

"Ezran, I hope you know I never meant to hurt you or Callum," Claudia said.

Ezran looked at Claudia carefully. She was backing away slowly as she spoke, pulling on the sleeves of her dress and twirling her long hair.

"It was scary, Claudia," he said, "how you acted." Ezran had never thought of Claudia as anything but a friend, but then she lied to him and Callum and attempted to capture them using dark magic. Then she tried to kidnap Zym. Ezran always looked for the best in people, but he didn't know what to think about Claudia anymore.

"I know," Claudia said. She looked genuinely remorseful. "And I am so sorry."

Ezran nodded silently. He appreciated the straightforward apology and the fact that Claudia didn't try to make any excuses. He decided to forgive her and clambered off the banther. Ezran hugged its bear-sized head.

"Thank you. Don't worry about me. I'll be safe," he said to the magnificent animal. The banther gave Ezran a quick lick, and bounded off.

Ezran joined Claudia on the street, and they walked together through the hustle and bustle. The townspeople were still recovering from the dragon attack, sweeping up ash, righting fallen signs, rebuilding roofs, and salvaging anything that hadn't been scorched by fire.

"I'm surprised to see you here," Claudia said. "And even more surprised you weren't that banther's dinner."

"I kind of have a way with animals," Ezran said. "And banthers are actually pretty friendly. They like praise, compliments, and a friendly scritch under the chin every now and then."

"Hey, that's like me!" Claudia said with a smile.

They continued to wander until they came to a stone tower, which had been partially destroyed in the dragon attack. The tower's delicate spire had broken off and lay on the ground in a heap of rubble.

"Whoa," Ezran said, staring at the structure.

"Do you wanna go up there?" Claudia asked.

Ezran nodded. Together, he and Claudia climbed the spiraling stairs up to the top of the tower. To Ezran's disbelief, the stairs ended in the open air, where the tower had broken off. The landing was a few stories up, with a sweeping view of the town and the mountain range in the distance.

Ezran and Claudia sat down together to survey the scene.

"So, Ezran, why are you here?" Claudia asked. "And by yourself?"

"I found out something. My dad—" Ezran started to say. He

closed his eyes, and shook his head, but couldn't find the words to complete his sentence.

"That's okay," Claudia said. "You don't have to talk about it if you don't want to." She put her hand on Ezran's shoulder. "I know it's not the same, but when I was a kid, my mom and dad split up. I remember hearing them fight a lot at night after we went to bed. And then one day things seemed different— really quiet and serious. My mom and dad said they needed to talk with me and Soren. They told us Mom was moving back to Del Bar, where her family was from. And then they said we had to choose." Claudia's voice cracked. "Me and Soren had to choose which parent we wanted to live with." Claudia started to cry. At first she wiped the tears away, but then she just let them flow.

Ezran looked in her eyes. There was wisdom and understanding in Claudia's words. He put his hand on her shoulder.

"And Soren chose Dad," Claudia said. "I couldn't believe it. How could I choose? How could I do that? Then my mom looked at my dad, and she came over to me and started wiping away my tears, even though she was crying too. And she told me to stay. She said I had to stay with Soren, that this was my home, and my brother and I needed each other. And then she left." Claudia was wringing her hands at the memory.

Ezran was shocked. Both his parents were gone now too, but not by any choice of their own. He imagined that a parent choosing to leave must feel terrible. "How could she do that, Claudia?" he asked. "Why would she leave you?"

"I think she needed to leave for herself," Claudia said. "To be happy, somehow. You might have noticed my dad is pretty intense."

Ezran still couldn't believe Claudia's mother would do that. It made him angry. "You must miss her," was all he said.

Claudia nodded. "Losing her has been the hardest thing that's ever happened to me," she said.

"When you grow up, sometimes there are changes you don't expect," Ezran said. "And you have to face things you're not ready for."

"Yeah. Yeah, it's hard," Claudia said.

"Callum told me that," Ezran said.

"You're so lucky to have a brother like Callum," Claudia said.

"I know," Ezran said, and immediately started crying. Claudia hugged him tight.

"And I'm lucky to have my brother," Claudia said. "Soren is a doof, but he's my doof! I know he would do anything to protect me, and I would do anything for him." Suddenly, Claudia got a far-off look in her eyes. Then she mumbled something to herself.

"What did you say?" Ezran asked. A little blue bird had jumped into his hands. Ezran ran his fingers along the bird's soft feathers.

"I was just thinking about Callum," Claudia said. "I know when he wakes up, he won't want to see me, but I want you to give him this."

Claudia pulled a little glass jar from her satchel. It was filled halfway with a yellow powder.

"Just mix it with water, and it will help Callum feel better."

Ezran smiled. "That's a really nice offer, Claudia," he said. "But I don't think Callum wants anything to do with dark magic."

"Well, let me just tell you how I make it," Claudia said. "First I squeeeeeeeze the essence out of fresh lemons! Then I dry it into a powder and mix it with sugar and some baking soda. I call it: Fizzlicious Lemonessence!"

Ezran laughed. "Well, Callum might try that after all," he said. "I'll give it to him. I wish I could give you something to help Soren."

"I think maybe you can help me, Ez," Claudia said.

Ezran looked at her.

"You don't just have a way with animals," Claudia said. "You can talk to them, can't you?"

Ezran hesitated, worried Claudia would judge him, but decided to confide in her anyway. "Yes—I can talk to them," he said.

"Great!" Claudia said. "I need you to help me find something in the forest . . . if you don't mind. If I can find milk-fruit, maybe I can help Soren."

Ezran had never heard anyone so excited about his ability to communicate with animals. But he wanted to help Claudia because he still cared about her. He stood up and extended his hand.

"Let's go down and find some milk-fruit," he said.

Claudia accepted his hand, and they climbed down the tower together.

"I was going to search for the milk-fruit by myself," she said as they started walking to the forest. "But I don't know exactly where to start. I was thinking, since you can talk to animals, maybe one could point us in the right direction?"

"Sure, Claudia," Ezran said. "I think pretty much any animal would help us with that. Of course, deer love milk-fruit, but I don't think there is any shortage."

"Oh, is that right?" Claudia asked. "That's so interesting. Deer love milk-fruit. Good to know."

"Everyone knows that, Claudia," Ezran said. It was weird that Claudia didn't know about deer and milk-fruit. Ezran thought even little tiny babies knew that. "Hey, why do you need the milk-fruit anyway?" Ezran asked. "How is it going to help Soren?"

"Oh, I just know about a spell that uses it for extra strength, that's all."

Ezran thought Claudia was talking really fast, but before he had time to think about it, they'd arrived at the edge of the forest, where a friendly squirrel sat nibbling on a chestnut. Ezran asked the squirrel about milk-fruit. Once the squirrel got over his initial surprise at a human who spoke squirrel, he told Ezran exactly where to go to find the best milk-fruit.

Ezran followed the directions. Soon he was leading Claudia into a lush mountainside grove bursting with flora and fauna.

"There, I see it," Claudia said. She was jumping up and down. "It's a milk-fruit bush."

Ezran thought Claudia was unusually happy to see milk-fruit. It was an uncommon plant, but not extremely rare. But Ezran immediately stopped worrying when he spotted a couple of deer grazing nearby.

"Look, Claudia! There's a family of deer. They must be here for the milk-fruit too."

"I see them," Claudia said. "Wow, you weren't kidding. Those little creatures do love milk-fruit." She turned to Ezran. "Thank you so much for guiding me here," she said. "I don't want to waste any more of your time. I'm sure Callum needs you. Do you know the way back?"

Ezran really wanted to spend a few more minutes with the deer, but Claudia was right. He did have to get back to Callum. "I'll be fine, Claudia," he said. "I've got plenty of friends to help me if I get lost." He smiled at a hummingbird fluttering nearby.

"And Ezran, I'm so sorry. I'm sorry if the things I did before were frightening or confusing," Claudia said. She knelt to keep eye contact with him. "I care about you and Callum a lot. I hope you can forgive me?"

Ezran smiled. He had forgiven her back when she first apologized. "I know you're sorry," he said. Then he turned and headed back toward town.

CHAPTER 32
head, hand,
and heart

Callum wandered alone in the vast, windy darkness,
looking this way and that. There was nothing but
blackness all around. Then he turned a corner and
found himself standing next to Captain Villads.

"Ahoy, Callum! I heard ye be needing a boat," Villads
whispered.

"Am I be needing a boat?" Callum asked. He had no idea what
he needed in this strange place.

"You am! For yer voyage," the captain said. He put one arm
around Callum's shoulders. "Into yer own heart and mind. It be
dangerous there."

Callum looked around and realized he was back on the
Ruthless. He didn't know how he'd gotten there, but he was glad
to be out on the sea again. "Let's hope the weather stays nice," he

said in his best pirate voice. A second later, rain started to pour, and waves crashed all around him. Apparently, the voyage into his heart and mind was a voyage into a terrible, violent storm.

Captain Villads was screaming and laughing, spinning the ship's wheel like a madman. "Hoist the mainsail!" the captain yelled over the storm.

"What?" Callum asked. "But I don't know how to do that."

"It's yer journey," Villads said. "You be the sail, and I'll hoist ye."

Suddenly, Callum realized his arms were tied to ropes. Captain Villads began hoisting up the ropes.

"Find the wind, boy," Villads said. "Be like the wind."

Callum felt his body getting puffier and puffier and larger and larger. When he looked down, he realized he had completely transformed and become the mainsail of the *Ruthless*. Callum felt so uncomfortable. His body was bloated like an overblown balloon about to pop. This was not how he'd imagined it would feel to connect to the Sky arcanum. The wild wind pushed his body/sail in whatever direction it chose. He writhed against the wind, trying to capture its power to steer the boat. But his efforts only seemed to make the wind stronger and angrier at him.

Callum exhaled deeply, and the wind released him back to his human form on the deck of the ship. He clutched the railing while giant waves tossed the boat. Captain Villads was nowhere to be seen, so Callum grabbed the wheel, which was spinning out of control.

Suddenly, Callum was outside the storm looking in at the

Ruthless. He watched the boat toss about the sea with his own bloated body as the mainsail. Then he felt his view of the scene retreat. He was farther and farther away from the storm, looking down on everything like it was contained in a glass globe. He watched the tiny Captain Villads, himself, and the boat all being dashed through the powerful storm inside the globe.

Then, before he could stop himself, Callum lifted the globe into the air and smashed it down to the ground, just as he had done with the primal stone when Zym was born. For a few moments, the shards of the globe remained on the ground. Then the pieces began to twirl around and gather together, reassembling themselves. At the last moment, a gush of wind sucked Callum inside, and he found himself back at sea.

The *Ruthless* had been destroyed. Callum was hanging on to a piece of wood, trying to stay afloat in the great foamy waves. He saw Captain Villads nearby in the water.

"Your conscience is a messy place, boy-o," Villads said merrily.

Berto appeared in the distance. As the parrot approached, Callum saw he had grown to a hundred times his normal size. The giant parrot gripped Captain Villads in his talons, carrying him away into the night.

"Villads out!" the captain called as he escaped the swirling seas.

This is one seriously weird dream, Callum thought. *How long had he been here?* Suddenly, it felt like days since Callum had seen Rayla or Ezran.

Callum gripped his piece of plywood so tightly that it broke.

He started to sink immediately—down, down, down through the thick water. Callum could see the surface fade into the distance. The moon above turned into a mere pinprick of light. There were flashes of lightning high above, but beneath the surface, it was quiet. *Maybe this was how Ezran felt when he was searching for the dragon egg underneath all that ice.*

Callum struggled to reach the surface, but it was no use. He seemed to have forgotten how to swim. He was doing everything wrong. He wanted to use the Sky arcanum to perform incredible magic. He wanted to connect to this mystical, ancient idea. But everything he tried moved him further from the goal. Callum was out of ideas. If a life of magic was going to be this hard, Callum wasn't sure he wanted it.

Callum's cheeks puffed out, and he released the little air he had remaining in his lungs. He watched air bubbles rise as he continued to sink into the darkness. Once Callum decided to stop struggling, the world around him became quiet and still and peaceful.

Then a soft voice spoke from the depths of the water.

"Breathe . . ." the voice said.

Callum knew that voice. He took a deep breath and opened his eyes.

"Breathe. Callum, you need to breathe," the voice said.

Callum found himself sitting on his bed back in Katolis. His mother was there with him, alive and beautiful. She was rubbing his back.

"You just need to breathe, sweetie," Queen Sarai said.

"But I feel so overwhelmed with everything," Callum said.

"I have so many thoughts, things racing through my head." He put his hands on his head, which was aching.

"Sometimes you just need to focus on the present, take a deep breath, and just be," his mother said. "Come on, try it."

Callum inhaled deeply through his nose, then let the air out slowly.

"Sometimes things can get so complicated that our minds can't quite sort them out alone," she said. She brushed some stray locks of hair away from his face. "But when you slow down and let yourself breathe, your spirit and your body can catch up with your mind, and help out."

"I just have to breathe?" Callum asked hopefully. He took a deep, clean inhale.

"To know something truly and deeply, you must know it with your head, hand, and heart . . . mind, body, and spirit." Queen Sarai leaned over and kissed Callum on his forehead.

"I love you with all of myself, and I always will," she said.

CHAPTER 33
I AM THE WING

Callum felt so warm and safe. His mother was alive! She was rocking him back and forth in her lap. She was speaking to him, but her words all melted together— he couldn't understand what she was saying. Then she began rocking him harder and faster. It was a little uncomfortable. "Mom, slow do—" he started to say.

"Callum, wake up! You've got to stay with me!" Rayla yelled. "Please come back. It doesn't matter what you did before. I just want you to be okay again."

Callum opened his eyes a tiny bit. *Why was his mother shaking him by the shoulders?*

"Oh," Callum mumbled.

It wasn't his mother shaking him, it was Rayla. Callum was on the floor of a cave, and the rune cube was on the ground next to him.

"Wake up!" Rayla repeated. "I can't lose you like this. You mean too much to me. Callum, I—"

Callum sat straight up and looked directly into Rayla's eyes.

"I'm awake!" he exclaimed. He put his hands to his cheeks—they felt warm. His body felt energized like after a good night's sleep. "What were you saying?"

But Rayla didn't respond to his question. Instead, she disentangled herself from Callum and stood up. She looked around the cave, at her feet, and outside. She looked in every direction but Callum's. She cleared her throat.

"Oh, look, you're awake now," Rayla said. "You're even looking cheery. And, is that a twinkle in your eye?"

Callum stayed very still as Rayla leaned her face close into his to examine the twinkle. "Oh, nope; that's not a twinkle, it's one of those sleep-crusties. Here, let me." Rayla swept the eye booger out with her index finger before Callum could stop her.

Callum shook his head to clear the last remaining fog from his dream. His dream! He sat up straighter.

"I have it! I understand the Sky arcanum!" Without waiting for a response, he hurried out of the cave.

Rayla, Zym, and Bait hurried after him.

"You understand the Sky arcanum now?" Rayla asked. She raised one eyebrow and cocked her head to the left.

"The arcanum isn't one simple thing," Callum said. His mind was racing, but his thoughts were as clear as they had ever been. "It's all the things. They just had to . . . come together, you know? It's like, when I had the primal stone, I held the power of the Sky in my hand, but now that's gone. But Rayla, the whole world is like a giant primal stone and we're inside it! I'm inside Sky magic, but it's also in me, with every breath I take." He walked toward the edge of the cliff.

"That kind of makes sense," Rayla said, coming up beside him.

"Yes! And I kept thinking about birds, and sails, and how they connect to the wind," Callum said. "And I thought I had to find my wings. But that's just it, I AM the wing!" It felt so good to say it, Callum repeated himself. "I AM THE WING!"

"That makes less sense," Rayla said. "But okay!"

I am the wing, I am the wing. Callum took a deep breath.

"Moment of truth. Let's see if I can really do this," he said. He closed his eyes, then traced the Aspiro rune in the air with his index finger. He waited for the feeling of the magic building inside him, as it had when he'd done the spell with the primal stone in hand.

One second passed, then two. Still no magic flicker. He held his breath.

Could he have fooled himself again?

He reset his shoulders and held his fingers out once more. *Breathe, Callum, breathe.* This time, instead of holding his breath, he let out a deep, slow exhale.

Suddenly a spark flew from the tip of Callum's finger. He felt his entire body melt into the air around him.

"*ASPIRO.*" Callum exhaled. He pushed all the air out of his lungs, and he could feel all the difference. It wasn't a normal breath. A powerful blast of wind erupted from his lips. The wind rushed around his ears and nipped at his cheeks.

Callum had done it—primal magic! He had figured out the Sky arcanum!

The magic wind swirled and grew stronger. Callum closed his eyes and grinned as it gusted around him. This felt right. *This* was his destiny. He soaked it all in, feeling more like himself than he ever had before. The connection he felt with each and every breath to the vastness of the sky itself was undeniable. He understood it deeply, with his mind, his body, and his spirit—his head, hand, and heart.

When he'd had enough, Callum let the magic gently die down. Now that he knew he could do that, he was sure he'd be doing it again soon. He took one last deep breath, then opened his eyes. There was still a huge grin on his face.

But immediately, his joy turned to confusion. Ezran was walking up the path to the cave with a large, very strong-looking man trailing a few feet behind him.

Rayla ran over to them. "Ezran, you're back!" She hugged him.

"He was gone?" Callum asked. *How long had he been asleep?*

Ezran beamed at his brother. "Callum, you figured it out! You can do magic again!" he said. "I knew it would happen."

"That's incredible, Prince Callum," Corvus said.

"Thanks," Callum said. "Um, who are you?"

"You missed a few things while you were out," Rayla said. "This is Corvus. He's on our side now."

"I've always been on the same side," Corvus said. "I serve the young king."

"What?" asked Callum, furrowing his brow. Then realization dawned on him. He turned to Ezran.

"I know about Dad," Ezran said.

Callum looked at his feet. "I don't know what to say. I'm so sorry that I didn't tell you," he said. "I tried to, but I just couldn't."

Ezran didn't answer. He just wrapped his arms around his brother.

All the animals had cleared out of the grove except for one young fawn. Claudia sat cross-legged on the ground, and the fawn approached her curiously. She offered it a milk-fruit.

As it enjoyed the fruit, Claudia stroked the baby deer's head gently. It was sweet and innocent. A beautiful tawny fawn with lovely white spots. It lifted its chin so Claudia could scratch underneath. A single tear trickled down Claudia's face.

"I'm sorry, little one. But you are agile, young, and alive," she said. Claudia touched the deer on its soft nose. "And I need you."

The deer gazed up at her with its milky-brown eyes. Her heart began to melt, but she closed her eyes and thought of Soren. She loved her brother so much.

With her eyes still closed, Claudia thought of her father. She remembered as a small child accidentally eavesdropping on an argument Viren was having with "the old one." She had snuck into Kpp'Ar's "puzzle house" and was hiding in one of the passages when she overheard the angry yelling. She could still hear her father shouting at Kpp'Ar, "I will do anything to protect my family—however dangerous! However vile!" Little Claudia was scared, but she knew her father loved them more than anything.

Claudia opened her eyes again.

Then she did what she had to do. She wrapped her bare hands around the fawn's neck, attempting to snap the bones, to kill it quickly and minimize its suffering. But Claudia had never killed an animal this size before, and she wasn't strong enough to make a clean kill. The fawn thrashed about, kicking its legs in a panic, milk-fruit spewing from its soft muzzle.

Would it ever die? How long could this baby animal possibly struggle? Just as Claudia thought she might have to let the deer go, it gasped its last breath. Claudia held the still-warm fawn in her arms, trying not to look at its glassy eyes.

With a shaking hand, Claudia found the proper page in her spell book and began chanting, "Nekorb eht laeh dna wolf, evila dna gnuoy eliga tserof fo doolbefil!"

Almost immediately, Claudia felt overcome by a power she had never felt before. Her entire body was possessed with the lifeblood of the now-dead fawn. She left the young animal on the forest floor and turned toward the town.

Walking felt like floating. Claudia had never felt so alive and so energized. She barely noticed the townspeople staring at her as she glided through the streets. When she burst through the hospital doors, Claudia's eyes were ablaze, and her entire body vibrated softly.

"You can't be in here," the town doctor yelled.

Claudia brushed by her.

"The patient needs rest," the doctor insisted.

Claudia shoved the doctor to the ground and entered Soren's room. A glowing aura burst from her every pore. She was invincible.

"Claudia? Wh-what are you doing?" Soren asked. He sounded worried—scared even—but she ignored him. She grabbed Soren in her electrified hands and pushed the healing energy into his broken body.

Soren began to scream. His body convulsed as the magic surged through him. He rose into the air above the hospital bed.

Claudia watched Soren's agony, but she didn't waver for a moment. *It's working! It's working!* Nothing else mattered.

When she'd filled his body with magic, Claudia stepped back, and Soren slammed down onto the bed again. Claudia could feel the eyes of the doctors and nurses on her, but she didn't care.

Finally, it was over. Claudia slumped to the ground, spent. She was too tired to speak.

"Hey. What's this?" Soren asked. "I can move my toes. I CAN MOVE MY TOES! I forgot how much I love wiggling them. I can feel again! I can feel my knees, and my strong powerful thighs." Soren grabbed his own thighs in admiration. "And my ribs—OHH!! I broke ribs, didn't I? It's horrible! I can feel again! Ahhh!"

Claudia could hear his excitement and she knew her spell had worked, but she was too exhausted to respond. Her dad had warned her to use dark magic sparingly. The very process could deplete a human being. Of course, her father was correct, but Soren had been in a dire situation. If there had ever been a time to use powerful magic, this was it.

"Claudia?" Soren said. "Claudia, are you okay?"

She picked her head up to look at her brother, whose huge grin collapsed into a frown when he saw her face.

"Your hair," Soren said. "Look, look at your hair."

"I can't see my own hair, Soren," Claudia mumbled.

"It's white—white like an elf's," Soren said. "Well, at least part of it is."

Claudia caught a glimpse of herself in the glass of a medicine cabinet. There was a three-inch-wide white streak through her otherwise black hair.

"You're going to be better now," she said. "That's all that matters."

CHAPTER 34
SMOKE AND
MOONSHADOWS

Outside the mouth of the cave, Ezran watched the sun setting. On the one hand, he was relieved that Callum was recovering and would be able to continue the journey to Xadia. On the other hand, he felt a lump of dread in his chest because his own situation had changed. He knew he could not continue on to Xadia with Callum, Rayla, and Zym. He was the King of Katolis, and his responsibility was to his people.

Ezran was trying to think of a way to break this news when Rayla burst out of the cave, smiling for the first time in a while.

"Everything's packed, and everyone's healthy!" Rayla said. "And we're just a few hours from the border of Xadia."

"Packed and ready," Callum said, emerging from the cave. "Let's do this."

But Ezran didn't return their smiles. He inhaled deeply and turned to Rayla and Callum.

"I'm not coming with you," he said. He wanted to look away, but he forced himself to hold their gaze.

Callum and Rayla seemed stunned into silence. Ezran felt he should explain his decision.

"Callum," he said, "when you told me that assassins were coming for Dad, I ran away and hid in the walls." Ezran felt ashamed thinking about it now.

"With a healthy stash of jelly tarts, as I recall," Callum said.

Was Callum not taking this decision seriously?

"Yeah. And when I found out Dad was gone forever, I ran away again," Ezran said. "I've been running away from things my whole life. But I can't run away from growing up."

Callum put an arm around Ezran's shoulders. "Now that you're King Ezran, are you going to say wise things like that all the time?"

Ezran didn't like the way Callum was joking around with him. This moment was the most serious moment of his life. He stared into his brother's eyes. "I'm not kidding, Callum. When you grow up, you have to face things you're not ready for," he said.

"Wait, what?" Callum asked.

"I'm not going with you to Xadia," Ezran repeated. "I must face my responsibility. Now that I'm king, I'll return to Katolis. Maybe I can help the world better from the throne than if I went with you. I'll do whatever I can to stop the war."

"But Ezran, returning Zym to his mother is the world's best hope," Rayla said.

"I know that, Rayla," Ezran said. "And you two will do that. You'll find his mom, and Zym will take his place in Xadia. Just like I have to take my place in Katolis."

"Ezran—" Callum started to say.

Ezran could tell his brother would try to stop him. "I wish I could go with you, Callum. But I can't. You and Rayla have to do this without me."

"I'll travel with the king and keep him safe," Corvus said.

"Ezran. Are you sure?" Rayla asked.

"I'll miss you, Rayla," Ezran said. "But I'll see you again, I promise."

"And you're sure you can keep Corvus safe from the banthers, right?" Rayla smiled and ruffled his hair.

"As soon as Zym is home, I'll come back to help you," Callum said. "I love you."

"I love you too, big brother," Ezran said. He hugged Callum. Then he bent down to say goodbye to Zym. "I'm so proud of you, little guy. You're going to grow up so strong, and good," he said. "I'm sorry I couldn't help you learn to fly, but I know you'll get it soon."

Ezran hugged Zym quickly. Then he picked up Bait and walked away before Zym could see the tears falling from his face. *Don't look back, don't look back.*

But Ezran couldn't stand it. He turned around for one last look at his friends and family. Rayla and Callum were waving, but Zym didn't understand goodbye. He was running after Ezran.

"I wish you could come with me too, but you need to go be with your mom," Ezran told the little dragon, patting him on his head. "That's your home. Both of us need to go home."

Zym didn't understand. He started to whine.

"Callum? Can you help?" Ezran asked. He didn't want to cry in front of Zym.

Callum hurried over and picked up Zym. He held the baby dragon tight, and Ezran turned back around to start the journey to Katolis.

Ezran sighed. He'd imagined that teaching Zym to fly would be only the first of his adventures with the Dragon Prince. He'd dreamed about growing up with Zym in Xadia, meeting all the magical creatures. But here he was, holding Bait and walking with Corvus. He would never live in Xadia. He would take the throne of his dead father.

It was nighttime in Katolis. The stars shone brightly amid a smattering of clouds.

Viren walked onto Harrow's balcony. He carried a large bundle under his arm and wore a scowl on his face. The caterpillar was wrapped around his ear.

"You tried to win over the other humans with loyalty and friendship, but they ignored you," Aaravos whispered into his ear.

Viren knelt on the balcony and unrolled the heavy bundle. It contained the four unique elven weapons, each of which had belonged to one of the deceased Moonshadow elf assassins. Viren had sharpened the blades immaculately. The shining silver glinted in the moonlight. Next to each weapon, he placed a small circular bowl. Each bowl held the ashes of one of the fallen elves.

If Viren had any second thoughts, the caterpillar in his ear squelched them.

"Those who fail tests of love are simple animals," Aaravos whispered. "They deserve to be motivated by fear."

Viren said nothing. Instead, he pulled a blood candle from his robes. With a snap of his fingers, he lit the wick. Then Viren took a pinch of ash from the first container and sprinkled it over the lit candle. The flame turned from gold to purple.

Viren began to chant: "Nissassa ykoms niaga esir nellaf fo hsa."

He gently blew on the flame. As the smoke billowed out, it took the form of one of the deceased Moonshadow assassins. The inky shape picked up her weapon. Viren repeated the spell three more times until the smoky forms of all four assassins stood before him.

Viren stood back and admired his handiwork.

"Bring terror to Del Bar!" he yelled. "To Neolandia! To Evenere! And to Duren!"

One by one, the smoke forms spirited off the balcony into the night. As the spell's energy dissipated, Viren felt his face transform. Deep-set wrinkles etched themselves into his skin— he could feel the grooves in his forehead. He rubbed his eyes and knew from experience that dark craters of exhaustion surrounded them. Though he ritually erased the effects of dark magic every morning, the frightening features seemed to reclaim his face more cruelly each time he used his dark power.

For a moment, he thought of his beautiful young daughter. He never wanted her to look this way or to feel this level of exhaustion. She didn't know what lay ahead of her. He would try to protect her for as long as possible. He pulled his hood up around his face so no one could see him in his present state.

Viren returned to his study and locked the door behind him.

"You're in danger," Aaravos hissed in his ear, not a minute later.

The hairs on Viren's arm stood on end, and his eyes darted back and forth.

"They've come for you," Aaravos said through the caterpillar. "Do as I tell you. Prepare for battle."

Viren grabbed ingredients from his desk drawers, shelves, and cabinets. Then he turned to the door and, with a flourish, expanded his cane into a full staff.

No sooner did he have the staff in hand than he heard pounding on his chamber door. Guards rattled the golden handle.

"Lord Viren! Open up, by order of the high council!" a guard shouted.

"Well?" Aaravos laughed. "Open it for them!"

Viren waved his hand, and the door exploded outward into the hall. The force of the explosion blasted a cadre of guards to the floor. The surviving guards gathered themselves together and poured into the room, swords drawn. Viren waved his staff to send energy blasts at them. He felt intense energy and power filling him up. He could sense his movements and actions being gently directed. Viren did not feel controlled, but he understood that somehow, invisible strings connected him with the Startouch elf.

Meanwhile deep beneath the castle, in the mirror, Aaravos appeared energized and transformed, almost floating. Though his actual location was a mystery even to him, there was no denying that in this moment he was in a way present and completely connected to Viren. He mirrored Viren's movements, creating runes on his side of the mirror, and releasing them and their powerful effects through his counterpart.

Viren cast spell after spell. He watched with glee as the guards fell. Just as he'd knocked out most of the guards in the room, archers arrived as backup for the soldiers. Viren slammed one into the sheep-girl painting, knocking it ajar, slightly off its hinges. He rushed over to close the painting door—it was the hidden passage to his secret chambers—but he was interrupted by a shout.

"Surrender, Viren!" Opeli called out. She must have walked in behind the archers.

Viren turned to confront his challenger, but the voice in his ear halted him. "Stop," Aaravos said suddenly. "It's over."

"But I can destroy them all," Viren said. He was on a rampage. He couldn't stop now. "I have all the power I need!" After the dark ritual earlier this evening, and this supercharged melee, Viren felt unstoppable. It seemed unnecessary to relinquish his power now.

"STOP!" Aaravos ordered. Viren saw he was encircled by archers.

"You're completely surrounded, Viren," Opeli said. "Give

yourself up—don't make me give the order. These guards are prepared to take you alive or dead."

It didn't surprise Viren in the least that Opeli was willing to execute him. Viren reluctantly dropped his staff. The guards rushed to apprehend him.

"You've betrayed me," Viren muttered to Aaravos.

"No. I will stay with you," Aaravos said.

Then the sticky talking Star caterpillar crawled deep into Viren's ear.

Was this how it would end for him? Opeli would have him executed for treason if no one stopped her. Who could help him now? He had known from the beginning he couldn't count on Aaravos.

"Claudia," Viren murmured.

"What's that, traitor?" Opeli shouted.

Viren said nothing. If Claudia returned, she would come to his rescue.

His daughter was his only chance now.

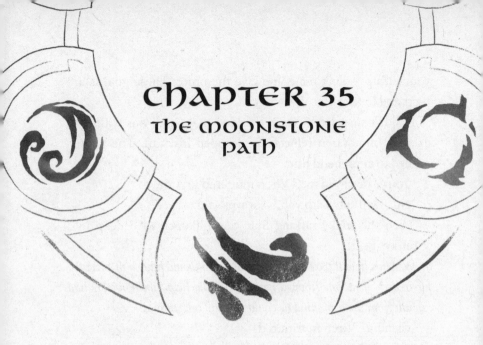

Chapter 35
The Moonstone Path

Callum kept his mouth shut, but it was taking longer to get to the Xadian border than Rayla had predicted. The journey gave him time to worry about Ezran. Would Ezran and Corvus make it back to Katolis? If they did, who would be there to greet them? Viren? That wouldn't be good.

Callum shook his head. There was no use worrying about things he couldn't control.

He followed Rayla through a narrow canyon. It was so dark he had a hard time believing Rayla could navigate.

"This is it," Rayla said. "This canyon leads to the Moonstone Path."

"Wow," Callum said. "I can't believe that we're almost to Xadia." But he was only excited for a moment. "We came this far, and Ez isn't with us."

Zym made a soft whining sound. Callum had carried Zym in his arms most of the way to the path. The baby dragon hadn't recovered from losing Ezran. He was clutching Callum tightly and had buried his head in Callum's chest.

"I know," Rayla said. "But we can't think about that now. Ezran's doing the right thing, and so are we."

They came around a final turn in the canyon, which opened onto the border. Callum gasped.

At this spot, the border was an enormous field of cooled, cracked lava. The cracks glowed an ominous red. Xadia was visible far across the lava, but the field stretched for miles to both the north and south. Clearly there was no going around.

"One simply walks into Xadia, huh?" Callum said. He raised an eyebrow at Rayla. *Might as well start walking, then.* He lifted a foot to step onto a rock.

"Hold on there!" Rayla said. She yanked him back to solid ground. "There's sort of a trick to it." Rayla picked up a stone and tossed it on the rock Callum had almost stepped on. The rock instantly sank down into the liquid magma below. Callum gulped.

"Not all the rocks sink that quickly," Rayla explained. "A few will let us stand on them long enough to walk across. Those special stones were enchanted and marked with hidden runes centuries ago, and the path has been a closely guarded secret. We call it the Moonstone Path."

"Okay, great," Callum said. There was at least a fighting chance of making it across. "So how do we know—"

"Patience, friend," Rayla said. She pointed in the direction of the moon, which was hiding behind a cloud. "Patience."

A moment later, the breeze blew the clouds away and the moon emerged. Callum's eyes grew wide as runes appeared on some of the rocks before them. They glowed, reflecting the moonlight.

"Oh, I get it," he said, marveling at the eerie yet beautiful sight before them. "The Moonstone Path." The rocks with runes created a safe route across the lava field.

He tentatively stepped on the closest Moon-marked rock. It began to sink, but much more slowly than that first rock he'd nearly stepped on. He smiled.

Slowly, they began to pick their way across, the marked stones sinking behind them.

The trio moved at a steady pace, but the path was slow going. Soon Callum, Rayla, and Zym found themselves far out on the lava field. The other side was within sight, but still quite far away.

"The sky's getting lighter. We need to hurry," Rayla said. "If the sun rises, we won't be able to see the moon runes anymore."

They started to move faster. Callum could still see the runes, but he had to strain his eyes. He stepped from one safe rock to the next, but each time, as soon as he landed, the rune faded before his eyes.

He looked up. The sun was now peeking through the crack of the canyon up ahead. Time was just about up.

"Run!" Callum shouted.

Callum, Rayla, and Zym ran as fast as they could, racing against the sunrise. But before they reached the end of the path, the runes disappeared entirely. The trio stood frozen and helpless on a single rock as it slowly started to sink.

Ezran and Corvus walked side by side through the forest to Katolis. Ezran tried to imagine what he would encounter there. He was looking forward to seeing his old friend Opeli, and he wouldn't mind getting his hands on a jelly tart.

Suddenly, Ezran's heart skipped a few beats. He forgot all about Katolis and tarts. Zym needed him. He could sense it. Ezran stood very still.

"What's wrong?" Corvus asked. "Why are you stopping?"

"I can see something," Ezran said. "Something that's not here."

"What are you talking about?" Corvus asked.

"They're in trouble," Ezran said. "They can't get to Xadia." He closed his eyes. "I can feel a connection to Zym as if we were in the same place! He's reaching out to me right now. He's scared," Ezran said. "It's okay, Zym! You're going to be okay. We'll get through this together." Determination surged through Ezran. It was his job to guide the tiny dragon home after all.

"Corvus," Ezran said. "I need to try something that might seem a little strange. You need to trust me."

"You're the king," Corvus said. "Whatever you need."

"Kneel down," Ezran said.

Corvus immediately obeyed. Ezran awkwardly scrambled onto his shoulders. Corvus stood up.

"Okay, Zym, you can do this. You need to block the light," Ezran shouted through space and time to the tiny dragon. Then he spread his arms and slowly moved them up and down as if they were wings.

Zym stared across the Moonstone Path. He wasn't sure why Callum and Rayla had stopped, but he knew they were all in trouble. They had to get to the other side of this river of lava. This, he was sure of. And it seemed that the problem was the sun.

Zym scampered over to Callum and climbed onto his head. From this height, he could see that the sun was rising over a rocky structure. Right now, the rocks blocked the full brightness of the sun. But it wouldn't be long before the sun was fully risen.

"Zym? What are you doing?" Callum asked.

An idea suddenly popped into Zym's head. If he could fly across the lava and land on the rocks, maybe he could block the sun and help his friends.

But Zym didn't know how to fly. He wished he'd practiced more with Ezran. Maybe taken the lessons with Phoe-Phoe a little more seriously.

Where was Ezran? Zym needed him so badly.

And then, with his feet on Callum's shoulders, Zym felt a strange sensation. It was as if a piece of his soul raced out of his body and then—BLAM!—joined another soul. He was with Ezran! Somehow, their souls were together, joined in an unknown part of the universe.

With his eyes closed, Zym saw Ezran spread his arms wide. Zym did the same. He unfurled his wings.

Then Ezran raised his arms up and down. Zym did the same with his wings.

You can do it. You can do it. Zym felt Ezran's words of encouragement flow through him.

There was no time to lose. Before he could think twice about it, Zym opened his eyes. He flapped his wings harder than he thought was possible. Then he leaped.

He was flying! He was really flying! Zym felt a big smile spread across his face as the wind breezed past him.

"He's flying! He's trying to block the sun!" Rayla shouted.

Zym heard Callum and Rayla cheering him on as he soared through the sky.

He was almost to the edge of the lava river when he noticed he wasn't as high as before. He flapped harder, but he only dropped lower to the ground. It didn't matter how hard he flapped. He wasn't strong enough.

Zym was going to fail everyone. Rayla, Callum, Ezran. Even Bait would be disappointed. And Zym would never meet his mother.

He stopped flapping so hard. It didn't matter anymore.

"ASPIRO!"

A tremendous gust of wind lifted Zym up into the air. He continued flapping, but this time he was gaining height. The winds from Callum's spell were pushing him upward.

Zym was high up now. He could feel the sun on his face. Seconds later, he arrived at the crack in the rocks where the sunlight shone through. He threw his head back in triumph and spread his small wings to block the sun.

In Zym's long shadow, the light of the moon activated the runes on the path.

"There's the path again," Rayla said. "Run!"

Zym heard Rayla and Callum sprinting across the path. At last, he heard Callum cry, "We did it! We made it across!"

Zym drifted down to meet Rayla and Callum on the Xadian side of the border. Then he folded his wings back.

Zym was a dragon now.

CHAPTER 36
INTO XADIA

General Amaya stared at the Breach from the human side. She didn't know how much longer the Breach would hold, and she could feel Lieutenant Fen's onion breath on her neck.

"General Amaya, we're running out of time. I strongly recommend we gather the battalion and abandon the fortress," Lieutenant Fen signed.

Amaya scowled. *Abandon* wasn't a word in her vocabulary. There was too much at stake. She'd put off the search for her beloved nephews and left Viren in charge of Katolis. All this to maintain the fortress at the Breach.

For generations, the Breach had been the only way for humans to cross the border to Xadia. And for all these generations, the Breach had remained safe and secure. If they lost control of the border crossing, it could be used by Xadian forces to launch massive attacks on the human kingdoms. Amaya would not let it fall under her watch. She was not about to walk away . . . not from the Breach anyway. Amaya turned away from Fen.

"General!" he shouted.

Amaya continued to walk away, but she could feel the thud of Lieutenant Fen's footsteps pounding behind her. She kept marching as he ran even faster to overtake her. Now he was facing her. She couldn't help but read his lips.

"General, the Sunfire elves have already taken over the outpost on the Xadian side of the Breach."

This was the last piece of news she wanted. Amaya stopped. She didn't want to have this conversation, but now she had no choice.

"If the elves mount an attack, we just don't have the numbers to hold this fortress," Fen said. "*When* the elves mount an attack, I should say."

"We do not abandon our post," Amaya signed.

She started to walk away when another soldier ran up to them.

"General Amaya, I'm sorry to interrupt. But someone has arrived."

Amaya turned in the direction the soldier was pointing. She saw a figure walking onto the battlement. She'd recognize the walk of that man anywhere! He was walking toward her slowly—too slowly for Amaya's taste.

She hurried over to Gren and scooped him up into one of her famous bear hugs. Amaya could get by without a translator, but communication would be much smoother with Gren to sign and speak at the same time.

Plus, she'd missed his cheerful, freckled smile terribly. But for some reason his boyish face was covered in the beginnings of a beard.

"What's this?" Amaya signed, stroking the growing stubble.

"I couldn't shave," Gren signed back. "I'll shave as soon as I can so you can read my lips. We have a lot to catch up on."

"I'm sorry to interrupt," Lieutenant Fen said, "but where are the reinforcements we requested? We sent many messages to Lord Viren."

"No reinforcements are coming," Gren signed. "That's one of the things we need to discuss. Lord Viren has been arrested for treason. He also held me prisoner, which is why I couldn't shave."

Amaya rolled her eyes. But in case Gren needed clarification on her feelings, she signed, "How shocking," with extra energy in her sarcastic hands. Even if Viren's treason wasn't surprising, it put Amaya in a more difficult position. Without reinforcements, they could not defend the Breach. She signed as much to Gren and Fen.

"Lieutenant, you are right—we can't defend the Breach." Fen seemed satisfied to have won the argument, but Amaya continued. "But I won't abandon it either. Our only option is to destroy it."

General Amaya thought quickly. "We'll set up explosives at a half dozen detonation points and connect them with a single cable. We will trigger the explosion with the cable from our side of the Breach and bring down an impassable wall of flowing lava."

Amaya, Gren, Fen, and a group of troops moved to the river of lava to set up the defensive explosion. Amaya worked with Gren to stuff barrels of explosives up into the rocks just above the secret path to Xadia. Nearby, her troops did the same. They had to be incredibly careful in their placement. If the explosives were a few inches too close to the magma, a stray ember could ignite the explosives prematurely.

After about thirty minutes, the troops waved their hands to signal that the explosives were in place.

"The cable," Amaya signed.

Fen passed Amaya a cable. She attached it to the last barrel in the chain.

"It's done," Amaya signed. "Let's go!"

The group hurried down the path to the human side of the Breach. Fen rolled the long cable out behind them. Amaya, Gren, and Fen stood just inside the gate that led to the secret path. A few soldiers stood nearby, cable in hand. They looked to Amaya.

"On your command, we'll pull the cable and detonate the barrels," Fen signed.

"And a thousand tons of rock and lava will seal the Breach forever," Amaya signed back. She dropped her hand, giving the command.

"Pull!" Gren shouted.

Fen yanked the cable with all his might. Nothing happened. He pulled again. This time, the cable snaked back toward them, and they could see it had been severed. Its end was glowing red hot.

Amaya whipped her head around. She could see the Sunfire

knight standing in the middle of the Breach path in the distance. She held the opposite end of the cable she had just cut in one hand, and in the other was the glowing Sunforge blade. A sneer crossed her face.

"Now what?!" Fen shouted. "The trigger's been disabled."

Amaya shook her head. Of course, Fen was panicking.

"Someone has to go out there and set them off," she signed. "I'll do it myself." She mounted her horse. She would charge the Breach and set off those explosives on her own.

Gren was running toward her, waving his arms. She paused.

"But Amaya. You won't survive," Gren signed.

Amaya looked at Gren. "But the rest of you will," she signed. The general grabbed a nearby torch—she would need it to ignite the barrels. Then she gave Gren the best smile she could muster, and galloped off.

Amaya and her horse raced toward the Xadian side of the Breach. As she neared the explosives, torch in hand, she could see the Sunfire knight standing directly in her path. The knight's eyes were narrowed, and her sword was drawn.

Amaya charged the knight and her glowing blade. But as Amaya approached, the knight dug her heels in and brandished her weapon. Amaya tried to leap over the knight on horseback, but the Sunforge blade singed the horse's flank.

The horse screamed in agony. Its body twisted and contorted in pain and it collapsed onto its side. The torch flew out of Amaya's hand, and she watched in desperation as it tumbled off the edge of the ravine. Now she had no way to light those barrels.

Nevertheless, she ran toward the first barrel and began to

climb. But before she could get to it, the knight yanked her to the ground. Amaya stepped forward, within the knight's reach. She grabbed the hilt of the knight's glowing Sunforge blade and ripped it away from her. Then she kicked the Sunfire knight back and clambered up to the barrel of explosives.

Amaya gave one last look across the Breach. She caught Gren's eye and nodded.

Then she plunged the Sunforge blade into the barrel to ignite the explosives.

Amaya planted her shield down as close to the cliff wall as she could, and braced herself behind it. She shuddered at the huge initial explosion. Then she felt each successive barrel blow, one after the other.

Success! Torrents of lava flowed over what was once the path, making passage impossible.

Amaya clutched her scorched shield, happy to have succeeded and surprised to be alive. She looked around, surveying her options on what to do from here. Her eyes settled on the Sunfire knight. She was nearby, barely hanging on to a ledge. She was moments away from plummeting into the lava far below.

Amaya hurried to the ledge and crouched down. She narrowed her eyes at her enemy. It could all be over in an instant. A simple shove would send the knight to her death.

But instead of shoving the knight, Amaya reached her hand out.

The Sunfire knight frowned and refused Amaya's hand. But Amaya had made up her mind. She reached down farther, grabbed the Sunfire knight's wrist, and pulled her to safety.

Within seconds, a group of Sunfire elves arrived on the scene and surrounded Amaya. They didn't seem to care that she had just saved their leader.

The knight looked away as the elves apprehended Amaya.

Amaya held her head high as they tackled her and tied her up. She had done what she had come to do. Katolis was safe . . . for now.

As the sun rose over the small town, Claudia helped Soren out of the hospital. She couldn't believe the doctors and nurses had allowed him to spend another night there after the whole dark magic healing fiasco. But they seemed to like Soren there. Claudia had slept on a nearby bench, outside.

Soren was hobbling on crutches, but his new lease on life seemed to have drained out of him.

"We both failed our secret missions, Claudia," Soren said. "What's Dad going to say when we show up empty-handed?"

This fact had occurred to Claudia as well. She wasn't looking forward to returning to Katolis. Their dad was going to be super furious. But there was no reason to upset Soren. He needed to focus on getting better.

"We're both alive, Soren," she said. "That's the important thing. And we're not coming back empty-handed." She waved something in front of Soren's face. "It's the horn you cut off the dragon!"

Soren eyes widened. He admired the dragon horn, and then he looked off into the sky. "Guess what, Claudia. Inspiration has found me," he said. Then Soren's expression changed to what Claudia had now learned to recognize as his "poem face":

> *Failed missions, mad dad.*
> *But dragon horn means magic.*
> *Maybe Dad not mad?*

Claudia beamed as she counted the syllables. Five-seven-five! Soren was unpredictable in the best ways.

"Yes!! That was amazing! A perfect haiku." She threw herself on Soren in a bear hug, nearly knocking him over in the process.

They would be able to reunite Zym with his mother any day now! In the early morning light, Rayla looked around at the rises in the canyon; she was practically bursting to show Callum what lay beyond. She spun around to face Callum and Zym and threw out her arms.

"Well, welcome to Xadi—"

A gasp from Callum cut her off. He was staring at something behind Rayla, his eyes wide.

She turned back around. *It's just rocks.*

Wait. That wasn't a rock. Rayla's heart skipped a beat.

"Oh no, oh no, oh no, oh no," she muttered to herself. "How could you have been so stupid, Rayla?!"

There, on the top of a small rise in the distance, silhouetted by the rising sun, was Sol Regem. This ancient dragon was known to all in Xadia. He had once symbolized all that was beautiful and glorious about Xadia. That was, until a human mage burned out his eyes hundreds of years ago. Now he roamed the Xadian border, blinded and bitter.

Sol Regem represented the rage between Xadia and the human kingdoms. And he was standing in the way of Zym returning to his mother.

Sol Regem might let an elf and a dragon through to Xadia, Rayla reasoned. But a human?

Rayla looked over at Callum. She hoped he was ready to do more magic.

ABOUT THE AUTHORS

Aaron Ehasz grew up in Baltimore, Maryland. He studied philosophy in college with the obvious goal of one day making cartoons and video games. Aaron was the head writer of the beloved series *Avatar: The Last Airbender* and is co-creator of *The Dragon Prince*.

Melanie McGanney Ehasz grew up in New York City, surrounded by books and tall buildings, and has a master's degree in English literature.

Aaron and Melanie live with three children and two fur children in Santa Monica, California, where they are surrounded by books and palm trees.